A Haunted Twist of Fate

A HAUNTED TWIST OF FATE

STACEY COVERSTONE

FIVE STAR

A part of Gale, Cengage Learning

Detroit • New York • San Francisco • New Haven, Conn • Waterville, Maine • London

GALE
CENGAGE Learning®

Set in 11 pt. Plantin.

LIBRARY OF CONGRESS CATALOGING-IN-PUBLICATION DATA

Coverstone, Stacey.
    A haunted twist of fate / Stacey Coverstone. — 1st ed.
      p. cm.
    ISBN-13: 978-1-4328-2541-6 (hardcover)
    ISBN-10: 1-4328-2541-0 (hardcover)
    1. Widows—Fiction. 2. Black Hills (S.D. and Wyo.)—Fiction. I.
  Title.
  PS3603.O88828H38 2011
  813'.6—dc23   2011032933

First Edition. First Printing: December 2011.
Published in 2011 in conjunction with Tekno Books.

Printed in the United States of America
1 2 3 4 5 6 7 15 14 13 12 11

To my husband, Paul—the love of my life.

Thank you to Julie Lence, my awesome critique partner, for your friendship and your talent.

ONE

"Shhhaaay."

The voice whispered across the air, nudging Shay Brennan awake.

"Who's there?" she mumbled groggily, while rolling onto her side. The springs of the old iron bed squeaked under her weight. The voice came again, soft, lilting in her ear.

"Shhhaaay."

Fingernails stroked her jaw. A palm caressed her cheek. Eyes popping open, Shay jolted up and bumped the back of her head on the bars of the headboard. Her back rigid, she scooted to a sitting position and glanced around the room, clutching the downy pillow to her chest.

Thoughts scattered and fuzzy, it took a moment for her to remember where she was. It was the first night sleeping in the Buckhorn Saloon, an 1885 Hill City establishment located in the historic section of town on the original Main Street. She'd walked past it a week ago. Having seen a *For Sale* sign in the window, she'd made an offer on a whim and closed on the legendary South Dakota property this afternoon.

"Who's there?" she repeated, touching her cheek and blinking several times as her eyes adjusted to the darkness of the bedroom. Goose bumps prickled her arms, and a chill crept across her nape. A sliver of moonlight shone through the thin curtains hanging at the window she realized she'd forgotten to close before retiring.

"Shay."

The voice spoke clear and strong this time, with more force. Her attention flew to the foot of the bed, where a gray mist began to take shape. With her heart lodged in her throat, Shay was barely able to breathe. Her body began to quake, and she bit back a scream when the unearthly figure of a female materialized.

"Help . . . me," the woman whispered, outstretching an arm.

Shay pressed her back against the headboard. Completely awake now, all of her senses were acutely alert. Fully formed, the body looked solid, like a live human being. But she knew that couldn't be possible. She'd locked her door. She would have heard the hundred-year-old wood creak open if someone had tried to come inside. Sneaking a glance at the door, she saw that the old-fashioned skeleton key was still in the keyhole.

I must be dreaming, she thought, shaking her head. The face staring back at her was pale and . . . seemed not of this earth. *She looks like a . . .*

"There's no such thing as ghosts," she said aloud.

The apparition searched her face with piercing blue eyes that seemed to peer into the depths of Shay's soul.

"Who are you?" she finally whispered, when she realized the person was not going away. Fingers splayed over her heart; she could feel the organ jumping inside her chest.

Noting the white petticoat and V-shaped corset that closed in the front with ribbon ties, the woman appeared to be dressed in Victorian undergarments. Her hair was blonde, piled on top of her head with long curls streaming down her back. And those eyes . . . they were as vivid as any Shay had ever seen.

The woman touched her neck with delicate fingers and began to softly moan. With her face twisting in pain, the moans eerily engulfed the bedroom, sending ice-cold shivers racing down Shay's spine. Within moments, the moaning turned to weeping, and the cries were so distressing and full of sadness that Shay suddenly felt overwhelmed by a deep depression and an odd sense of regret.

"Help . . . me," the figure pleaded again.

Shay loosened the death grip on her pillow. "How can I help? Who are you?"

It was then that she noticed the black-and-blue marks on the woman's neck. Her gaze moved again to those vivid eyes, and without warning, Shay's throat closed up. It felt like she was being choked. Invisible hands were around her neck, and frigid fingers pressed into her flesh, making it a struggle to breathe. The pressure on her throat was intense for a few seconds before it let up.

Coughing, Shay gasped for air, and when she looked up again, the manifestation had disappeared.

"What . . . the hell . . . just happened?" She stroked her sore neck with trembling hands.

She'd barely had time to process what had just transpired when an urgent knocking came from downstairs. Was that the sound of the ancient oil furnace kicking on? She angled her head and listened carefully while inhaling deeply in order to will her skipping heartbeat back into rhythm.

It sounded more like someone pounding on the front door. Squinting at the clock on the bedside table, Shay swore under her breath.

"Who would be at my door at midnight?"

The rapping stopped. But after a moment's respite, it started up again.

"Damn." She flipped on the table lamp, swung her legs off the bed, and threw on some jeans and shimmied into a T-shirt. The plank floor was cold on her bare feet. A chill nipped the air as she unlocked the bedroom door and stepped into the hallway, switching on the light. The pounding continued as she eased down the oak staircase, craning her neck over her shoulder, feeling like someone was watching her.

"I'm coming!" she shouted while striding across the hardwood, weaving between the round gaming tables original to the saloon, and past the long paneled mahogany bar, which was polished to a splendid shine. Turning her head, she jumped when she caught her reflection in the large gilded mirror above the bar. Her body jerked a second time when her gaze flew up and met the glassy eyes of a stuffed elk head hanging over the mirror.

The thought of a stranger pounding on her door at this hour sped up the pulse of her heart more than it was already racing. Could it be a drunkard at the wrong place? The cops? Stopping at the front door and inhaling deeply, she hollered, "Who's there?"

The knocking halted. It was an indecent hour to be calling on a person. Someone had better be dead, she thought crossly. Tossing a glance back up the stairs, she realized the pun she'd made. She had the distinct feeling someone *was* dead. Very dead.

"It's Colt Morgan," answered the voice from the other side of the door.

Colt Morgan? The real-estate broker? Shay peeked out from behind the heavy maroon curtain covering the glass-paneled door.

Sure enough, there stood the man who had been the listing agent on the property—a tall drink of water in a cowboy hat.

Two

Shay unlocked the door, and a cool breeze swept in. Her head tilted. Confused, she said, "Can I help you?" It felt like a cloud had settled over her brain. Had she really just seen a ghost in her room? And why was this handsome man standing at her door at midnight?

Despite the early hour, Colt Morgan's green eyes sparkled beneath his brown Stetson. As if suddenly remembering his manners, he jerked the hat off his head to uncover sandy-colored hair and held the hat at his chest.

"Sorry to bother you, Miss Brennan," he drawled, shifting from one foot to the other.

"Please. You can call me Shay."

Soft-spoken, and offering a smile that lit up his tanned face, he nodded and repeated, "Okay. Shay."

"Yes, Mr. Morgan. It's pretty late. What can I do for you?" The man's rugged attractiveness nearly took her breath away, even at this hour, under the dim glow of her porch light. But she couldn't fathom why he was bothering her at this ungodly time of night.

Today at the closing, she'd caught herself staring at his handsome face, thinking he reminded her of someone, but she couldn't put her finger on who. It hadn't been until later when she was having dinner alone that it occurred to her. He looked like George Strait, the country singer. He had the same strong jaw, twinkling eyes, and crooked grin. She didn't know much about country music, but she'd seen a concert poster of the singer somewhere, not long ago. Where had it been? Iowa?

Snapping back from her musings, Shay realized she probably looked a sight and suddenly felt self-conscious. She wasn't wearing any makeup, or a bra under the T-shirt. No doubt, her long hair was messed up from restless tossing and turning in bed—the way she slept most nights.

"You can call me Colt, ma'am," he said, interrupting her thoughts.

"All right. Now that we have the introductions made, Colt, would you mind telling me why you're standing at my door at midnight?"

"Of course." He cleared his throat. "Someone walking past the saloon a while ago claimed to see water running under the door here." They both glanced down at the same time. "This fellow said he knew I was the agent who'd listed the place, so that's the reason he called me. I thought I'd better come check it out."

Colt stared at the ground again and then scratched his head. "The ground isn't even wet. I don't see any traces of water."

"That's because there are none," she said, wondering what was really going on. She didn't like pranks being pulled on her, especially at this hour by men she didn't know.

He sighed, seeming embarrassed and confused. "I guess it was a false alarm."

"Guess so." His eyes were hypnotic, but she refused to be drawn into them. She'd had enough of men and their lying, manipulative ways to last a lifetime—even the good-looking ones.

"So, everything else is okay over here?" He peered around her shoulder into the dimly lit room behind her.

Uncomprehending, she said, "What could be wrong? I don't understand."

He raked a hand through his hair. "Well, this might sound crazy, but that same man told me he saw . . ."

"Saw what?" she prodded. The vision of the woman she thought she'd seen upstairs replayed through her mind.

After a moment's hesitation, Colt chuckled. "Ah, never mind. The guy might have been drunk and was imagining things. Come to think of it, his voice did sound slurred." He chewed his lower lip and then said, "Forget I mentioned anything."

Shay had a feeling. She wondered if this "drunkard" had seen the ghost who had appeared in her room. Maybe he'd seen the spirit through her window from down on the street. It crossed her mind to tell Colt about the woman, but then thought better of it. He'd probably think she was insane. Or plastered like the guy who'd called him. Besides, maybe she had imagined the whole thing. There weren't any such things as ghosts.

"So, you're okay?" Colt repeated, plopping his hat back on.

"Yes. I'm fine. I appreciate your coming over in the middle of the night. That was real neighborly of you." Even though his appearance and the story seemed suspicious, there was no need for her to be rude.

He grinned and the awkward tension between them dissolved. "Just taking care of my client, Shay. That's my job. But you're welcome. Is that lock strong?" He was referring to her front-door lock, which he jiggled.

"Yes. The building inspector went over the entire building with a fine-toothed comb. This place is as secure as a bank vault."

"Sure. I remember reading the inspector's report. Since everything seems to be in order here, I'll be on my way. I apologize for waking you." He touched a finger to the brim of his Stetson and turned to leave. Then he snapped his fingers.

"There's some paperwork I forgot to give you today at the closing. Would you like to meet me for breakfast in the morning? I could give it to you then."

Could that be true? For the second time, Shay wondered if the story about the water had been some kind of excuse. Maybe he'd taken a liking to her at the closing and had simply wanted to see her again. Although she had sworn off men, she was flattered if that was the case, although waking her at midnight was probably not the smartest way to get on her good side.

Colt was the only person she knew in town, and eating alone was starting to get old, so she decided to accept his invitation.

"That'll be nice. I've been going stag a lot lately."

"I wasn't sure if you knew anyone in Hill City yet. We can meet at the Golden Spike diner. It's right here on Main Street, down a block."

"I know it."

"They make the best blueberry pancakes in town. You like blueberry pancakes?"

She nodded. "Yes. What time should we meet?"

He glanced at his watch. "Does eight o'clock work for you?"

"Sure. Eight works."

Grinning, he said, "Well, good night. Again, sorry for bothering you."

"No problem. It's nice to know people look out for each other here. You don't find that so much where I come from. Good night."

She watched him saunter to his pickup, admiring the snug way his Levi's fit his long legs and cupped his backside. As the truck pulled away from the curb, a hand shot out the window and waved. Shay waved back and then closed the door, locking it securely behind her.

As she crept past the tables and started up the stairs, she stopped and turned. She smelled the sweet aroma of cigar smoke and could swear she heard the faint sound of shuffling cards.

THREE

As he was driving home from the Buckhorn, Colt recalled how rattled that caller had been; the one who'd claimed there was water running out from under the door of the Buckhorn. Colt had thought the story believable, considering how old the saloon was. That's why he'd rushed right over. One of those ancient pipes could bust at any time, no matter what the inspector had told Shay. The second part of the story was what had Colt flummoxed. The guy had also vowed he'd seen a woman in white walk straight through the front door.

Normally, Colt would have laughed that one off. But the call had woken him from a strange dream he'd been having, where he'd pictured a strangling in one of the upstairs rooms of the Buckhorn. He'd recognized the room from when he'd listed the property. For some unexplainable reason, he'd awakened knowing that room was the same one his client, Shay Brennan, was sleeping in tonight.

The dream had seemed so real—nothing he'd ever experienced before. In fact, when the phone had jingled and he'd jolted up in bed he'd realized he'd been coated in a cold sweat.

The call had been a peculiar coincidence, but it'd turned out to be a convenient excuse for Colt to go over and check on Shay and make sure she was okay. Although he was rarely afraid of anything, the dream had spooked him.

Halting at a red light, he recalled the look on her face when she opened the door to him. She could have cussed him out or

17

bitten off his head for waking her in the middle of the night. He would have deserved it if she had, even if he'd only been trying to do the right thing. She must have realized that, because she'd been obliging and good-natured, even as he offered her what now seemed like a lame story for stopping by.

What *had* that been about anyway? Colt wondered, realizing he hadn't even taken down the caller's name, just jumped in the truck and driven to the Buckhorn. Guess he'd never know who'd been pulling his leg, or why. But better some midnight joke than a saloon full of water, even if he didn't cotton to being roused from bed at that hour.

"You're listening to KPOC, ninety-three-point-one, and that was Carrie Underwood singing 'Angel Take the Wheel,' " the DJ on the radio said. "Coming up in the next hour, we'll be playing Blake Shelton's new song, plus we'll have some Tim McGraw, and an oldie from Lee Ann Rimes. So don't go away."

Colt punched the off button and rubbed a knuckle over his eyes. Cool air blew across his face through the open window. He'd be lucky if he got back to sleep before one-thirty. Once he was awakened in the night and his mind started cranking out thoughts, he had a hard time shutting it down again.

For instance, tomorrow morning he had to get to the office early to fax a contract to someone on the East Coast. Then, he needed to pull some listings for a couple who were relocating to Hill City. He had to remember to call Lisa to set up an appraisal for Pete Johnson. Then meet Shay at eight for breakfast . . .

"Aw, damn," he groaned.

Why the hell had he asked her to breakfast? He had a rule about mixing business with pleasure, especially with pretty clients. He should have told Shay he'd either have the papers mailed to her or delivered.

Colt lightly banged his fist against the steering wheel, wondering why his gut was twisting in knots. Was the Mexican food he'd had for supper wreaking havoc on him? Or, could it be that Shay Brennan's smile and her kind, easygoing nature had stirred him in ways he hadn't been stirred in years? That kind of feeling wasn't anything he needed. He'd been doing just fine the way life was.

The light turned green and he pressed slowly on the gas pedal. The town was dead. It was nice. Peaceful. Gave him time to think without the usual distractions of work and demanding clients. And his family, who, for several years now, had been trying to set him up with eligible ladies.

His late wife, Denise, had been the love of his life. When she'd died ten years ago, a part of him had died with her. Eventually, he'd learned to manage his grief, but he still maintained the notion he'd never find anyone as perfect for him as Denise had been.

Before she'd passed, she'd made him promise he'd find love again. She'd told him she didn't want him to grow old alone. He'd promised, to appease her, but he'd known it would be a pledge he wouldn't keep. It had been many years before he'd been able to think about dating another woman, let alone give his love to someone else. Losing Denise had shattered his heart in ways he'd never imagined possible. That kind of pain was not something he ever planned to go through again.

A few years ago, when his family found out he'd started dating again, they'd been eager to help—even though he'd insisted he wasn't interested in any permanent relationship.

Mama only had his best interests at heart when she'd introduce him to "a real sweet gal" she knew from the bank or had met at the grocery store. As did his brother, who'd talk him into going to the bar with him on Ladies' Night every once in a while. But, no woman out there could hold a candle to Denise, so Colt was not interested in trying to find one.

Hell. He wasn't just tired of looking, he eventually became fed up with the whole damned dating scene. Of women who were divorced a couple of times over, with a few kids, looking for someone to provide for them. Of young, high-maintenance gals who were interested in a sugar daddy, and the high-powered career women who wouldn't get off the cell phone long enough to have a real conversation. Of the ones from church who expected a ring and a wedding date after the first kiss. Of the girls he'd meet in bars who wanted nothing more than a one-night stand.

It wasn't as if he was a saint. Far from it. He'd slept with a few women over the years, mainly those he'd picked up at Ladies' Night. He was a man with needs and urges, after all. But he'd felt disgusted with himself the next morning, once the hangover had worn off. That wasn't who he was, or the kind of woman he wanted—even for the short run.

The muscle in Colt's jaw twitched when his thoughts took him back to that lady, Ann, he'd dated for several months. She'd been crazy for him, but there'd been no emotional ties on his part. Even when he'd known it was going nowhere, he'd continued to call her when his physical appetites had needed to be satisfied. After finally growing a conscience and breaking it off for good, she'd called him for days afterward, pleading to know what she'd done wrong, and he'd felt like a shit for having used her that way.

Life, he'd decided, was easier without a woman in it. His pickup was reliable. Work was a sure thing. Family he could count on. At forty years old, love the second time around . . . it didn't seem to be in the cards. And that was okay with him.

He pulled into his driveway and cut off the truck's motor, thinking about Shay Brennan again. She didn't seem to fit the mold of the women he'd met the past few years. There was something about her . . . something different.

Ah, hell. Maybe breaking his rule and having breakfast with her might not be such a bad thing after all.

FOUR

Shay walked into the Golden Spike at eight on the dot and spied Colt sitting at a table for two next to the window. As she approached, he stood and pulled out the chair for her.

"Good mornin'." His smile was dazzling, but she was determined not to allow his good-ol'-boy charm to get to her.

"Thank you," she said, as he scooted her in. "Good morning to you, too."

When he returned to his seat, he pointed out the mug of steaming coffee in front of her. "I ordered you a cup. I noticed you were drinking coffee yesterday at the closing."

"Thanks." She stirred a packet of sugar into the mug. "I admit I'm a coffee fanatic. I don't smoke or drink, so it's my one vice. Although I know caffeine's not good for you."

Chuckling, he said, "If that's your only weakness, I wouldn't be too concerned. You're as fit and as healthy looking as any I've seen."

The comment and his focused gaze were not lost on Shay, but she let both pass as the waitress appeared and took their orders. Blueberry pancakes and bacon for both. When the waitress left, Colt said, "You must have gotten back to sleep okay last night. You look refreshed and very nice this morning."

"Thank you." His gaze, though direct, was friendly, not lecherous.

"That blouse goes well with your auburn hair," he continued. "And it brings out the green flecks in your hazel eyes."

Shay took a sip of coffee and smiled, wondering if he was for real or if that was just his salesman personality shining through. Men didn't normally notice such things as whether the color of clothing set off a woman's hair. At least none of the men she'd known in her thirty-three years. Unless they were gay. She scrutinized him closely. Nah. This guy was definitely not gay.

It was a nice change to be given a compliment, especially since she'd gotten up early to figure out what outfit to wear and to wash and dry her hair so it shined. She didn't exactly know why it made a difference, but she'd wanted to make a better impression today than she had last night. After several changes of clothes, she'd finally decided on the emerald-colored blouse and jeans, which, she guessed, had been a good choice.

"You have a charming way about you, Mr. Morgan. I guess chivalry is not dead in the American West." Her gaze narrowed playfully.

"Ah, I've never thought of myself as charming. I'm just a guy who's honest to a fault. And remember, it's Colt. Not Mr. Morgan."

Handsome. Engaging. And polite. She glanced at the ring finger on his left hand. No wedding band. It made no difference to her, but why wasn't he taken?

"I'm not married," he said, grinning. "In case you wondered."

Her cheeks began to burn. Could he read her mind? Of course not. He'd followed her gaze to his hand. He was easygoing and had a sense of humor, too.

"I'm not married either," she said, lowering her gaze to the coffee cup, and then wondering why she'd offered that information.

"I know. I wouldn't have asked you on a date if you were."

The wall she'd been building around her heart for some time now flew up. "What do you mean, a date? I thought you had some paperwork to give me."

"Uh, that's right. I do." He slipped a thin envelope out of his pocket and handed it to her, then leaned back in his chair, looking sheepish, but eyes still twinkling like stars. "I suppose having breakfast together *could* be considered a date, by some," he said.

Their hot plates were delivered, briefly interrupting the conversation.

"I'm starving," Shay admitted, drenching the pancakes with syrup and stuffing a forkful into her mouth. She was glad for the distraction, because the banter on whether this was a date or not was not something she wanted to pursue.

Colt ate a strip of bacon and said, "I like a woman who isn't afraid to eat in front of a man. So many ladies eat like little birds, picking and nibbling and only ordering lettuce." He shook his head, as if he didn't understand it.

"I don't have that problem," Shay replied. "Life is too short to nibble and pick."

"That's a philosophy more ladies should adopt."

It didn't take either of them long to devour the food, after which they requested refills on their coffees.

"You're not from South Dakota," Colt said. It was a statement, not a question. He sipped his brew, obviously waiting for her to share something about herself.

Comfortable enough with him and finding no reason not to chat, she decided to give the abbreviated version of her life so far.

"No, I'm not. I grew up in the Midwest. My father was very wealthy—a self-made millionaire a couple of times over. He died about fourteen months ago. My mother passed away six months before him. I have no brothers or sisters, so everything—his entire fortune was left to me."

She gauged his reaction while silently wondering why the inheritance had been the first thing she'd mentioned. Since her father's death, she hadn't told anyone about that. It was weird, since being the daughter of affluent parents had caused her so many problems with men. Why had she opened up about that to this man? It seemed her mouth had a mind of its own.

"I'm sorry," he said. "Not that your father left you a fortune, but that he's passed on. And your mother, too."

She smiled, understanding his meaning and relieved that he hadn't even flinched when she'd mentioned the money. Had she unconsciously been testing him? If so, it was with good reason.

"Thank you. Anyway, after Dad died, I decided to quit my job, pack a couple of suitcases, and travel out west. I needed to get out of Illinois, and I've been fascinated with the west since I was a child. I was hoping the wide open skies, rugged mountains, and sun-soaked deserts would somehow help me come to terms with being an orphan."

Her gaze dropped to her lap for a moment. "That's how it felt at the time," she continued. "With both my parents gone and no siblings or extended family to lean on, I felt so alone. Being on the road this past year has given me time to grieve, but more importantly, I've also realized just how precious life is. I've learned not to take one moment of it for granted."

When her gaze reconnected with his, she saw compassion behind his eyes—and concurrence. Still, she internally questioned why she'd spilled so much to him so early. After what she'd been through with her last two relationships, where both men got close to her because they were in love with wealth, it was not like her to trust so easily. But something about Colt Morgan set her at ease. She decided not to worry about it, since this was nothing more than a business breakfast anyway.

"How did you end up here in Hill City?" he wanted to know.

"A gift-store clerk in Rapid City told me I had to visit Deadwood and check out the casinos. But I'm not into gambling. I prefer history and getting off the beaten path—taking the road less traveled, you might say. I skirted Deadwood and came to Hill City instead. I don't regret the decision."

"Me either," he replied, appearing more interested as they conversed. "Then you saw the *For Sale* sign in the window of the Buckhorn and . . ."

"The rest you know." She finished the last of her coffee. "It was a good deal. I had the money, and I was drawn to the saloon. It might sound strange, but from the moment I saw it, I felt like I belonged there. Besides, this seems like a good town in which to put down some roots. I don't plan on returning to Illinois. There's nothing back there for me anymore."

"What are you going to do with the place?"

"It's a historical landmark, so it must remain what it is—an Old West saloon. I wouldn't want to change that about it, but I might redecorate the upstairs bedrooms and eventually open as a bed and breakfast. Or I might just live there. There's a bathroom at the end of the hall on the second floor, and someone, at some time, turned a small room downstairs into a kitchen with the basic necessities, so it's perfectly livable the way it is. This has all happened so fast, I haven't had time to make plans, to be honest."

When the waitress brought the check, Colt snatched it and pulled out his wallet to leave a tip on the table. He rose and pulled out Shay's chair.

His lips nearly grazed her neck when he leaned in and whispered, "I hope you don't change the Buckhorn too much. The spirits might not like it."

Shay's jaw went slack. She felt the pulse in her neck begin to throb. "What made you say—?"

"The sun's shining," he broke in. "Wait for me outside. I'll pay the bill and then we can take a walk. I have something to tell you that you may find interesting."

FIVE

When Colt stepped outside the restaurant, Shay whirled.

"What did you mean when you said the spirits might not like it?"

He'd meant to capture her attention. Mission accomplished. "Let's walk," he said, moving in the direction of the saloon.

Standing so near to her got his heart racing like a thorough-bred horse. Though not intentionally, the moment his eyes had opened this morning, she had been on his mind.

Last night when he'd gone to check on her, Shay had been just another client he was helping, albeit a beautiful, intriguing client. But, this morning, when he was putting his boots on, he'd realized something had changed. Odd as it seemed, he'd felt a strong connection to her, as if an invisible string tied them together. And he'd been eager to see her again.

He was a sensible man, and love had not been in his vocabulary or on his radar for many years. But this feeling nagged at him—the feeling that they'd been destined to meet. He'd never experienced anything like it before, not even when he'd met Denise. The sensation made him feel more alive than he'd felt in years. But then, wasn't sexual attraction supposed to make a man feel alive? Maybe that's all it was. Either way, he'd wanted to see her and find out.

"What do you have to tell me?" she asked, keeping up with his long-legged strides. They passed by a few of the gift shops and tourist traps that comprised the historic Main Street.

Not wanting to frighten her off so soon by thinking he was a nut, he carefully considered how to frame his words. Clearly, he hadn't thought this through before opening his big mouth.

"Colt?"

A sideways glance showed him she was getting antsy. Shay's mouth was pursed and her pretty hazel eyes were enlarged.

"Are you going to tell me what you meant back there?"

"Yep." He kept walking.

Sighing, she bunched her shoulders and spread her hands out, palms up. "When? At the turn of the century?"

It didn't take long to walk the block to the Buckhorn. They stopped in front. "Can we go inside?" he asked, facing her.

"Okay. Sure." Shay dug the key out of her purse, stuck it in the lock and pushed the door open, stepping in first. As soon as Colt entered, an icy chill slithered across his neck and crept down his back—same as the first and last times he'd been in here.

Laying her purse on a game table, Shay pulled out two chairs and offered him a seat. "Now that we're here, will you please tell me what's going on, Colt?"

They sat and he peered around the large room that he'd been told had barely changed since it was built in 1885. A large gilded mirror hung on one wall. An upright piano sat against a back wall. Brass foot rails ran the length of the bar with a row of spittoons spaced along the floor. No doubt the gambling tables, like the one they were sitting at, had seen many hands of poker dealt out through the years.

"Let me ask you a question, Shay," he began. "Didn't you wonder why you were able to close on this deal so quickly and at such a good price? Everything in here is original. No rodent or insect infestations. It's a good, solid building. And it's a piece of Hill City history. The asking price should have been much higher."

She considered the question. "It did cross my mind to ask, but, in the end, the answer wouldn't have mattered. The saloon spoke to me. I knew I had to own it. I was glad it happened so fast, and I was pleased with the price."

When he remained mute, she said, "How did you come to be the listing agent for it? Do you know the former owner?" He nodded, and she prodded further. "I did wonder why I hadn't met the owner and that he didn't attend the closing."

Colt met her inquisitive gaze. "He's an old man of eighty-five. His name is Frank Averill, and he's sick. He and my grandfather were best friends. That's how I got the listing. Frank's grandfather, Dean Averill, built the Buckhorn in eighteen eighty-five at a time when tin mining dominated the area. Hill City flourished, as did this saloon."

Shay's soft-looking lips curved into a smile and she seemed to relax, probably glad for the knowledge.

"That's interesting. I'd planned on looking into the history of the building. So, it's been in Mr. Averill's family all these years?"

"Yep. Frank's father kept it up as a saloon while Frank was growing up. When the elder Averill died, Frank took over for a few years before going into the hardware business."

Shay's expression grew serious again. "That's well and fine, but you still haven't told me what you meant back at the diner. You mentioned something about spirits."

Their gazes latched. Colt folded his hands in front of him. "It's been rumored, ever since anyone can remember, that this saloon is haunted. In fact, I think that's the real reason Frank closed down the place. I can remember my granddaddy telling me of Frank's claims that there are several entities hanging around here."

She didn't say anything, but her pupils grew large, and he knew he'd struck a nerve.

"I've known Frank Averill my entire life," he went on. "He

was always a tough guy, not easily intimidated and certainly not afraid of anything or anyone. In fact, he and Granddaddy told me plenty of stories about the fistfights they would get into and the trouble they caused. But Frank must have believed there is something here, and I get the impression he had some bad experiences when he ran the place."

"Go on."

"I didn't mention it last night when I came over, but I'd been having a dream when that guy called and woke me up. I dreamt that someone was being strangled, upstairs in your bedroom."

Shay's hand flew to her mouth and she gasped.

"I don't mean to scare you. When that anonymous caller told me water was running under your front door, it was such an odd coincidence. I knew you were alone in here. I'm not the kind of man who scares easily either, but that dream was so real. I wanted to make sure you were okay."

"You said upstairs in my bedroom," Shay said quietly.

His gaze drifted to the staircase. "Yes. I saw the bedroom clearly in my dream. I recognized it from when I toured the building before I listed it. Iron bed. Green-and-pink floral wallpaper. An antique bureau in the corner. A brick fireplace on one wall with an oak mantel. Tall windows overlooking the street."

"Yes," she exclaimed. "That's my room. I was sleeping there last night. But how did you know?"

"It was just a feeling."

He didn't want to tell her he'd *known* she'd been sleeping in that particular room. How he'd known, he had no clue. Just that somehow, in his soul, he'd *felt* her there.

"Do you think I'm as crazy as a bedbug?" He chuckled nervously.

"No. Not at all."

He saw her bottom lip quivering. Seemed her mind was working. Sensing she was holding back some news of her own, Colt asked, "Do you have something you want to share with me?"

She nodded and blurted, "Yes. I think I saw one of those spirits last night, right before you stopped by."

He leaned forward, propped on his elbows. "Tell me."

Inhaling deeply, Shay explained what she thought she'd seen, including black-and-blue bruising around the woman's neck. When she finished, she said, "What's happening, Colt? Do you believe it's a coincidence?"

"No. I don't know how to explain it, but there has to be something more to this than chance. I'm a practical man—a South Dakotan cowboy born and bred. I heard the stories about ghosts haunting this town as I was growing up. To be honest, I've never believed in ghosts and I still don't. But I've never had that kind of dream before either."

Shay's hypnotic eyes delved into his, causing him to grow hard and weak at the same time.

"So, you're saying you do believe I saw a ghost?" she asked, seeming unsure.

He didn't know her from Adam, and she could be as nutty as a fruitcake, but he didn't think so. Something hinted she was telling the truth, at least about what she *thought* she'd seen.

Although he knew ghosts did not exist, what reason would she have for lying?

Colt reached out and placed his hand over hers. "I believe, Shay, what we've got here is some kind of a haunted twist of fate."

Six

As Shay explored the basement later that afternoon, digging through boxes and crates to see what kinds of old treasures she could find, she thought about Colt and their exchange earlier that morning. For some reason, they'd trusted each other with confidentialities that would have normally had one or the other calling the sheriff—or someone with a straitjacket. She wondered why that was.

Recalling his words, *a haunted twist of fate,* gave her the willies. Was it possible that a spirit from beyond had somehow brought the two of them together? He'd suggested that, in a roundabout way. She didn't know him from a hole in the wall. He could be as mad as a hatter.

Despite her reservations about getting involved with anyone, she did like him. He seemed to like her, too. Before they'd parted, he'd asked her out tonight—to a chuck wagon supper and cowboy music show, of all places. If she was going to be a local, he'd teased, there was no time like the present to start acting like one. And he'd thought she'd enjoy meeting some people since she was new in town. His kindness had touched her. And it was true. She'd been feeling lonely since hitting the road a year ago and would be glad to meet some friendly people from the place she now called home.

One year ago, she never would have imagined ending up in a small town in South Dakota, living in a historic saloon, coming face-to-face with an apparition (if that's what she'd been) and getting to know a real cowboy.

Shay had no idea what to think about ghosts and Colt's dream. What was even more disconcerting than him dreaming someone was being strangled in her bedroom was that she'd felt hands on her neck for those few seconds while in the presence of the blonde woman. And she'd felt they'd been her hands wrapped around her throat.

What did any of it mean? Why was Colt even involved? Was it because he was a friend of the former owner? It was a mystery, but one that wouldn't be solved today.

She went back to her exploration.

Opening the lid of a cardboard box, Shay discovered it was full of dusty bottles. Carefully removing them one by one, she held each up to the single bulb hanging from the ceiling, which didn't offer much light. Most were beer bottles, but there were a few labeled *Sarsaparilla.* Other amber-tinted bottles carried peeling whiskey labels. Deciding they'd look good upstairs as decor on the shelves behind the bar, she began to wipe them down with a rag.

Touching the bottles carried her back in time. What kind of men had bellied up to the Buckhorn's bar and slapped down their coins, requesting a beer or a whiskey? Miners and gamblers? Lawmen and gunfighters? Had there been killers amongst the patrons of the saloon during its heyday? Shay had no doubt. Every territory in the west had been wild in the 1800s, with the Black Hills being one of the wildest. Everyone from Bill Hickok to Calamity Jane had frequented the saloons in Deadwood. They'd probably spent time in Hill City during their travels as well.

Thinking about the men who had drunk their libations here piqued her curiosity about the women of that time period. Had saloon girls worked at the Buckhorn, singing, dancing with the patrons, and flirting with them, coaxing them into buying more drinks? Could the bedrooms upstairs have been used for prostitution? The possible scenarios got her blood to pumping. She'd have to do some research.

Thinking about doing research brought the pretty face of the blonde to mind again. Had she been a saloon girl? Or had she sold her body to survive? She'd looked so young and innocent. The only thing Shay knew was that she'd reached out, begging for help.

That was the strange thing she couldn't stop thinking about. What kind of assistance did the woman need? How did one go about helping a dead person, anyway? Maybe she was stuck in limbo waiting to go into the light. There were a lot of TV programs showing mediums doing this sort of thing—guiding ghosts into the light. Shay had never been interested in those shows before. Now she wished she'd watched a few of them so she'd know what to do.

She was gently placing the polished bottles back inside the box when she heard footsteps above her. It sounded like someone was running across the floor upstairs. Cocking her head, she jumped when a peal of laughter rang out from the top of the stairs.

"Who's there?" she called.

Carefully lowering the last bottle into the box, she began advancing up the creaky basement steps and had the weirdest sensation that someone was watching her. The hairs on her arm stood on end.

Twirling, she lost her hold on the rickety handrail and stumbled, but was able to catch herself before falling.

"That was a close one," she said aloud, while placing a palm over her thumping heart.

Feminine giggles startled her. It was as if the giggling bounced off the walls from all directions, like surround sound. Her head jerked up just as the door at the top of the stairs slammed shut.

"Colt?" she called as she crept the rest of the way up the steps. Her fingers clutched the doorknob and she tried to rattle it, but it was as if the door was frozen shut. "Someone please let me out," she hollered, shaking the knob. It didn't budge. Perspiration beaded her forehead as she shook it several more times.

More footsteps plodded in front of the door on the other side and stopped. A shadow moved under the crack in the door. Shay held her breath and placed her ear against the wood. Again, it was as if eyes were boring into her back, but she was afraid to turn around. Strongly sensing a male presence close by, she wrinkled her nose, smelling something rank—like a dead animal.

"This isn't funny," she screamed, while banging on the door with the palm of her hand.

The vein in her neck pulsed. More rattling of the knob did nothing. She removed her hand and listened again. The laughter faded into nothingness. The footsteps padded away. An eerie silence filled the space around her.

When a hand suddenly yanked her hair, Shay shrieked and instinctively grabbed for the knob again and pulled hard. This time the door sprang open and she fell through it onto the floor. Flipping onto her back, she kicked the door shut with her foot.

Stumbling to her feet, she locked the door, planted her back against it, took a couple of deep breaths, and heard her cell phone ringing. She'd left her purse upstairs in the bedroom. With rubbery legs that shook like gelatin, she took the stairs two at a time and answered her phone on the fifth ring.

"Hello." With ragged breathing and her heart beating erratically, Shay wilted onto the bed.

"Hey. Sounds like you've been running. What's wrong?"

Though scared out of her wits, she smiled, picturing Colt's

open face. When she'd given him her cell phone number this morning, she hadn't expected a call so soon. But she sure was glad to hear his voice.

"You won't believe what just happened to me," she exclaimed.

"What?"

"Your grandfather's friend, Frank . . . he's so right. There is definitely more than one spirit in this saloon." Shay proceeded to tell Colt what had just happened. "There's a very angry ghost in the basement," she said, "and he just scared the crap out of me."

"Do you want me to run over? I can, if you don't want to be alone."

A knight in shining armor coming to her rescue was a sweet gesture, but she just wasn't that kind of woman. She'd been independent for a long time and had learned men, with the exception of her dad, were not to be counted on. Unfortunately, she'd trusted and been let down too many times. She'd gotten used to handling life on her own.

"Hopefully that horrible thing will stay in the basement," she said, finally catching her breath and remembering the horrid smell. "I locked the door and I don't plan on returning any time soon."

After asking Colt to hold, she listened and heard no more noises downstairs, and informed him that all was quiet again.

"I'm okay now," she answered in truth, although the presence in the basement *had* frightened her. "I think these ghosts are testing the waters—playing with me. I guess it's been a long time since a living person has spent any time here. They probably feel I'm invading their space."

Colt chuckled. "Maybe." She could imagine him shaking his head, but she hoped he'd be shaking it because he admired her courage and not because he thought her foolish or making things up. Oh, well. It didn't matter what he thought of her anyway.

"I'm looking forward to this evening," she said honestly, wanting to change the subject. She placed a hand over her chest and felt her heart rate had completely returned to normal.

"Me, too. I'll pick you up at five. In the meantime, if you need anything at all, call me. I mean that. I'm here at your service."

"All right."

"You sure you'll be okay this afternoon?"

"Yes, but thanks for being on the other end of the phone at the right time. See you tonight."

She flipped her phone shut and decided to take a hot bath. As outdated as the bathroom was, she was simply happy to have one that functioned. The room was small and the old-fashioned claw-foot tub had been stained from years of nonuse. But she'd cleaned it with bleach first thing yesterday and it looked new again. A bath would settle her raw nerves.

Strolling out of the bedroom to go draw the water, Shay heard a rustling sound behind her. She paused and peeked back around the door into the room. The curtain on the window waved like a flag, despite there being no breeze.

SEVEN

When Colt knocked on the door at five o'clock sharp, Shay was not surprised. She'd guessed he'd be on time. It was refreshing to meet a man who was punctual—not that she was keeping a list of things she liked about him.

Her breath hitched when she opened the door. Dressed in black Levi's, a black-and-white-plaid shirt, cowboy boots and a black Stetson, he looked every bit the essence of western masculinity. When he smiled and cocked his hat with the tip of his finger in greeting, she literally thought she might swoon.

Feeling as nervous as a girl about to go on her first date, she felt her face heat when his gaze slid up and down her body, taking in every inch of her and apparently enjoying what he saw.

Winking, he said, "You look beautiful, Shay."

Not knowing what one wore to a chuck wagon supper, she'd chosen a denim skirt, a white fitted T-shirt, and a pair of cowboy boots she'd purchased at the boot shop down the street after her bath. She was also wearing a western belt with a silver buckle and rhinestones, and dangling earrings. She didn't want to stand out as the outsider she knew she was and hoped this outfit was appropriate, and not over the top.

"Thank you. Do you think people will believe I'm a local?" she asked.

"Yep. The only thing missing is a cowboy hat. We'll take care of that later."

We? She wondered at his turn of phrase as she locked up.

"Any more unusual occurrences after I called this afternoon?" he asked.

"No. I guess the ghosts wore themselves out earlier."

He escorted her to his pickup truck and opened the door for her. Nice. She noticed the name of his business printed on the side—*Morgan Realty.*

"How long have you sold real estate?" she asked once she'd gotten situated and he'd climbed into the driver's seat and backed away from the curb. She was hoping to guess his age without coming straight out and asking him. She believed he was older than she was, but she wasn't sure how much older.

"About ten years."

"And before that?"

"I've been involved in my family's ranching business since I was a kid." He kept his gaze focused on the road as he talked and drove. "I graduated college with a business management degree, concentrating on agriculture, and was a labor agency manager for a couple of years. Then my folks lost their ranch manager, so I did that for about seven years before deciding to get into real estate."

"Hmmm." She quickly did the math.

He slid a sly grin at her. "I turned forty this year, in case you were wondering."

There he goes again, reading my mind. "Are you sure you're not psychic, Colt? I was putting the numbers together."

He laughed. "If I was psychic, I wouldn't be curious about your age, Shay."

She smiled. "You know it's not polite to ask a woman how old she is."

"Yes, ma'am. That's why you have to throw me a bone."

"I'm thirty-three."

"And never been married?"

She shook her head, not wanting to get into all that. "No. I came close, but that was a long time ago. What about you?"

Colt stopped at the light then made a right turn out of town, and before long, they were traveling down a gravel road.

He hadn't answered her question, and she was beginning to think he wasn't planning on replying when he finally said, "I was married once. She passed away."

Shay's heart dropped. "Oh, Colt. I'm sorry for your loss."

"Thank you. I appreciate that," he said, glancing her way. "It was a long time ago, too."

She wondered why he hadn't remarried, but thought she'd already pried enough. She hoped she'd get to know more about him as the night went on. He was an interesting man. Face close to the glass window, she peered out at the magnificent Black Hills, for which the area got its name, and totally switched the topic.

"The hills take my breath away, Colt. It feels like we're in another land, or time. I never believed they were really so black until I saw them for myself. This area is so unique and sort of mysterious. You're lucky to have grown up here."

"Yes, I guess I am. I've been around a bit, and this is as good a place as any to live."

Turning off the gravel road, he drove under a wooden entrance with a sign reading *Double M Ranch,* and she sat up straighter, gazing at the pastures on both sides of the road and the buildings ahead.

Colt parked at a hitching rail in a gravel parking lot that was full of cars and shut off the motor. "We're here. I hope you're hungry. You ever try buffalo meat before?"

"No!" Her mouth gaped. "That's what they serve here?"

"That, along with pulled pork sandwiches, seasoned potatoes, cowboy beans, biscuits, applesauce, fresh lemonade and homemade ice cream. Do you think you have room for all that?"

Shay patted her stomach. "I know so. I'm not one of those

little birds. Remember? Besides, I skipped lunch today."

"Now I see how you stay so thin," he said, jumping out and slamming his door. "You shouldn't skip lunch." He came around and opened hers and took her hand to assist her out.

"Thanks." She noticed his gaze landed squarely on her legs as she smoothed down her skirt, and she felt her cheeks flame. "This is a neat place," she said, glancing around and taken with the looks of the ranch.

Guests were strolling along wooden sidewalks of what was built to resemble an Old West town. Feeling like they'd stepped back into another time period, her gaze shifted from building to building. She noted a gift shop, a bank, a candy store, a blacksmith's shop, a schoolhouse, a small chapel, and several other authentic looking western storefronts lined up side by side. There was even a stage stop with a stagecoach parked in front of it. Nearby in a corral, miniature goats, miniature horses, and miniature donkeys were being petted and manhandled by enthusiastic children. There was also a playground full of slides, swings and bridges that dozens of kids were climbing on.

"Nice, isn't it?" Colt guided her toward a huge red barn where, she assumed, supper and the music show took place.

"This is not at all what I expected," she admitted, as they stepped inside and she gazed about.

"What did you expect?"

"I have no idea. But this looks really fun."

The barn was huge and packed with people laughing and chattering as silverware clattered. The delicious smells wafting through the air caused Shay's stomach to grumble.

Tables covered in red-and-white-checked tablecloths were lined up family style below a big stage, with long benches as seats. Stuffed heads of game and deer antlers decorated the walls, and hay bales were scattered around.

They approached a podium, where the hostess, an older, attractive woman wearing a cowboy hat, boots, and fringed leather vest and skirt greeted them with a huge smile.

"Hello, sweetheart," she said, grabbing Colt around the shoulders and leaving a big red lipstick stain on his smooth cheek.

Shay threw him a wide-eyed look. Sheepishly, he made the introductions as he pulled a hankie from his back pocket and swiped his cheek. "Shay, I'd like you to meet . . . my mama, Hannah Morgan. Mama, this is Shay Brennan. She's the lady who just bought the Buckhorn Saloon."

"Pleased to meet you, honey," Hannah said, smashing Shay to her expansive bosom.

"Your mother?" Shay's mouth opened and closed like a goldfish's as Hannah set her back. Then she remembered the sign they'd driven under. "The Double M," she mused, pointing an accusatory finger at Colt. "Would that happen to stand for Morgan and Morgan?"

"It would," Hannah said with pride. "I'm one Morgan, and Colt's daddy is the other. I'm the brains of the operation, and Chet's the brawn."

Laughing, Shay rolled her eyes playfully at Colt. "You ambushed me. This is your family's business you told me about."

He nodded and blushed, which she found endearing.

"Aren't you a pretty thing?" Hannah said, sliding her gaze up and down. "She sure is a pretty thing, Colt."

"Yes, Mama. I completely agree."

Feeling like a doll on display, Shay felt herself warming again as Colt joined his mother with his own intense gaze.

"Come this way," Hannah said, grabbing Shay's hand and leading them to one of the tables in front, closest to the stage. "I'm giving you two the best seats in the house. That's one of the benefits of being related to the owners."

Colt placed his fingers at the small of Shay's back and

whispered in her ear, "I bet you've never met a man's folks on the first date before."

A tingle raced from the spot where he touched her out to every nerve ending in her body. "This is our second date," she reminded him before thinking. "Breakfast was the first, you said."

"That's right." He grinned. "In that case, it was about time you met my mama."

EIGHT

After supper, the Double M Cowboy Band took to the stage and performed a rousing hour of current country songs, authentic cowboy music, and comedy. Shay recognized a couple of the old-time tunes as ones made famous by Roy Rogers.

One corner of the barn was designated as the dance floor, and lots of couples, as well as children, took to the floor as the band played both fast tunes and ballads.

When one slow song started up, Hannah magically appeared and nudged Shay and Colt onto the dance floor and then stood by, watching them with a smile plastered on her face.

"I think Mama likes you," Colt said, squeezing Shay tight.

"I like her, too."

Dancing in his arms sent a river of shivers cascading down her spine. He held her in the traditional way, with one hand at the small of her back and his other arm stretched out, clasping her hand in his. He was a good dancer. They didn't speak anymore while the music played; just swayed in rhythm, bodies pressed together. She hadn't expected to feel such a rush of emotion or any kind of sexual stirring when she agreed to come with him tonight—or when they took to the floor. However, as her loins began to ache, and her body trembled with longing, she became aware of what a powerful aphrodisiac music was.

She hated for the song to end. When it did, Colt walked her back to their seats and said, "Thank you for the dance, ma'am. I enjoyed it very much." Even the way he called her "ma'am" in that smooth drawl involuntarily sent her senses reeling. Northern men had nothing over a western gentleman.

As if the entire evening hadn't already taken her by surprise, she received yet another shock when the MC of the show called Colt up to the stage minutes later.

When she tossed Colt a questioning look, he simply grinned and strode up the steps onto the stage and picked up an acoustic guitar that was propped against a speaker.

As he straddled a wooden stool and adjusted a microphone stand, the MC, a handsome man with silver hair looking to be in his sixties, clapped Colt on the back.

"Performing our finale tonight for you folks," he announced to the crowd, "is my eldest son, Colt Morgan, singing that pretty little song by King George, 'Blue Clear Sky,' accompanied by the Double M Cowboy Band. Come on now. Let's hear it for Colt and the boys."

As applause thundered in her ears, Shay smiled and shook her head in amazement. Colt played guitar and was a singer? The evening couldn't have gotten any more perfect. *And* he was singing a George Strait song? The coincidences were beginning to pile up like pancakes.

The room hushed when the band began. Colt stared directly into her eyes, and her heart melted as the lyrics took on a beautiful meaning with him singing them to her. His voice was as smooth as silk, and his gaze was powerful and passionate. It seemed they were the only two people in the room. Not once did his eyes waver from hers during the entire song. Shay's heart pounded so hard, she thought for sure he'd be able see it beating through her shirt, even from up on stage.

When the performance ended, she joined the other guests in a standing ovation and he took off his cowboy hat and waved it in the air as thanks.

"Thank you for joining us tonight," Colt's father hollered

into the mike, as the band began playing its swan song. "We sure enjoyed having you at the Double M. Come back and see us again real soon. Good night!"

The crowd around her began dispersing, but Shay barely noticed. Her eyes were only for Colt, who shook hands with his dad then strolled off the stage and sidled up next to her. Flashing a boyishly shy smile, he waited for her to speak first.

"That was a bombshell I didn't expect," she said, still fluttering with emotion. "That song was wonderful. Do you sing with the band often?"

"Not as often as I used to. I felt inspired tonight."

His deep gaze was evidence that she'd been his inspiration. After only two short days, she knew it would be easy to fall for this charming man. But she wouldn't let it happen. This had been a fun night, but that's all it could be. She'd been burned before. There was no way she was going to touch a hot stove again.

"Are you going to introduce us to your friend, Colt?" a man said, breaking in. He had the same build and sandy hair color as Colt, and Shay recognized him as the band's drummer. Colt's father also sneaked up, appearing at his side.

"Shay, this is my kid brother, Brady, and"—he looked over his shoulder—"my dad, Chet. Dad. Brady. I'd like you to meet Shay Brennan."

Both men greeted her with grins as mischievous as Colt's and pumped her hand with vigor, one after the other.

"That was a terrific show," she told them, "and the food was out of this world. I had no idea this was your family business when I accepted Colt's invitation to dinner, or supper, as you call it out here."

Chet laughed. "He didn't tell you this was our ranch?"

"No." She nudged Colt's shoulder. "I didn't know he could sing or play the guitar either."

"Colt's one of those guys that don't say much," Brady offered, winking. "It takes him a while to warm up to people."

"Is that so?" She met Colt's steady gaze. "He's done a pretty good job getting to know me so far."

Brady's eyebrow arched. "Then you must be easy to get along with. How long have you two known each other?"

"Two days," Shay answered.

The expressions on both men's faces showed their obvious astonishment. Brady elbowed Colt in the ribs and said, "Fast work, brother."

"What are we discussing over here?" Hannah swooped in to interrupt the joshing and gave Colt and Brady each a kiss on the cheek. "Nice singing, Colt. Good drumming, Brady."

"What about me, Hannah banana?" Chet gave her his whiskered cheek and she pecked it like a chicken pecked the ground.

"Good show, sweetie. As usual. And please don't call me Hannah banana in front of Colt's friend." She gave his arm a spirited smack. "She'll think we're silly children, as opposed to the sophisticated hillbillies we really are."

That was the last thing Shay was thinking. She was enamored by the genuine love and devotion that radiated between Colt and his family. It made her long for her own loving parents and the camaraderie of a family she no longer had.

"I think it's a sweet nickname," she said.

"See? She thinks it's sweet," Chet teased.

They all laughed. "You two want to come over to the house for some coffee?" Hannah asked.

Colt answered without asking Shay, but she didn't mind. As much as she would have enjoyed getting to know his family, there was no point in pretending this was something it wasn't—or that it was bound for something more. Tonight had simply been a casual date.

"Thanks for the invite, Mama," Colt replied, placing his hand at Shay's waist. "But I think we'll pass this time."

Hannah gave him a knowing nod and a wink. Shay felt the urge to tell her not to get her hopes up, so she wouldn't be let down when she discovered they weren't dating. But, that was up to Colt.

"Okay, you kids run on then. It was a real pleasure to meet you, Shay. I hope to see you again soon." She took her hands and squeezed.

"Thank you, Mrs. Morgan. Mr. Morgan, Brady. I've enjoyed meeting all of you, and I had so much fun tonight. You have a great setup here."

She and Colt said their good-byes and stepped outside. The temperature had dropped. "It's cool," she said, shivering.

"Will this help?" He wrapped an arm around her shoulders and they walked to his pickup that way. It had been a long time since she'd been touched by a man, or felt a strong arm around her. It felt good.

She glanced at his profile. She'd have to stay firm in her convictions if she was to escape Colt's charismatic ways.

Once she was in the truck and he'd shut the door behind her, he got into the driver's seat and said, "Let me get this thing started up and I'll turn on the heat."

You already have, she thought, wishing he weren't so damned sexy.

NINE

The moon was floating high in the sky when they returned to the Buckhorn. Colt held the passenger door open and offered Shay a hand. He couldn't help but admire her shapely legs once more as she swung them out of the truck.

It was hard to comprehend, and completely unexpected, but the woman had done something to him. There hadn't been this spark with anyone, this tug on his heart—not since Denise. What was even funnier than feeling this way so fast was that he believed Denise would have liked Shay.

In fact, he believed Denise had been telepathically communicating with him all day. He never would have admitted such a ridiculous thing to anyone, but he swore he'd heard her voice speaking to him clearly in his head. It had been as if she'd been sitting next to him, urging him to go for it—to pursue Shay. That kind of thing had never happened to him before. He'd tried to tell himself he was imagining it, but her words had echoed in his mind all day that she didn't want him to grow old alone.

If anyone had asked him, Colt would have said love didn't happen so fast. Even with Denise, it had taken over a year for him to tell her he loved her. But, from the first moment he touched Shay, he physically desired her. Did that make it love? More likely the churning he felt in his gut and the fire that burned in his loins was lust, or infatuation. When he touched her, electricity raced through his body, lighting up his insides like a Christmas tree. He wanted to kiss her and hold her, but that didn't mean he was falling in love. Love was a tricky business. Business he didn't need to get mixed up in. That fact aside, he was a man, with a man's needs. Sex was a different animal from love.

The two of them stood next to the truck with her back pressed against the passenger door. She fumbled with the latch on her purse then fished out her keys. "Found them," she said, jingling them.

When her chin lifted and she peered up at him, the moonlight danced on her face. Her eyes sparkled and her skin shimmered, like an angel. He had the strongest yearning to cup her cheek in his palm and slide his fingers under her hair and over her slender neck. The craving for her was nearly uncontrollable.

"What would you say to inviting me in for a nightcap?" he asked quietly.

The question seemed to have taken her off guard. "I . . . I don't have a living room, or even a comfortable place to sit and talk," she said, apologizing, "but I guess you could come inside, if you don't mind sitting at the bar."

Not at all ready to say good night yet, he nodded and slipped his hand into hers, and they stepped onto the sidewalk. His mouth went dry as sawdust, and his groin swelled with anticipation, but another peculiar sensation suddenly swept over him.

Feeling eyes upon him, he looked up and glimpsed what he thought was someone standing in the second-floor window. Was it a woman? Wearing her underwear or a nightgown? Her penetrating gaze slowly shifted from the street to Colt. But the moment their lines of vision connected, she disappeared in front of his eyes—and he marveled at whether he'd only imagined her.

"Shay, is that your bedroom window?" he asked, pointing.

"Yes. Why?"

"I think I just saw . . ."

"What?" Her gaze flew to the window. "Did you see the woman I told you about?"

He shook his head, not wanting to admit it. "Maybe. I don't know. It was probably the curtain moving in the breeze, and the light from the street lamp reflecting in the glass."

Shay squeezed his hand and expelled a long breath. "You can tell me the truth. If she'd show herself to you, you'd know I'm not crazy."

"I don't think you're crazy," he said, while deep down, he was thinking that verdict was still out with the jury. He took the keys from her hand and felt his erection wither. "Let's go inside and we'll talk about what you think is happening here."

After Colt unlocked the front door, Shay flicked the inside switch and the saloon was bathed in light. "At least it's bright in here," he said, closing the door behind them. "Ghosts do their haunting in the dark, right?" His attempt at joking fell flat, because Shay acted as if she hadn't heard.

"Would you like some coffee?" she said, seeming distracted. "I can put a pot on."

"Don't make it special for me. I'm strictly a morning coffee drinker."

"I don't need it this time of night either," she said, glancing around the room. Rooted to her spot, she suddenly seemed edgy—and understandably so. The hair had stood up on the back of his neck the moment they'd walked in.

"We're not alone in here," he stated.

"So, it's not just me. You sense them, too?"

Colt angled his head and listened to the murmuring that sounded like distant thunder. "Yeah. Feels like this room is crowded with people. I can almost feel them moving around us." He sniffed the air. "Do you smell that?"

Snuggling against his shoulder, Shay replied, "Cigar smoke. I smelled it yesterday, too."

They stood as still as statues. He heard what sounded like poker chips clinking together on the game tables. When the piano in the back suddenly plinked out a few notes, his spine grew rigid and sweat started trickling down his back. What was going on here?

Shay wedged herself into his chest. As he held her secure in his arms, he could feel her heart beating in rhythm against his. The staccato rasps of their breathing seemed to be the only living noises in the room.

There was no such thing as ghosts, Colt reminded himself. *There has to be an explanation for the smells, the sounds, the feeling . . .*

Shay suddenly grew stiff in his embrace and whispered, "Do you sense him?"

Colt nodded. As much as he didn't want to believe, he was sure a powerful presence had entered the room. One that was asserting itself in a formidable manner. What felt like a dense blanket of fog surrounded them, bringing with it the stench of something rotten like seaweed or spoilt food. Pressure on his chest made Colt suck in a sharp intake of air. He was acutely aware that whatever was in the room with them was of a sinister nature.

"He's pure evil," Shay whispered, her voice barely audible.

Colt grasped at his throat. Before he had time to reply or react, his throat began to close and tighten, as if someone was stuffing a rag into his windpipe. That was impossible. Only Shay was in the room. Her hands were at her sides.

"Colt! What's wrong?" She hit him on the back a couple of times and screamed into the air, "Stop it! Leave him alone!"

The weight of the invisible hands immediately lifted and his throat reopened. Whatever Colt thought he'd felt in the room disappeared in an instant, along with the awful smell.

"Are you okay?" Shay's eyes were bulging with terror, and her hands clutched at his arms in a death grip.

"I'm fine," he answered, rubbing his throat gingerly and gazing around. "Who were you calling out to just now?"

"The ghost. I wanted him to stop hurting you. I guess it worked."

"Guess so." Colt had no idea what he'd experienced, but there had to be some logical explanation. There was no such thing as ghosts. He stared at Shay, trying to figure it out, as her pretty hazel eyes reflected back at him.

"That's one ghost with anger management issues," she said, apparently trying to lighten the mood. "He's definitely upset about something. Maybe he doesn't like that I've moved in. Tomorrow I'm going to start researching the history of this saloon. I want to know who the woman upstairs is, and who this scary guy is, and whether they have some connection."

Colt nodded, still in disbelief about what seemed to have happened. He'd felt hands on his neck. He'd smelled cigar smoke and heard poker chips clinking. He'd heard the piano play on its own, and he'd felt something ominous around them. What it all meant was anyone's guess.

"I don't think you should stay here alone tonight. It's not safe. That goon might hurt you." As soon as the words left his mouth, he wished he could reel them back in. What was he saying? That he believed a ghost had throttled him and might do the same to her? It wasn't possible. Saying things like that would only serve to keep her illusions alive.

"All he did was pull at my hair in the basement today."

She nibbled her bottom lip, giving Colt the distinct feeling she was holding something back. "What is it?" he asked.

"The night you had the dream about someone being strangled in my room . . ."

"Yes?"

"It really happened to me. Someone choked me, exactly like you were choked just now. But I'm sure the one who did this to you is different from the one who did it to me. That one was a female. This one's aura definitely feels masculine."

Aura? Colt said nothing. What *could* he say? He didn't believe in auras or psychics or a bunch of mumbo jumbo about ghosts. Still, he'd had that creepy dream, and weird things were happening. They were discussing dead people as if they were talking about Sunday dinner. Were they both nuts?

All he'd wanted to do was come inside and steal a kiss or two. This evening wasn't turning out the way he'd hoped.

"Are you okay?" she asked.

"I'm fine." He noticed her gaze took on a faraway look. "What about you?"

"Colt, this is my home now," she said. "Last year I ran away when Dad died because the pain was too great. I felt so alone. I've had some setbacks in the last few years, and I've let fear rule my life. I have to be in control here. This is *my* home, not *theirs.*"

Turning in a full circle, she called into the air, "You hear that, whoever you are? You don't belong here anymore. You're not going to frighten me, and you're not about to run me out! So leave or get used to it, because I'm your new roommate!"

Colt spun Shay toward him and grinned. He didn't know much about her, but he liked what he saw so far. He liked her spunk, and she was very easy on the eyes. When he dipped his fingers under her hair and moved his hand across the back of her neck, he felt her quiver beneath his touch.

"Shay Brennan. Ghost buster," he drawled.

Her bright smile stoked the fire that had already ignited in his belly. With both hands planted on the sides of her face, he drew her close and kissed her. A spark kindled the moment their lips pressed together, and Colt enveloped her into his embrace, wanting to crush her with his heat. As his mouth eagerly played with hers and their tongues darted and flicked, his groin hardened again and throbbed inside his jeans.

When their lips finally parted, he rasped, "Maybe you should come home with me tonight."

TEN

Shay unraveled herself from his arms. "I don't sleep with men on the first date."

"It's our second, remember?"

Tempted to crack a smile, she refrained, finding his wit humorous but nonetheless feeling insulted that he'd think she'd be that easy. Backing up, she folded her arms over her chest to send him a message.

With a hangdog expression covering his smooth face, he moved forward and caressed her hair with the palm of his hand. "I'm coming on too strong, huh?"

"You think?" Her eyebrow lifted and she backed up again.

He flashed a toothy grin. "I'm sorry, Shay. What I meant was maybe you shouldn't be alone tonight, with what just happened."

"I think you meant exactly what you said."

Smiling, he admitted, "I got carried away. It's been quite a while since I . . ."

"Please. Spare me the details." She threw her hand into the air, uninterested in hearing about his love life. "I really enjoyed our time together tonight, but we barely know each other. I like you, but this is moving too fast for me. Besides, as you can see, I'm living in a saloon full of ghosts. That's taking precedence right now."

His gaze dropped to the floor for a moment. "I know. I'm not looking to be involved in a permanent relationship, but I'm not going to say I regret kissing you."

She was glad to hear that, about the kissing part. She hadn't regretted it either. But, what did he mean by not being interested in a relationship? That he'd only wanted to sleep with her tonight? No strings attached? She wasn't like that. A one-night stand years ago had been one too many, and two disastrous relationships after that were exactly why she couldn't let this go further. Colt was nice, but Gary and Tom had seemed nice, too. Both of them had fooled her into thinking they loved her when all they'd cared about had been her father's money. She wouldn't open her heart to that kind of betrayal again.

When Colt stepped back and said, "I withdraw the invitation to stay at my place tonight," she tilted her head in question. That had been a quick change of mind. Probably because she hadn't jumped at the chance to hop in bed with him.

Nevertheless, she chuckled and felt her body relax. "Is that so?"

He smiled a lopsided smile. "Yeah. I do have a guest room you could stay in, but the first time you spend the night with me, it's going to be *your* idea. And you *won't* be sleeping in the extra room. You'll be in my bed, with me all night."

Shay stared at him for what seemed like an eternity. What a cocky son of a gun he was. The look behind those green eyes was one of confidence and pure determination. He was obviously a guy who knew what he wanted and had the patience to wait for it. He came on strong, but his honesty was refreshing. A burning sensation spread through her torso, and her heart picked up its pace. Without thinking, she lifted the Stetson off his head and plowed her hand through his hair, and replied, "You've got yourself a deal, cowboy."

Colt took the hat from her hand and set it back on his head, then put his hands on her hips and gave her one more peck on the lips. He turned and strutted to the front door.

"I think we'd better call it a night, darlin', before I do something I *will* regret. I'm going home to take a cold shower."

The joke was the perfect ending to the evening. She laughed and gently pushed him out the door. Feeling a little confused, she was relieved that the pressure to make love was off, but she was also sorry to see him go.

"I did have a good time tonight, Colt. Thank you."

He tipped his hat. "As did I."

"Ghosts and all?"

He hesitated before answering, "Ghosts and all. I'll see you again soon."

"All right."

"Promise you'll call if those . . . well, if you get scared. Anytime day or night. I'll come runnin' if you need me."

She liked that and had no doubt he meant it. "Okay. I promise."

"Night."

"Good night."

After sauntering to his truck, he opened the door and stood on the running board staring back at her. She was thinking about how he'd called her darlin'. No one had ever called her that before. "What?" she asked, torn from her thought.

"You're awfully pretty standing there in the moonlight."

A thrill of emotion coursed through her. She smiled and waved good-bye.

After watching his taillights disappear down the street, she locked up and headed to the kitchen for a glass of water, with her head dizzy with conflicting sensations. She'd had a great time tonight, enjoyed being with Colt and meeting his family, who seemed absolutely normal and fun. But she knew all too well that looks could be deceiving. She'd learned that the hard way, having been engaged twice—only to learn the truth about the intentions of both men, just in the nick of time.

Something hinted Colt was nothing like either Gary or Tom, but his good looks and pleasant personality would not be enough to make her want to take another chance on love. Or to jump into bed with him.

She flipped on the kitchen light. This room was also in need of a modern update, but it was functional and included the basics, which was all she required.

After filling a glass with tap water, she exited the kitchen and walked past the piano. Stopping, she plunked a few of the keys with her finger. It was obviously out of tune, sounding tinny. She wondered whether the piano had been here as long as the saloon.

"Which one of you spirits was playing this a while ago?" she asked rhetorically.

Her gaze drifted across the room. Both she and Colt had smelled the cigar smoke and heard poker chips clinking together on the tables. It had been just like last night, when she'd heard the shuffling of cards out here. It was obvious the gambling hadn't stopped in this saloon simply because the players were dead. The game playing by those spirits minding their own business didn't bother her, but the bad guy was another story. What were his intentions?

Sensing no further danger tonight, and feeling uncharacteristically calm, she switched off the saloon lights and carried her glass upstairs to the bedroom. Even though he hadn't admitted it, she knew Colt had seen the apparition of the young woman in her window.

Would she still be there, waiting for her?

Eleven

With no more paranormal activity as distraction, Shay had gone to bed early, as she didn't have a television yet and had been too wound up to read. Along with dreams involving ghosts, Colt and his kiss had kept her tossing throughout the night.

Although not refreshed, she woke the next morning anxious to begin delving into the mystery of the ghostly woman's identity. She decided to begin her search at the historical society.

Shay had called the Hill City Visitors Center as soon as it had opened, and someone there had told her where the historical society was located—in a circa-1900 schoolhouse at the end of the street.

After coffee and a bagel, she started the short hike. The morning was crisp and sunny, which might have been the reason so many people had bounces in their steps. As strangers smiled and nodded good morning while passing her on the sidewalk, she had no regrets about the decision to settle here.

Of course, it wasn't just the friendly people that had her smiling. She'd had no idea she'd meet a man like Colt when she made the side trip to this town. Now that she had, she couldn't help but wonder if their meeting had been happenstance, or if there was more to their connection—as he'd suggested. Even though she tried, and knew it would be for the best, she couldn't get him, or his kiss, out of her mind.

Realizing she didn't even know which end of town Colt's office was located, she began paying attention as she passed by storefronts, hoping it was on this end of the street. Three blocks down she stopped in front of it.

Printed across the door was his name—*Morgan Realty*. No lights were on inside. His pickup wasn't parked on the street. She glanced at her watch. Eight-thirty. Maybe he was at the Golden Spike having pancakes. That image made her grin.

She considered leaving a note then decided against it. She didn't want to be pursued. However, if there ever were going to be any pursuing, he'd be the one to do it, not her.

Two more blocks down, the schoolhouse came into view. It was a charming two-story structure with Victorian architecture. Painted white, a bell tower protuded from the roof, and a wide bank of stairs led to the front door, with a sign above it reading *Hill City Historical Society and Museum*. A ramp for the disabled had been built on the side, she noticed.

Once Shay was inside, she was greeted by a curly-haired woman wearing wire-rimmed glasses, a lavender blouse, a long denim skirt, and stodgy-looking shoes. The lady looked to be of retirement age, and was eager to be of assistance.

"Welcome. My name is Doris Rockwood. Are you here to visit the museum, or can I help you with something else?"

Shaking her extended hand, Shay introduced herself. "Hello. My name's Shay Brennan. I'm new in town. I just purchased the Buckhorn Saloon and I've come to see what kind of information I can find on the history of it."

"The saloon, you say?" The woman seemed intrigued. "Follow me, dear. I can steer you in the right direction."

"Wonderful. Thank you, Mrs. Rockwood."

"Please, call me Doris."

Shay had hoped finding some history on the saloon would be a fairly straightforward project, but this might be even easier than she'd expected. Her rib cage inflated with eagerness. But when Doris led her into a large back room, her lungs deflated.

Stacks and stacks of books filled floor-to-ceiling shelves.

How would she ever find what she was looking for in here?

Doris chuckled, evidently noticing Shay's dropped jaw. "Don't worry," she said. "I'll help you track down what you're looking for. Believe it or not, there's a method to the madness in here, and I'm one of the few people who knows how to decipher it."

Doris moved to a wooden cabinet that was sitting under a stained-glass window and began pulling out small drawers.

"Is that a card catalog?" Shay asked, stepping to her side.

"It sure is. There aren't many card catalogs in use anymore these days. Not since computers came on the scene. But this is a small town, and our organization is a nonprofit, so we don't have a lot of money to work with. We're supposed to be updating to computers within the next year or two, but for now, this is what we have to work with."

Shaking her head, Shay thought her desire to learn the history of the Buckhorn was a lost cause, but Doris started thumbing through cards and setting them on the tabletop next to her in quick order. "I was a librarian for forty-three years in Springfield, Illinois, before retiring here five years ago. I know what I'm doing."

"I grew up in Illinois, too," Shay said. "In a suburb near Chicago."

Doris stopped and cocked her head. "You don't say? Isn't that a coincidence?"

Guess it didn't matter much to Doris how Shay had come to reside in Hill City or why she'd wanted to buy the saloon, because she asked no questions and offered no further details on her own life in the Midwest. The glasses were perched on the tip of her nose, which was buried deep in the drawers of cards.

A half dozen cards later, Doris slammed the drawers shut,

snatched the cards off the table and said, "Come with me."

Shay was amazed when Doris started pulling material off the shelves and filling her arms.

"You can sit at one of these worktables," Doris said, referring to two long wooden tables. "There's a lot of light in this room, and the chairs are fairly comfortable."

Books bearing the titles *The History of Hill City, South Dakota*, and *Photographs and Residents of Early Hill City in the Black Hills* were unloaded onto the table where Shay had dropped her purse.

"Be right back," Doris chirped, trotting into an adjoining room. A few minutes later, she returned carrying a large binder in her hands. "This is full of newspapers dating back to the late eighteen eighties. Eighteen eighty-five was the year the Buckhorn was built, if memory serves."

"That's correct," Shay answered, thrilled with Doris's efficiency and helpfulness, and her knowledge about her adopted hometown.

Doris dropped the binder onto the table and it landed with a thud. Just like in a movie, dust spiraled into the air, causing Shay to sneeze.

Doris laughed. "As you can see, this binder hasn't seen the light of day in years. This one has newspaper articles from the years eighteen eighty-five and eighteen eighty-six, so I figured it's a good place for you to start. Good luck finding what you're looking for. I'll be in front, so yell if you need me."

Shay stopped her before she could leave the room. "Thank you so much for locating this material for me. It should keep me busy for a while. I wonder if I can bother you with one more request."

"Of course. That's what I'm here for. What is it you need?"

"Would you know if there is any information on . . . local ghosts?"

Without batting an eye, Doris replied, "It's common knowledge that there are ghosts roaming all over the Black Hills. Which ones are you specifically referring to?"

"Those haunting the Buckhorn Saloon."

Doris placed a finger on her lips and tapped while she contemplated. "Hmmm. I don't know anything about spirits in the saloon. Our local authors haven't written any books about them that I know of. Brenda Preston would probably be the person to talk to. Or Frank Averill. He could probably tell you some stories. His father owned the place, and his father before him, I believe."

"Yes, so I've been told. I hope to meet Mr. Averill when he's feeling better. I understand he's elderly and ill. I'm curious about Brenda Preston. Who is she?" Shay asked.

"A psychic medium. Quite a good one, from what I hear. I'll give you one of her business cards. I have a few in my desk."

TWELVE

A psychic? Shay chuckled and took a seat at the table as Doris walked briskly to the front room. She returned and handed Shay a colorful business card.

"Brenda lives right here in town," Doris said. "Her cell phone number is listed there."

"Thanks. I may give her a call if I don't come up with anything else. It might be interesting to see what she can tell me."

Doris left and Shay set the business card aside and started flipping through the pages of the book on the town history. The back cover noted the book had been written and published several years earlier by a local man.

Reading the history of the Lakota Indians and how Hill City started up and then grew and prospered due to tin mining kept her fascinated for close to forty minutes. After skimming through pages of old photos, she ran across a vintage photograph of the Buckhorn and felt like she'd hit pay dirt. Her heart began thumping as she read the inscription under the photo.

The Buckhorn Saloon, 1885. Owner Dean Averill.

A man stood in front of the building wearing a derby hat, but the photo had been taken from a distance and was not of good quality, so she couldn't see his face. A blurb followed the photograph, which she read out loud.

The Buckhorn Saloon was built and operated by Dean Aver-

ill, a former tin miner who was one of the first in Hill City to strike it rich. The bar served such customers as fur trappers, cowboys, miners, gold prospectors, gamblers and lawmen. The whiskey served in the early days was strong stuff, a combination of raw alcohol, burnt sugar and chewing tobacco. Cactus wine, made from a mix of tequila and peyote tea was popular, as well as something called a Mule Skinner, which was made with whiskey and blackberry liquor. Rye and bourbon were also popular drinks, and beer was served in high volume, though not ice cold as it is today. Sometimes a barkeeper watered down the liquor with turpentine, ammonia, gunpowder or cayenne pepper. It packed a wallop either way.

Poker and faro were known to be played in the Buckhorn, as well as dice games. Mixing alcohol and gambling, no doubt, could result in some deadly gunplay. Professional gamblers quickly learned to protect their assets by honing their six-shooter skills at the same time as their gambling abilities.

Aside from the usual drinking and game playing that went on at this well-known Black Hills saloon, dancing girls were said to have entertained the patrons, catering to them twenty-four hours a day, seven days a week. These girls sang, played piano, and danced with the customers, dressed in somewhat revealing dresses with feather boas. It is likely some of them occasionally doubled as prostitutes, which could be the reason there are several bedrooms on the second floor of this establishment, which still stands today.

Turning the page, Shay peered at the first of two photos. It seemed to have been taken just inside the front door of the saloon, because it captured the tables in the middle of the room as well as the mahogany bar with the mirror above. Men in cowboy hats were lined up at the bar with their heads turned, staring solemnly into the camera.

She was astounded to discover the room had hardly changed

through the decades. The caption under this photo read *Opening Day at Buckhorn Saloon, March 1, 1885.*

The black-and-white photo at the bottom of the page was grainy, but Shay could tell the snapshot was of the piano, standing in the same spot at the back of the room where it stood now. Several saloon girls leaned against it, with one sitting on the bench with her legs crossed.

Shay held the book close to her eyes and squinted, trying to distinguish whether one of the girls was her visiting ghost. Unfortunately, because of the poor quality of the photograph, there was no way to tell. They all looked young.

"Darn." She'd thought she'd been onto something there.

She closed her eyes and placed her hand on the page over the photo, hoping a sixth sense would reveal if one of the girls in the picture might be the spirit.

"Having any luck?"

Shay's eyes flew open and she felt her cheeks heat with embarrassment. She hadn't heard Doris enter the room. Doris stood in front of her with a comical expression on her face. Feeling like an idiot, Shay slapped the book shut.

"Some," she answered, smiling and opening the second book.

When Shay's cell phone blared from inside her purse, Doris frowned and pointed to a sign on the wall.

Please Turn Off Cell Phones

"I'm sorry," Shay apologized, whipping the phone out and flipping it open. "I'll go outside," she whispered, passing Doris on her way to the front door. As she walked through the main reception area, she noticed there wasn't another soul in the place so it seemed silly to be whispering.

"Hello," she answered, once outside and standing on the steps.

"How are ya?" a deep voice drawled.

She felt her face light up. "I'm fine, Colt. How are you?"

"Great, now that I've heard your voice."

"That's a sweet thing for you to say." She pictured his crooked smile and green eyes and delicious lips, and felt her hormones begin to rage.

"I'm a sweet guy," he replied. Clearing his voice, he went on. "Unfortunately, that's not the reason I'm calling. Where are you right now?"

"The historical center. I've started doing some research on the saloon. Where are you?"

"Standing outside your place." Something in his tone changed. "I stopped by to see you and . . . well, you'd better scoot on down here."

"What is it, Colt? Is there a problem?"

"Yeah, there is. Not to scare you, but hurry over if you can."

"Sure. I'll be right there."

THIRTEEN

"I have to go," Shay told Doris, when she swooped back into the room. "There's some kind of emergency."

"Oh, my," Doris said. "Go on. I'll put these things away for you."

"I appreciate that. I plan on coming back soon, today if possible. Depends on what's going on at my place. Can you keep the materials out front for me?"

"Of course. I'd be glad to."

"Thank you."

Shay dashed outside and vigorously walked the five blocks to the Buckhorn. Colt was leaning against the old hitching rail that was in front of her building. He bounded up when she approached and greeted her again. "Hi. You made it here fast."

"Hi." Catching her breath, her head bobbed up and down, scanning the building. "What's going on, Colt? I thought the place was on fire or something."

Slipping his hand inside hers like it belonged there, he led her to the front door and pointed at the glass-paned window. "Take a look at that."

Condensation fogged the window at eye level, as if someone had blown on it in the dead of winter, and the warm breath had steamed up the glass. A word, spelled backwards, was written in the condensation.

H C T I B

Shay gasped and her fist flew to her mouth. If the vulgar

69

word wasn't enough to shake her, the fact that it wasn't cold out, *and* the condensation was on the inside of the window, not on the outside, did cause her pause—and concern.

Colt touched her arm. "Who do you think would have done that?"

She met his curious gaze. "I have no idea. It wasn't there when I left this morning. I would have seen it when I locked the door."

"Not necessarily," he said, tapping on the glass. "That velvet curtain would have covered it up. You wouldn't have seen it from the inside."

She dug the keys out of her purse and unlocked the door then pushed the curtain back. The word *BITCH* glowered at her in big letters.

"Only someone from inside the saloon could have done this," she said, uncomprehending.

Colt didn't respond, but she could see his mind working, probably questioning how that was possible, unless . . .

"You don't think *I* did this, do you?" she snapped. The nip in her voice hadn't been intentional, but noticing his furrowed brow had made her feel the need to defend herself. Maybe he thought she was orchestrating this ghost business herself. Loss and grief affected people in different ways. Maybe he thought she was someone creating this situation for attention.

Colt replied, "Of course not, Shay."

His tone was unconvincing. His eyes narrowed. "I'm just wondering which of the undead in this saloon wrote it."

It was obvious he had reservations about her and her sanity. She took a deep breath and bit her tongue so she wouldn't say something she'd be sorry for later. "It doesn't matter whether you believe there are spirits in here or not. I didn't write this. There's no other explanation other than supernatural."

Shrugging, he said, "It's not for me to say. I've never believed in ghosts, but I'm willing to give you the benefit of the doubt. I don't take you for a psycho."

"Gee, thanks." Shay rolled her eyes and stared at the window, thinking.

"I hate to say it," Colt continued, "but whoever left this is sending you a clear message."

She shuddered. "It has to be the spirit from the basement. But, who is he and why is he trying to scare me? So I'll leave? I'm not going to leave, no matter what he does."

"Maybe you *should* think about selling," Colt said. "You've been through enough in your life, from what you told me, and especially this past year or two. I can relist the property, and you can find yourself a little house here in town. I have several listings that would be perfect for you."

Her ire was slowing rising. What did he know about what she'd gone through in her life, and what would be perfect for her? She hadn't shared much of anything with him, except for the fact that she came from money—which had been a mistake—and that she'd had some trouble with past relationships. He seemed anxious for her to put the saloon up for sale. Did he have another buyer in mind? Someone willing to pay more so he'd earn a bigger commission?

"No, Colt. I'm not leaving," she said to end that conversation. "I'm going to get to the bottom of this and put a stop to it somehow."

They stood staring at the word for a moment and then she wiped it away with her hand.

"Do you know a woman by the name of Brenda Preston?" she asked.

The discomfort that washed over his face was subtle, but noticeable, all the same. The corner of his mouth twitched and he sighed.

"Yep. She lives right here in town, and, as a matter of fact, I went to school with her."

"Oh. Then you know she's a psychic?"

"Who told you that?"

"Doris Rockwood. She's a volunteer at the historical society. She helped me find some books on the history of Hill City, and when I told her about the ghosts haunting me, she suggested I speak to this woman, Brenda Preston."

"You told a stranger about the ghosts?"

She gathered by his tone that he wouldn't have made that choice. "Yes. There are stacks and stacks of material in that place. There's no way I could find what I was looking for without assistance, so I told her so she'd be able to help. That's her job."

He shrugged again. "Did you find anything?"

"Some old photos of the Buckhorn. It hasn't changed one bit since eighteen eighty-five," she answered, still amazed about that. "Even the piano looks to be the same one. There was a photo of some saloon girls standing in front of it, and I was hoping to see the blonde girl among them, but the picture wasn't clear. Oh! And there was a photo of the saloon when it first opened, with Dean Averill standing in front of it, but it was taken too far away to see his face. That was disappointing."

Colt rubbed a hand across his smooth-shaven chin. "I imagine Frank will have a picture of his grandfather, if you want to see what he looked like."

Shay grew excited. "That's what I was thinking, too. I'd like to meet Mr. Averill. Do you have any idea when he'll be able to receive visitors?"

"I'll drop by and check on him. He has a live-in nurse to care for him. I'll find out how he's doing and let you know."

She touched his arm. "Thanks. I can probably learn more from him than any books I could read. Does he still live at home?"

Colt nodded. "Yes. He refuses to be put into a nursing home. Says he'll die if he goes to one. I'm afraid his time is running out anyway."

"You said he has a nurse. Doesn't he have any family to help out? No children?"

"His wife passed on about twelve years back. They had a child, a daughter, as I recall, but she's also gone. I don't know the whole story, but ever since I've known Frank, I've never heard him speak of her. I believe she died many years ago."

"That's sad. It's nice of you to look out for him."

Colt smiled. "I do it because of my granddaddy. They were best friends their whole life. Besides, Frank is a real nice fellow. He's always been good to me."

A moment of silence filled the space between them before she confessed, "I walked by your office this morning."

His face brightened. "I'd meant to tell you where it was so you could come by sometime. I'll give you the grand tour next time you stop."

"We can go now if you're headed that way. There's nothing to be done about this message, and I'd like to go back to the historical society and dig around a little more. Your office is on the way."

"Yes, it is. We'll walk together."

She relocked the saloon door and they started down the sidewalk. "What about your truck?" she asked, glancing back to see it was parked at the curb.

"I'll pick it up later."

He took her hand again and held it as they strolled. It was warm and he held tight, like he didn't want to let go. Despite what she'd told herself about not getting involved, his strong hand holding hers was comforting and sent the butterflies fluttering around her stomach again.

When they entered his office, he shut the door behind them

and pulled down the shade on the door. Before she realized what was happening, he'd swept her off her feet and into his arms and carried her to his desk, where he sat her down on top.

"What on earth are you doing?" she lightheartedly cried.

"You'll find out in about two seconds."

Fourteen

Colt held onto her shoulders to keep her from tipping back and leaned in and planted a soft kiss on her lips. There was no way he was not going to take advantage of an empty office.

"You taste good," he said.

"You taste like maple syrup."

Licking his lips, he grinned and replied, "Blueberry pancakes."

"Do you eat pancakes every morning?"

"Nearly."

He kissed her again, parting her moist lips with his tongue, and began to feel the swell of arousal when she responded with her own tongue. It was she who stopped and shot a glance over his shoulder.

"Someone could walk in any minute," she said, pushing her hand into his chest.

"That's why I pulled the shade and locked the door. To keep the pests out."

"Don't you have a secretary?"

"Yeah. She's off this morning. Doctor's appointment."

He leaned in again, but she wiggled around him and hopped off the desktop.

"I need to leave."

He groaned with disappointment.

"I have more research to do," she said, smoothing her hair with a hand. Her mouth had become a thin line, and her brows knitted together.

"I'm sorry, Shay. I'm coming on too strong again."

Her halfhearted smile spoke of uncertainty, while her lips and tongue had been very decisive. "Nothing gets past you, does it?" she said.

Ah. Sarcasm. "I think you liked it as much as I did," he challenged.

She sighed. "I never said I didn't like it. I said I have to go." She pushed by him.

She was flustered, which meant she was definitely interested. That he could live with. "I'd like to invite you over to my house tonight. We can have supper together. Do you have any plans?"

Hand on the doorknob, her hesitancy lasted several seconds. "No."

"Then it's a date?"

She made him suffer in silence for a few seconds more before craning her neck around. "Supper at your house is not a date."

"Whatever." As he was writing out directions to his residence, she asked, "Are there going to be any surprises in store for me, like there were last night? Will there be more members of your family jumping out of the closets?"

He handed her the paper with the address on it and shook his head. "No more ambushes. It'll just be you and me this evening. I promise."

"Okay."

His groin grew hard again, seeing her lips crack a smile and imagining the possibilities.

"What time should I be there?" she asked, turning the knob.

"It's locked, remember?" He stepped forward and flipped the lock. "How about six?"

"Okay. See you then."

He tugged on the bottom of the shade, letting it snap to the top of the window. Sunlight was pouring onto the sidewalk where he followed her outside.

"Do you like Italian?" he asked, reaching for her hand, but missing it when she moved it on purpose.

"It's one of my favorites."

"Italian it is, then."

Their gazes locked, and then she waved good-bye without another word.

He took a stance in the middle of the sidewalk and watched her move down the block. The woman had an ideal body. She was petite, with curves in all the right places. Her auburn hair was shiny and soft. Her hazel eyes sparkled when she smiled, and she had the face of an angel.

Physically, Shay was everything he longed for in a woman. Though the sexual attraction hit a 10.0 on the Richter scale, he was beginning to realize there was more to her than physical appeal. There was no denying the emotional connection he felt with her. He didn't understand it, or how it had happened, but he believed they'd been destined to meet. Despite what he'd told her about not wanting to get involved in a relationship, he hadn't felt this happy in years. For the first time in a long time, he could almost see himself dating a woman more than a couple of times. Maybe even settling down again.

How would he be able to accomplish anything the rest of the day, when all he'd be thinking about was seeing her tonight?

With Shay on his mind, he stepped back into his office and picked up the desk phone to check his messages. He'd just eaten breakfast, but food had nothing to do with the insatiable hunger aroused in his gut.

"You're back." Doris greeted Shay when she walked in. "Is everything okay at home?"

Shay didn't want to explain about the writing on the window. Doris probably wouldn't believe it anyway. For now, it would be her and Colt's secret. "Yes. Everything's fine," she answered, suddenly remembering to turn off her cell phone.

Doris pulled the huge binder and books out from under the reception countertop. "Here you go."

"Thanks. I'll take these to the back room and get back to work."

"Let me know if you need me to look up anything else," Doris called to her back.

Settling in and opening the second book, Shay skimmed the table of contents. A chapter titled *Census* caught her eye. When she flipped to that section, she was pleasantly surprised to find Hill City residents for the years 1885 through 1890, listed in columns. It only took a few moments to go down the row of last names beginning with "A" since it was alphabetical. There was Frank Averill's grandfather's name and occupation included for the year 1885.

Dean Henry Averill. Saloon Owner.

The name *Cynthia Sarah Averill* was located above Dean's name, with occupation listed as *Wife*. No other Averills. Shay wondered about the name of the female who'd appeared in her bedroom. She'd asked her name that night, but had received no response.

This book included a wealth of photographs from the early days of Hill City. There were some photos of people, but most of the pictures were of buildings in chronological order as the town sprang up. Again, she was pleased to find some more pictures of the Buckhorn, showing both the inside and outside of the building. One shot was of the bartender standing in front of the gilded mirror pouring drinks for a row of customers.

Shay pulled the book closer. This picture was clear. The bartender was looking straight at the camera smiling. Short haircut parted on the side, a bushy mustache, wearing a dark vest over a long-sleeved shirt and an apron at his waist. Could this be Dean Averill? Chances were the owner had also tended his own bar. She stared at the photo for a couple of minutes questioning whether his supernatural footsteps had been some she'd heard walking the halls of the saloon at night.

An hour had passed by the time she finished going through the book looking at all the photos. Disappointingly, none were of the young blonde. Needing a break, Shay stood up and stretched and then took the book to the front to ask Doris if she could make a copy of the snapshot of the bartender. She wanted to have it, if and when she got to visit Frank Averill.

Returning to the table, she opened the binder and began the daunting task of reading through newspaper articles from the *Hill City Pioneer.* Not sure how to go about this search, she started with the March 1885 papers, since that was when the Buckhorn had opened. She would search for headlines that mentioned the business and any of its patrons or employees, especially the saloon girls.

After two hours of reading about unusual deaths, the amount of snow that fell on a particular day, the election of the sheriff (John Manning, with his brother Thomas and cousin Pat acting as deputies), reports of Indian attacks, a recent trip to Deadwood by a Mrs. Antoinette Ogden, and a variety of other interesting stories about Hill City and its former inhabitants, Shay had not found anything she didn't already know about the Buckhorn.

Weary and cross-eyed, she marked the spot where she left off and closed the binder, returning it to Doris up front.

"I'll keep it here under the counter until next time," Doris pleasantly told her.

Stomach grumbling because she'd worked through lunch, Shay said good-bye and started the short trek home.

Fifteen

After Colt finished showing several homes to the couple relocating from Ohio, and agreed to show them a few more tomorrow, he drove to Frank Averill's house. Last time he'd seen him, Frank had looked to be at death's door, but Colt had seen the man go through a spell like this before and come out fresh as a daisy on the other end of it.

The nurse swung open the door on the first knock.

"Where the hell have you been the past couple of days?" she said, not bothering to lower her voice. "He's been asking for you."

Opal was a heavyset woman with a no-nonsense attitude and either a bosom too large for her nurse's uniform, or a uniform too small for her bosom. Colt wasn't sure which. Her hair was as short as a man's, and she cussed like a sailor. She was a tough bird, but Frank seemed to like her.

"Nice to see you, too, Opal."

Colt strode down the hallway toward the bedroom, but was brought to a standstill when Opal stuck her arm out and karate chopped him in the stomach.

"Watch it, Opal," he complained, flinching. "Your arm's as thick as a slab of beef and twice as dangerous." He'd learned through trial and error that the best way to communicate with her was the way *she* communicated.

Opal smiled, flashing him canine teeth that looked as razor

sharp as a vampire's. "Sorry, Colton. Don't know my own strength."

"Don't call me that," he warned good-naturedly. "I haven't been called Colton since I sat in the principal's office in high school."

She grinned. "I like to rile you up. It makes my day. You need to come around more often."

"I'll see what I can do to accommodate you from now on. Now, tell me why Frank's been asking for me. What's wrong with him?"

"He's dying, fool."

Colt rolled his eyes. "I mean, specifically, today. Is he any worse than last time I was here?"

"Not worse. About the same. But he's been hallucinating some, calling out a lot of names. Yours, mostly."

Sighing, Colt said, "You have my cell phone number, Opal. If he wanted to see me, you should have called. I told you to call anytime day or night if he needs me."

She shrugged. "I figured you'd be by sooner or later."

Colt stepped around her, which was not easy to do in the narrow hall, and entered Frank's bedroom. Frank lay in his hospital bed, propped up on some pillows, and appeared to be asleep. Colt waited beside the bed, staring into Frank's ashen face, noting the once-strong body that was now skeletal, and remembering the fun times he'd spent with his granddaddy and Frank as a boy growing up. They'd taken him hunting, fishing, on excursions to Deadwood, and he'd even drunk his first beer with them on a camping trip.

His mental wanderings were interrupted when Opal entered the room and thudded to the other side of the bed. She jiggled Frank's arm to wake him.

"You don't have to do that," Colt whispered, frowning. "I can see he needs his rest."

"He'll get all the rest he needs when he's six feet under."

"Good Lord, Opal, but you're over the top at times. For the life of me, I can't figure out how you manage to land any nursing jobs at all with that smart mouth of yours."

She grinned again. "A lot of people like my outgoing personality, *Colton*. But, mostly, I *land* jobs, as you call it, because I'm dedicated to my patients, *and* I'm the best damned nurse in all of South Dakota."

He shrugged. "If you say so."

"Colt? Is that you?"

Frank stirred and opened his eyes, but seemed to have trouble focusing. Colt clamped a gentle hand on his arm.

"It's me, Frank."

"I'm here, too, Frank," Opal said, lightly taking his other arm. "I'm going to check your blood pressure again, honey."

"Okay."

Colt watched in astonishment at the gentle way in which Opal handled Frank. The tone of her voice had even changed. She sounded . . . sweet.

"It's just fine," she told Frank after she'd listened and removed the cuff. Opal wrote the number down in a notebook and then looked at her watch and excused herself. "I'll leave you two boys to your privacy. I've got my soap to watch anyway."

Once she'd left the room, Colt noticed Frank's eyes were fully open and his gaze steady.

"I don't know how you put up with that woman," Colt chuckled. "She's as rough as a cob."

Frank smiled. "Opal ain't so bad. She keeps me laughing. That lady can tell some real humdingers."

"I'll bet. Well, laughing is a good thing," Colt replied. "Can I get you anything? A glass of water?" He noticed a full pitcher sitting on the dresser.

Frank waved it off. "Nah, I'm fine. But I wouldn't mind rattling these old bones a bit." When he tried to scoot himself up, Colt lifted Frank by the waist so he was comfortably sitting up straight. He felt light as a feather.

"Thank you, Colt. That's better," Frank said. "Get tired of lying down all the time. Wish I could go outside and take a walk now and then. But my bones would probably break if I put any pressure on my feet."

Colt took a seat in a straight-back chair that was next to the bed, thinking how it must be hell to become old and decrepit. Worse yet, Frank was alone, with no one but a surly nurse as a companion.

"How's the lady who bought my saloon?" Frank asked, out of the blue.

Caught off guard, Colt answered, "She's real nice. Her name's Shay Brennan. As a matter of fact, she'd like to meet you sometime, when you're up to having visitors."

"Why is that?"

"Well, I guess she just wants to meet the man who owned the property before her. And I believe she's interested in the history of the building."

Frank's piercing gaze showed intrigue. "Has she experienced anything peculiar going on in there?"

Colt hesitated before answering. He didn't know the true reasons for Frank shutting down the business years ago when he was a younger man. His granddaddy had hinted it had something to do with supernatural occurrences, but Frank had never confided in Colt.

"Yes, sir, she has," he confessed. "But you probably already knew that."

A strange cackle erupted from Frank's throat, sending a jolt through Colt, and then Frank's skinny arm reached out and he snatched at the air, grabbing for Colt's sleeve. Colt stood up and leaned against the bed railing. Frank tugged on his shirtsleeve.

"Bring her by tomorrow," he croaked.

"You sure you're strong enough?"

"Bring her," Frank repeated.

"Yes, sir. I'll do that."

When Frank lay back against the pillow and closed his eyes, Colt patted his arm. "I'll see you tomorrow, Frank. You rest now."

A slight nod ended the conversation.

"I'll be back sometime tomorrow," Colt told Opal as he sauntered through the living room and flung open the front door. "And I'm bringing a visitor, so I want you to be on your best behavior. Okay?"

Engrossed in her soap opera and the handful of cheese curls she was crunching, Opal grunted her good-bye.

Sixteen

Shay found Colt's house with ease that evening. As she pulled into the paved driveway and ran her gaze over the property, she was pleased with the looks of it. It was an older two-story home with vinyl siding, a front porch with white railing, and a nicely manicured lawn. A large tree shaded the side yard. Flowerbeds or hanging plants would have brightened the exterior, but all in all, it was very nice. It was simply missing a woman's touch.

Colt stepped outside and waved her in. The sight of him caused heat to race through her veins. He looked so good in tight jeans and a T-shirt that showed off his muscular arms. Too good. Had she made a mistake in coming here? Time would tell.

"Hi," she said, strolling up the steps. "Nice to see you."

When he planted a welcome kiss on her lips, that pleasant burning sensation began to swell in her again. She was determined not to have sex with Colt, but that didn't mean she was immune to his charming advances. Every move he made, each slow smile, the way he walked, the way he talked, how he touched her—everything about him oozed masculine sexuality.

His gaze moved up and down her body. "You sure look beautiful tonight, Shay. And you smell good, too."

"Thank you."

"Come in. I'll show you around."

"This is for you." She handed him the bottle of wine she'd bought, thinking it would go well with Italian food.

"I appreciate that, darlin'," he said, flashing her that crooked smile and causing her breath to hitch at being called the pet name again. Like a puppet head on a string, her gaze landed on his backside as he led the way in. Denim jeans had never looked so fine on a man.

The interior of his house felt warm and cozy. As he gave her the dollar tour, she noted hardwood floors throughout and neutral paint on the walls. In the living room, the furniture was dark leather, worn in and very comfy-looking. A flat-screen television hung above the chunky mantle of a stone fireplace. Imagining them curled up in front of a blazing fire on a cold wintry evening set her heart dancing, but she quickly tried to erase the thought.

A sturdy oak table, four chairs and a hutch were the only furniture in the formal dining room. An outdated chandelier was suspended over the table, and a couple of oil paintings hung on the walls.

"I never use this room," he said, as they walked through it into the eat-in kitchen.

She had expected an old-fashioned kitchen in need of modernization, but was pleasantly surprised to walk into a room with cherry cabinets, gleaming granite countertops, and stainless-steel appliances. A center island and a table with built-in banquette seating under a bay window highlighted the space. He set the wine on the island.

Noticeably missing were the savory smells of Italian food simmering on the stove. Shay wondered whether he'd changed his mind about cooking for her and they'd be going out to supper instead. That would be disappointing, because she'd wanted to see what kind of a chef he was. She expected there was nothing this man couldn't do.

"Your kitchen is beautiful," she gushed. "Was it like this when you purchased the house?"

"No. The house had been a foreclosure, so we got it at a bargain price. The interior was in pretty bad shape at the time, but the bones of the place were good. I pretty much had the whole thing gutted inside and we started over. The kitchen was the last room to be done. It was Denise's dream kitchen. But, unfortunately, she got sick and didn't have much of an opportunity to use it."

Shay's heart went out to Colt. This was the most—actually *all* he'd said about his wife, and she sensed he'd truly loved her. As fast as he'd brought her up, however, he changed the subject just as quick.

"That's it, except for my bedroom, which is upstairs." With a devilish grin, he reminded her, "But you can't see that tonight."

"Why? Do you have clothes strewn all over the floor and an unmade bed?"

Laughing, he replied, "No. Because *I* invited you over this evening. Have you forgotten what I said about you sleeping in my bed?"

"Not at all." She *had* remembered, and was glad the tour didn't include the bedroom. Anyway, she'd hoped he'd forgotten that conversation. Imagining herself in bed with him was dangerous. Temptation could only lead to making decisions she'd regret later. The subject needed to be changed—fast. "How long have you lived here?"

Before he could answer, the doorbell rang and he said, "Excuse me."

She followed him into the front room where he opened the door to a pizza delivery boy.

"Thanks," he said, handing the young man some cash and telling him to keep the change. As he carried the pizza box and a plastic sack to the kitchen, he smiled and said, "You told me you like Italian, right?" He placed the pizza box on the stove then pulled a large bowl of salad out of the plastic bag and set it on the island.

She had to grin as he removed two plates from the kitchen cabinet.

"I'm not much of a cook," he admitted while pulling a bottle of ranch dressing from the fridge. "Hope you don't mind. Do you like ranch?" he asked.

"Yes," she laughed, having received her answer about whether he was a good cook or not.

He eyeballed the bottle of wine then said, "I'm sure that wine is delicious, but pizza goes great with beer. Want one?"

"Sure. We can save the wine for another time."

"Now you're talking. For another time," he repeated, winking.

He poured two ice-cold beers into tall glasses. As he offered her a stool at the island and a slice of pepperoni pizza on her plate, it was strange, but she felt like they were a couple. There was no pretense surrounding Colt. What you saw was what you got—and that's what she liked about him. After worrying how the evening would go, she was starting to relax.

"I saw Frank today," he said between bites. "He'd like to meet you."

"Really? That's great. How's he feeling?"

"He's weak, but still hanging in there. He asked me to bring you by tomorrow. I have some houses to show in the morning, but will you be available early afternoon?"

"Sure. Any time is fine. I can't wait to talk to him. Do you think he'll be able to shed some light on my . . . situation?"

Colt shrugged. "The paranormal is not a topic I've heard him speak of, but you're a persuasive lady. If he has something to say, I have no doubt you can get him to open up."

She smiled, taking that as a compliment.

They adjourned to the living room after they'd finished their pizza and salads, and Colt put on a CD of soft music. A button on the wall lowered the lights in the room. For a good ol' boy, as he liked to call himself, she was starting to believe he was really a hardcore romantic.

He lowered her onto the sofa and any predetermined notions about not making out with him tonight flew out the window when he held her face in his hands and they started to kiss.

Seventeen

It took every bit of willpower Shay could muster to break away from Colt. It hadn't taken long for his hands to start roaming, and she was losing strength to resist.

"It's getting a little hot in here," she said, sitting up. With his well-muscled body pressed to hers, she'd felt like a teenager making out, but it had started to get intense. It was time to put the brakes on Colt. She'd promised herself before she drove over here that no matter how attracted she was, or how she longed for intimacy, she wouldn't have sex with him tonight, and she meant to stick to her word.

"I think we both need to take a cold shower tonight," she said, attempting a joke.

"That's going to be a problem for you since the Buckhorn only has a tub," he smiled. "We can shower here, together," he replied, obviously not giving up. She knew he probably would strip out of his clothes in record time if she'd agree to take a shower with him.

She stood and adjusted her shirt, which he'd started to unbutton, and smoothed down her flyaway hair. It was time to go before things really got out of hand. "Thanks for having me over, but I'd better be going."

With her loins on fire, she grabbed her purse off the chair where she'd tossed it when she'd arrived and strode to the door. The need to get out of there as fast as possible had her shaking. Hand on the doorknob, she turned and asked, "What time will you be picking me up tomorrow to go to Frank's?"

Colt stood up. His shirt had pulled out of his jeans and he swayed a little, like he was drunk. She knew he wasn't, but he was staring at her with that deep and powerful look in his eye.

"I want to make love to you," he said softly.

She nodded. "I know. That's why I'm leaving." Her heart pounded with an insane rhythm. She wanted him to make love to her, she realized. But it was too soon to trust. Too soon to give herself to any man. "What time tomorrow?" she repeated, feeling a howl working its way into her throat.

He shoved his hands into his pockets and looked like a little boy who'd had his candy taken away. "I should be done with my clients by one o'clock. I'll come by the saloon right after."

"Okay. See you then." She opened the door herself, and when he followed her onto the porch, she bolted down the steps before she could change her mind about leaving.

Shay went straight into the bathroom once she got home and cleansed away her makeup and brushed her teeth. The face in the mirror reflected a woman she hadn't seen in many years, but had somehow found again. The move west had been the first big step toward healing. Deciding to put down roots and then meeting Colt had been unexpected treasures.

Walking away from him tonight had been difficult. She felt happy when she was near him. But could happiness last? She knew it to be fleeting. Both love and family had been ripped from her, leaving her heart battered and wounded. It wasn't easy to depend on anyone or to have faith in a happy ending anymore. It would be especially hard to trust Colt, since he'd told her he wasn't interested in a committed relationship. One-night stands or sex for the sport of it was not the way she was programmed.

Pushing Colt to the back of her mind, she tried to concentrate instead on meeting Frank Averill tomorrow. She sauntered into her bedroom—and a prickly feeling niggled beneath goose-fleshed skin.

There, hovering in front of the fireplace was the young blonde. The black-and-blue bruising around her neck was as clear as a picture. She stared at Shay, not speaking.

Quickly gathering her wits about her, Shay knew she had to try communicating if she was to gain any information about the woman.

"Will you talk to me?" she asked.

The woman nodded slowly.

Good. She was still willing to communicate. And Shay was willing to forgive her for choking her before. "What's your name?" she said, trying not to move a muscle for fear of scaring her away.

The woman touched her neck, and her eyebrows drew together as she whispered, "Cal . . . lie."

Callie! So far so good. From the pained expression on her face, it must have hurt for her to speak. It was obvious from the dark bruises that she had probably been strangled.

"Callie, is there a way I can help you?"

She nodded and her form seemed to lighten in front of Shay's eyes, as if she was fading.

"Don't leave," Shay begged. "Please stay. Tell me what I can do." She inhaled deeply. "Did you write that word on my front door today?"

Callie shook her head with vehemence.

Shay exhaled. "I'm glad to hear that. Do you know who *did* write that word on the window?"

The spirit's blue eyes widened and she touched her neck again.

"Was it the same person who hurt you?"

She nodded again, and Shay felt excited that she was starting to get somewhere. Strangely, she didn't feel frightened at all now, only curious. In her enthusiasm, she took a step forward, but backed off when Callie's expression grew fearful.

"I'm sorry," Shay apologized, stopping in her tracks. "I won't come near you. I promise. Let me ask you about the person who hurt you. Does his spirit remain in this saloon?"

Callie's head bobbed up and down.

"Can you tell me his name?"

Before she could answer, Shay heard a crash downstairs and then footsteps plodding up the staircase. A lump formed in her throat, and her body went cold as she felt a presence approaching her bedroom door. Her fists clenched at her sides. This was definitely not one of the passive card-playing ghosts. Glancing at Callie, she saw the girl's eyes grow large in terror.

"Who is it?" Shay asked. "Who's out there?"

Callie seemed not to be paying attention to her. She appeared frozen, staring at the door, horrified.

"Who is it?" Shay repeated.

Staring at the open door, Callie's mouth opened and she whispered, "Ev . . . er . . . ett."

When the door slammed against the wall and invisible footsteps stomped across the threshold, Shay jumped and dashed to the other side of her bed. The booming steps caused the room to shake like it was under siege. Shay inched closer to the window, smelling the rotten odor, and knowing it was the same ghost from before. She glanced toward the fireplace and saw that Callie had dissipated.

Feeling completely alone and vulnerable, Shay chanted out loud, "He's dead. He's dead. He's dead." If she could convince herself the entity couldn't hurt her, she'd be okay. Her back was stiff against the windowsill. "Whoever . . . whatever it is, it's dead and it can't hurt me," she repeated.

As the presence drew nearer, the air grew thick and cold as

ice. Shay yelled, "Everett! I know it's you. Leave me alone!"

The window at her back slammed up violently and she screamed. Twisting her head around, she saw the two-story drop to the concrete sidewalk below and felt nonexistent hands pushing on her chest. Wind coming from nowhere whipped her hair around to slap in her face.

"God, help me!" she cried, grasping onto the thin curtains as her feet slid out from beneath her. She was being lifted into the air! Two feet off the floor, she screamed out the window, "Someone, help me!"

When flames suddenly blazed and exploded in the fireplace, whatever held Shay let loose and she crashed to the floor. In an instant, the sulfuric smell disappeared and the ominous pressure that had filled the room was gone.

Shay crawled to the bed and laid her head against the mattress, drawing in shallow breaths. Her heart felt like it was going to burst out of her chest. When she sensed someone watching her, she raised her head and saw Callie standing before her.

"Did you start that fire?"

The woman nodded.

"Thank you."

And Callie disappeared again.

EIGHTEEN

Shay scurried onto the bed and dug through her purse for her cell phone. "Please, Colt. Please answer your phone," she prayed aloud while punching in his number with a quivering hand.

"Morgan Realty."

Thank God. "Colt, it's me. I've just had another encounter. Actually, two encounters. The girl was here, and so was the evil male spirit. He almost pushed me out the window."

"What the hell? I'll be right over."

Click. The line went dead.

Shay grabbed her pillow and clutched it to her chest, her gaze darting around the room, expecting the entity to return and wreak more havoc. It was not out of the question. Ghosts could do whatever they wanted, whenever they wanted, apparently—including physical assault on live human beings.

"Callie? Are you still here?" she whispered.

There was no sign or sense of her. The room was quiet, and so was downstairs.

It seemed ages before Colt arrived. When he banged on the front door, Shay leapt off the bed and ran down the stairs, still trembling. When she flung open the door and saw his face etched with concern, she threw herself into his arms. He held her tight and sifted his fingers through her hair. Melting into his broad chest made her feel protected and safe. Slowly, as he held her, her pulse rate began to decrease. It wasn't until she finally eased out of the comfort of his embrace that they exchanged words.

"Tell me what happened."

Shay took his hand and led him through the saloon and up the staircase. "I'll show you."

When they reached the top of the stairs, probably sensing her apprehension, Colt stepped into the bedroom first, gazed around and announced, "It's clear. There's nothing in here."

She followed him in and told him of her experience. "As soon as I got home, I went straight into the bathroom. When I walked in here, Callie was standing in front of the fireplace."

"Who's Callie?"

"The young girl. She told me her name tonight. Do you recollect hearing the name before, in any of the ghost stories you heard growing up?"

"No. Guess she didn't tell you her last name."

"No, but her first name isn't that common. Maybe she's listed in the census I found in one of the books at the historical society."

He nodded. "On the phone you said *he* tried to push you out the window. Do you know who he is yet? Did the girl tell you his name, by any chance?"

"Yes." The adrenaline was still rushing through Shay's body. "I heard his footsteps pounding up the stairs and then he entered the room. That horrible smell filled the room and I knew it was Everett."

"Everett?"

"He's the one who strangled Callie."

"Wait a minute," Colt said, holding his hands up as if he was surrendering. "How do you know she was strangled? Did she tell you that, too?"

"No. But she kept touching her neck, and it has black-and-blue marks on it. I'm guessing that's how she died. I think she was murdered."

"Where did you come up with the name of Everett?"

"Callie spoke the name as he was entering the room. The expression on her face was one of complete terror."

"Did he show himself to you?"

Shay shook her head. "No. He never manifested. But he felt like the Hulk when he lifted me into the air over there." She walked to the window and her legs began to shake at the recollection.

"See this window?" she pointed. "It was closed, but Everett opened it and then he pushed me. I held onto the curtain as he was lifting me into the air."

Colt examined the curtain and saw where her fingernails had ripped the fabric.

"There wasn't anything I could do," she continued. "He was going to throw me out the window, but Callie saved my life. She started a fire in the fireplace, and he immediately let go and vanished."

Colt strode to the fireplace and knelt. "There aren't any logs in this fireplace. No ash. No sign of a fire."

She trotted to his side. "Callie made the fire start. I swear."

"There hasn't been a fire in this grate for years," Colt repeated. "Are you sure you weren't asleep and this was all a bad dream?"

Shay ground her teeth, realizing he was questioning her sanity again. "I saw it flaming. I heard it crackling. I felt its heat." She knew the octave of her voice was rising, but she hadn't been hallucinating. She didn't want him to think she was a raving lunatic. "How do you explain the tears in the curtains?" she asked. "He hoisted me into the air and was about to throw me out the window. I didn't dream that."

Colt stood up and put his arms around her again.

Pushing away, Shay searched his face and said, "Do you

believe me?"

He sighed and plowed a hand through his hair. "I've never held to the rumors about ghosts, but I *want* to believe you."

Her mouth stretched into a thin line. "Either you believe me or you don't, Colt. If you don't, then please leave. I'll deal with this myself—like I've dealt with all the other problems and heartbreaks in my life."

When his face softened and he reached out to gently push a strand of hair behind her ear, she struggled to hold back tears.

"I'm sorry. I want to believe you," he said. "None of this makes sense, but I don't know how to explain it logically. I'm thinking that dream I had must have been about you or this girl."

"Callie."

"Callie." Colt shook his head as if he was trying to put all the pieces together. "The hands around my throat yesterday felt real. We both saw the writing on the glass. You tell me you were almost tossed out the window tonight, and you've been seeing and speaking to a dead person. Unless you're as crazy as a loon, you're not imagining the things that have been happening to you."

With a hand on her arm, he assured, "Even if I hadn't experienced some of these things myself, I . . . I believe you."

She smiled and hugged him tight. "Thank you, Colt, because I needed to hear that, and I need you to help me unravel this mystery."

He set her back. "What mystery?"

"The mystery about who Callie and Everett were, and why Callie needs my help."

Colt grinned. "You mean I'll be Doctor Watson to your Sherlock Holmes?"

Shay's eyes lit up. She was learning he was good at turning around a stressful situation with humor. She played along. "Or

Frank Hardy to my Nancy Drew."

He snapped his fingers. "How about, I'll be Scooby Doo and you can be Daphne?"

"Why not Velma? She was the intelligent one."

"Because Daphne was the hot one with the red hair."

Shay rolled her eyes. "I can't argue with that."

They smiled at one another. "Feeling better?" he asked.

"Yes. But would you mind staying a while longer? I'm wound tight and still a little nervous."

"I thought you'd never ask." He eyed the one chair in the room and then the bed.

"I don't have a living room," she reminded him, following his gaze. "We'll have to sit on the bed."

"Or lie," he teased. Colt fluffed up the pillows and flopped onto the mattress, which squeaked under his weight. He lay back with his arms behind his head and stretched out his long legs.

"This is nice," he said. "Comfortable." He patted the bed with his hand, requesting her to join him.

When she curled up beside him, he placed his arm around her and she snuggled into his shoulder, sighed, and closed her eyes.

NINETEEN

Sitting on the edge of her bed the next morning, Colt jiggled Shay's arm to wake her. Her eyelids rolled open and she lazily said, "Good morning."

"Mornin', sleepy head."

She yawned. "What time is it?"

"Seven o'clock."

He'd been up for an hour watching her breathe. It'd been a long time since he'd awakened beside a woman. Nothing had happened last night except he'd stayed with her, and they'd both drifted off with her in his arms. This morning, watching her sleep had given him time to reflect, and a deep longing had washed over him. Studying Shay had reminded him of what he'd been missing for so many years—a soft body nudged against him in the mornings, warm breath on his neck; a woman to love and cherish.

He'd noticed she seemed to barely breathe when she slept. A quiet sleeper would be nice, he thought. Denise had been sweet as pie, and he'd loved her more than life itself, but she'd snored like a freight train throughout their entire marriage.

Another cute thing he saw while watching Shay was that she'd smiled in her sleep a couple of times. Maybe she'd been dreaming about him.

His reverie was broken when he saw her peek under the covers he'd tucked her into sometime in the night.

"All of my clothes are still on," she said, lifting one eyebrow.

"Everything except your shoes. You didn't think I'd take advantage of you in your sleep, did you?" He narrowed his eyes, teasing her. "I'm not that kind of guy. I want you to be fully coherent the first time I undress you."

Her eyes widened.

Damn. Why do I keep saying things like that to her?

The truth of the matter was he couldn't help it. Open mouth and insert foot. That's how it seemed to be when he was near her. Honest to a fault. That's the way he'd described himself to her when they'd first met, and the description fit him to a tee.

All he'd been thinking about was what it would be like to make love to her, and he had a damned hard time not hinting at it. She'd kept him in line so far, much to his chagrin, but patience was a virtue. Or so he'd been taught. Anyway, he'd meant what he'd told her. First time they made love, it would be *her* idea. That way she'd know he was in this for more than a one-night stand.

That confession sent shock waves through him. He didn't think he had it in him to take a chance at going the distance with another woman, but this woman seemed to be changing all that. She didn't seem too stoked about moving forward, however. Taking it slow was how he'd need to play it with her, if he wanted to prove he was different from the others who'd come and gone. Not knowing her full story, he still sensed she'd been hurt bad somewhere along the line.

"I'm gonna leave now," he said, cupping her face. "I'll be back around one to pick you up to go to Frank's."

She yawned and stretched like a cat. She was definitely more at ease this morning than she'd been last night at his place.

"Okay. I'm really looking forward to meeting Mr. Averill. Have fun showing your houses today."

"Showing houses is not fun," he said matter-of-factly. "It'll be especially hard to concentrate when all I'll be thinking about is seeing you this afternoon."

She propped up on one elbow and flashed him a slow smile. "You're a kind man, Colt Morgan. Thank you for staying with me last night. And for not trying anything."

"Don't think I didn't want to."

She grinned, and when she leaned forward to give him a soft kiss, he knew without a doubt that she was special. They both had morning breath, but it didn't matter to her.

"See you at one." He patted her arm, rose from the bed and exited the room, amazed that a woman could look as fresh as a daisy at that hour. "Are you coming down to lock up behind me?" he asked, stopping in the doorway.

"I'll go down soon. I want to lie here a minute more." She turned her head toward the window. "The sun feels good."

Colt let himself out and hadn't realized how disheveled he must look until an older couple wearing matching powder-blue sweat suits jogged past him on the sidewalk and then stopped and whirled around.

"Colt! What on earth are you doing out this hour of the morning?" the woman said.

It was Margaret and Bill, longtime friends of his folks. Margaret, a retired schoolteacher who had taught him in fifth grade, cast a suspicious glance at the saloon and then stared at his shirt, which was not tucked in. When her wary gaze moved to his face, he rubbed a hand over his cheeks and chin, feeling the five-o'clock shadow that covered them. Margaret still had a way of making him feel guilty, even at the age of forty. Like she'd caught him sticking his hand in the candy jar and was sorely disappointed in his behavior.

"Just visiting a friend," he drawled, skimming a hand through his hair, which felt like it was sticking up on end.

"Uh-huh," Margaret said with a tone he'd heard many times as a kid. "Hannah told me she met your *friend.*"

"Chet says she's real pretty," Bill added, smiling.

"No secrets around here," Colt mumbled.

"It's awfully early for a visit, Colton," Margaret stated.

"For heaven's sakes, Margie," Bill gently admonished. "Colt's a grown man of fifty. He's not your student anymore. Leave the poor guy alone."

"Forty," Colt said, clapping Bill on the shoulder. "I'm only forty, sir."

"Sorry 'bout that." Bill tugged on Margaret's arm and then waved to Colt. "Nice seeing you, but we've got to run."

He and Margaret broke out laughing at his pun. As they took up their jog again, Bill looked over his shoulder and winked and gave Colt a thumbs-up.

TWENTY

Shay stepped into the historical society later that morning to find someone other than Doris manning the front desk. A tall bald man greeted her. After Shay explained to him who she was, the man said, "I'm Bart Rockwood, Doris's husband. Doris is under the weather today, but she told me you might be in." He pulled out the books and the binder from below the counter where Doris had stored them.

"I hope it's nothing serious."

"She gets a migraine when a storm's on its way."

What was he talking about? She'd just walked to the old schoolhouse, and the sun was shining bright and there were no clouds in the sky. There was no sign of a storm.

"I don't need all the material today," she told him, ignoring the comment. "Just the one book for now. Thank you."

She took the book with the census list in it and headed for a chair in the corner, which sat underneath a window. Hoping to locate Callie and Everett, she began the daunting task of tracing her finger down each column, searching for their first names.

It didn't take long for her to become blurry-eyed and realizing this method wasn't going to work. The lists were alphabetical by last name. It would take forever to find Callie and Everett this way. The whole point was to discover their last names anyway. There had to be a better way.

Setting the book back on the counter in front of Mr. Rockwood, she asked, "Is there a cemetery in town?"

"Why sure. It's up on the hill, just east of here, about three blocks."

"Is it the only one in Hill City?"

"The churches have their own graveyards, of course, but the Black View is the only public cemetery. It's real pretty and peaceful up there."

Hmmm. This could start her on another wild goose chase, one as potentially daunting as the census lists. But, if Callie had been a saloon girl, chances were she was buried in the public cemetery, not one of the church's graveyards. It was worth a try to go check it out.

"The Black View has an old part and a new part," Mr. Rockwood advised. "The historic graves are in the back half, and the newer are in the front."

"Thank you, Mr. Rockwood. You've been a great help. Please tell Doris I hope she feels better."

Stepping out into the warm air and strolling east, Shay thought it would be a lot easier to wait until Callie manifested herself to her again. Then she could just ask what her last name was, why Everett had murdered her, and why she needed her help. But what if Callie didn't return for days? Or she was unable to speak next time she appeared? It seemed she had trouble getting her words out last night. Maybe she was losing her ability to communicate.

Besides, Shay was already caught up in the mystery, and she had nothing better to do with her time right now. She couldn't very well make plans to open a new business in the saloon as long as ghosts haunted the place. And even though she was rich, she had to do something with her life. A bed and breakfast seemed like a good idea in a tourist town.

If she helped Callie with her problem, whatever it was, she'd be helping herself as well. It was important to move forward and put the losses of her parents and the heartaches of her failed relationships behind her.

Shay strode to the Black View Cemetery, determined to find Callie and Everett's tombstones.

The cemetery was a short hike up a hill, as Mr. Rockwood had mentioned, and the view from the top was fabulous. Beyond were the jagged peaks of the Black Hills, for as far as the eye could travel. She guessed that's why the name Black View had been chosen for this spot.

What a pleasant place to spend eternity, she thought, glancing around. Towering trees shaded the entire property, making it feel more like a park than a graveyard.

She began wandering through the newer section, stopping to read monuments that stood out among others. Most were carved of marble or granite. Wooden fences or wrought-iron fence and rails surrounded headstones that were grouped together. Most sites looked to be well maintained, with flowers or other mementoes placed at the foot of the tombstones.

As she strolled, a green granite headstone caught her attention because of its unusual color. She went to investigate and was stunned to see the name *Morgan* engraved on it.

The breath caught in her throat as she stared at the inscription.

Denise Marie Morgan
Beloved Wife of Colton Morgan
Precious Daughter of Dennis and Nancy Green
Born: April 4, 1972 Died: December 15, 2000.

What a strange coincidence. Of all the graves in this cemetery, what are the odds I should find the grave of Colt's wife?

Shay stared at the stone, imagining the kind of woman Denise had been, and the type of life she and Colt had made together. Colt hadn't talked about her except to mention she'd gotten sick, but Shay sensed it had been a happy marriage.

She tilted her head and listened to the trilling of a bird. Looking up, she spied a pretty bluebird sitting on a nearby branch. The cemetery was totally quiet, except for the chirping. Not even a breeze stirred the leaves in the trees, she realized. It was slightly eerie, being completely alone up here, but the bird's joyful song helped alleviate her uneasiness—for a few moments.

As she started walking toward the back half of the cemetery, the little bird followed, flitting from one tree to another, continuing to sing its song. As Shay moved deeper into the cemetery, the bird flew with her. At one point, she stopped and the bird halted its chirping and hovered in front of her, flapping its wings. It seemed to stare right into her eyes.

"Go on, birdie," she said out loud. "Shoo. You're starting to creep me out a little."

Picking up her tempo, the beats of Shay's heart kept pace with her footsteps—as did the flapping of the bird's wings. She weaved between tombstones, watching the bluebird out of the corner of her eye, until she found herself in the historic section of the cemetery. Populated with older shade trees, this part of the graveyard was denser and darker than the front part. Spooky.

"Look at these old stones," she commented aloud, momentarily forgetting about the bothersome bird. Casually walking between the narrow rows, she saw dozens of flat headstones that were cracked and discolored or covered with algae. Most of the names had been worn down by weather and erosion. Some monuments were still partially readable, with years dating back to the early 1800s, while the faces of others were completely blank, having been worn completely off.

Undeterred, and with the sudden thrill of excitement, she began gliding from tombstone to tombstone, searching out the graves of Callie and Everett.

TWENTY-ONE

Shay checked each and every marker, imagining the lives of the people that lay in the graves. It had to have been a tough life back then, particularly for a woman. Over a hundred years ago, this area of the Black Hills would have been isolated and untamed, lacking any of the conveniences found in the cities back east.

Winters had to have been harsh, there would have been few ways to earn a living, and, from the records of history, Shay knew wild and dangerous men roamed the land, inflicting cruelty and pain wherever they went. It would have been a struggle just to survive another day. She wondered what kind of pain Callie had endured before Everett ended her life once and for all.

As she walked, reading every headstone that was decipherable, Shay got the distinct feeling someone was watching her. Several times, she looked over her shoulder, feeling eyes boring into her back, to find nothing, or no one there. Goose bumps rose on her arms and the hairs prickled on the back of her neck—feelings she'd been experiencing all too much in the last few days.

The bluebird was no longer singing. In fact, it was gone. Wishing the bird still there to keep her company, she called to it. "Where'd you go, little birdie? You can come back if you'd like. I won't tell you to shoo anymore."

A twig snapped about thirty feet away. Shay jerked her head

in that direction but saw no one. "Is someone there?" she called out tentatively.

With her heart in her throat, she questioned whether she should have come to this place alone. The cemetery was secluded. Sheltered amid the towering trees, she felt like she was in another world, far from civilization. A serial killer could be lurking behind the tombstones, poised to attack. She could lie for days, injured or dead, with no one knowing where to find her. This had been a bad idea.

Her gaze darted around while she willed herself to calm down and stop thinking crazy thoughts. "Mr. Rockwood knows I'm here," she reminded herself. "I'm not going to let some stupid noises scare me. I came here to locate those graves, and I'm not going to leave until I find them."

With a tingle racing up her spine, she continued examining headstones one by one, and her spirits lifted when she came to a fenced-in plot with four tombstones inside. Peering over the fence, the largest of the stones was clearly legible, bearing the names of both Dean and Cynthia Averill.

The marble monument was not embellished in any way, but it was also not a wooden marker like many in the graveyard. The names looked to be professionally engraved. No surprise there. After all, Dean Averill had owned the Buckhorn. He'd probably been one of the wealthiest men in Hill City at the time.

Cynthia had been born in 1864 and died in 1894. Shay quickly did the math. She'd been only twenty-nine at the time of her demise. Dean, on the other hand, had lived to be considerably older for the time period. The date of his death was 1910.

Shay tried to decipher the two stones to the right of the big one. They were little more than markers, and the carvings on them were illegible except for the words *God's Child* etched on one of them. Shay figured these two graves must be those of the children of Dean and Cynthia.

A fourth tombstone was of better quality than the others, and it looked to be newer. The name on it was *Marcus Dean Averill,* and he'd lived to be an old man of seventy.

Marcus must have been another of Dean's children. Maybe he was Frank Averill's father.

Perhaps the spot beside Marcus was reserved for Frank. Colt had said he'd been near death several times. She didn't know the man, but a deep sense of sadness swept over her unexpectedly at seeing the graves of his family lying before her.

As she stepped away from the Averill family plot, another chill danced across her neck and shimmied down her arms. A rustling in the trees above caused her to look up. Through the breaks in the trees, she saw dark clouds forming, blocking out the sun and blue sky. It looked like Mr. Rockwood had been right. Unbelievably, a storm seemed to be brewing.

With hurried steps, Shay tried to shake off the sensation that someone was watching her, and she continued progressing through the rows of graves. Despite the possibility of getting caught in a rainstorm, a feeling hinted for her not to quit looking for Callie's grave. Believing the "eyes" upon her might be Callie herself, guiding her, Shay closed her own eyes and said, "Callie, if you're here, please show me the way to your grave."

After a moment, compelled by some unknown force, Shay strode to the far corner of the graveyard. It didn't feel like Callie's spirit showing her the way. Nevertheless, it felt like the spirit of *someone.* Invisible hands propelled her forward.

There, by itself, stuck in a sad-looking patch of grass, was a small wooden marker. Shay knelt and traced the simple inscription with her finger.

Callie Hayes
Birth: 1865 Death: 1885

"Callie Hayes," she whispered with reverence. "You were just twenty years old when you died. Who buried you? Your friends from the saloon? Or was it your boss, Mr. Averill? Did you have any family in Hill City?"

A crack of lightning reverberated across the sky just then, followed by a boom of thunder, which caused Shay to jump. A few raindrops fell on her head. She stared into the ever-threatening sky.

"Great. This is just what I need. I'm going to get drenched."

Knowing she should leave now or get soaked but hesitant to go, she continued to speak to the stone. "Now that I know your full name, I'll help you any way I can. You just have to tell me what you need, Callie. What is it you want me to know? Was someone else involved in your murder besides Everett? Did he have a partner in crime? Were they punished for what they did to you? Maybe they were never caught, and you're seeking justice," she wondered.

When a voice growled in her ear, Shay screamed and stumbled to her feet.

"Who's there?" she called, spinning in a circle. A slow movement captured her attention from out of the corner of her eye. Something—or someone—*was* watching her, standing about fifty feet away. Her head pivoted, and her gaze landed on a shadow. Was it the branch of a tree, or was it a person? With eyes enlarging, she saw a dark figure slip behind a tombstone.

Taking in a lung full of air, Shay bolted in the opposite direction. Another crash of thunder shook the earth, and a lightning bolt struck the ground in front of her.

Shrieking, she flinched and kept running.

Out of nowhere, pounding footsteps rushed up behind her, causing her ears to pulsate. Cold breath teased her neck, and a male voice hissed around her head. Frightened out of her mind, she sprinted as fast as her legs would carry her, with her pulse throbbing in her veins—afraid to turn and look at what was bearing down on her.

Chest burning and legs about to give out from under her, running became even more difficult when the storm clouds cracked open and rain started to pour.

Slipping in the wet grass, Shay twisted her foot and cried out when she fell, landing hard on her arm. Sensing a presence near, she fought against the raging pain and fought to stand. When unseen arms hoisted her up, she found herself eye level with Denise Morgan's headstone and gulped.

As if that weren't strange enough, the little bluebird sat perched on top, with its beady eyes fixed on her.

With water streaming down Shay's face, she begged, "Who are you?" and then she felt the world go black.

TWENTY-TWO

When Shay woke up, she was lying on her back in damp grass, hair matted to her face, wet clothes clinging to her like a sodden second skin. But at least the storm had passed. Rolling onto her side, she winced when she moved her foot. Her ankle hurt, and so did the arm she'd fallen on, but there was no time to dwell on the pain. That was secondary to getting out of the graveyard before anything more bizarre happened.

She hauled herself to her feet and leaned on Denise Morgan's tombstone, keeping as much weight off the tender foot as possible. Glancing in every direction, the tension in her body melted when she realized the storm must have driven away whatever evil had been chasing her. Her fear subsided, and curiosity took a backseat to pain when she realized the bluebird was nowhere to be seen either.

With rays of sunlight pushing through the openings in the trees, Shay might have thought she'd imagined the storm, the bird, the dark figure, and the footsteps behind her, if not for being completely soaked. The cemetery was at peace again, the way a cemetery should be.

She hadn't found Everett's grave, but at least she knew Callie's full name now. That was good enough for one day. Shivering, she knew she somehow had to make it home on her injured foot and get into a hot bath before she caught her death from the cold.

She eased away from the granite headstone, putting most of

the weight on her uninjured foot, and limped slowly, managing to make it through the graveyard without slipping and falling again.

Her energy was zapped, but she still had close to eight blocks to walk to get home. Could she do it with pain shooting through her foot? Thinking of the daunting task ahead, tears welled in her eyes. She stopped and leaned against another headstone to rest a moment.

"You look as if you could use a hand," said a voice from behind her. Her heart leaped inside her chest, and she craned her head. An elderly man and woman had slipped up on either side of her, inquisitiveness etched on their lined faces.

"You must have gotten caught in that storm," the woman said. "My brother and I waited it out in our truck before coming up to visit our sister, Maude. You should have waited, too."

Shay forced a smile when she realized these were real people—not ghosts or evil shadow people—and they were older, nonthreatening people at that. "I didn't know it was going to rain when I walked here from town," she explained, shoving wet tresses out of her eyes. "I didn't bring an umbrella, and, unfortunately, I twisted my ankle."

"We're done visiting Maude. You can ride with us back to town," the woman said, linking her arm through Shay's. "Julian, take the lady's other arm," she told her brother, who jumped at her directive. "And both of you watch your step as we walk down the hill. We might all tumble down like Jack and Jill if we're not careful."

Back at the Buckhorn, Shay thanked the couple as she slid off the seat and out of their old Ford pickup.

"You sure you can get inside on your own?" asked the old lady, as she pulled the truck door shut. "That foot looks like it's starting to swell."

Shay nodded and waved. "I'll be okay. Thanks again."

Once she was inside the saloon, she limped to the kitchen and grabbed a bag of frozen peas out of the freezer for her sprained foot, and then hobbled up the stairs and ran a bath. As she collected dry clothes from her bedroom, she was grateful for the peace and quiet that greeted her. There'd been enough paranormal activity for one day, and she was exhausted.

After carefully climbing into the tub, she gently propped her leg on the rim and laid the peas across her ankle. Though it was throbbing, she was sure the foot wasn't broken. But it did feel strained. Hopefully the swelling would go down and there wouldn't be much bruising.

The hot water did its job and sent her body temperature skyrocketing back to normal. As she soaked, her pulse began to speed up again when she replayed the frightening things that had happened in the cemetery. She wondered what Colt would think when she told him later—*if* she told him at all. He didn't believe in the supernatural. Maybe he'd heard enough and would decide she *was* completely out of her mind, especially if she mentioned his wife's grave and the odd bird. He was her only friend in town, and she couldn't afford to lose him.

At one o'clock, Colt picked her up as planned, helped her into his truck when he saw she was limping, and they were on their way to Frank Averill's house. His heart rate increased as Shay related her experiences in the Black View Cemetery. Although he'd been a nonbeliever all his life, there was no way he could deny the things that were continuing to plague her.

"You're sure your foot isn't broken?" he asked, glancing at the ankle she'd wrapped in an Ace bandage.

"I'm sure. It feels a lot better now. I guess frozen peas really work on sprains."

He drove slowly through town, silent . . . considering all she'd told him. The entire story was incredible, but the one thing that had most captured his attention was the fact that she'd accidentally stumbled upon Denise's headstone. Once again, he didn't believe this incident had been rooted in chance, and that was because of the bluebird.

At first, Shay had been hesitant to tell the whole story, but as he prodded, she revealed that she'd come upon the headstone quite by accident. She'd mentioned being surprised to look up and see Denise's name, but hadn't asked much about Denise, and understandably so. If she hadn't mentioned the bluebird, he would have felt a lot more awkward talking about his wife, too. But the bird was something he simply couldn't ignore.

Clearing his throat, he said, "I want to tell you something. It may sound crazy, but . . ."

Shay interrupted him. "Colt, trust me. Nothing you say could sound crazy. You've listened to everything I've said and you haven't called the men in the white coats yet."

With his gaze on the road ahead, he stated, "Denise's animal totem was a bluebird."

When Shay didn't respond, he glanced sideways. She was turned in the seat, her body facing him, her forehead wrinkled in question.

"Do you know what an animal totem is?" he asked.

"I've heard the term. It has something to do with Native Americans, right?"

"Yes. A totem is symbolic. It can be the symbol of a tribe, a family or an individual. Native Americans believe animals hold special power and knowledge, and that each individual is connected with an animal that accompanies the person through life, acting as a guide. They call that animal a totem. Although a person may identify with different animal guides throughout his or her lifetime, it is one special totem animal that acts as the main guardian spirit for that person. The animal guide offers power and wisdom. Denise's guide, or totem, was the bluebird."

"Was Denise Native American?"

"No. But she underwent a variety of alternative treatments during her illness, and some of them were spiritual in nature. She had many Native American friends, and she respected the culture and beliefs."

"And Denise chose the bluebird as her totem?"

Colt could see Shay's interest was piqued. He shook his head. "The animal chooses the person, not the other way around. Every animal has its own special power and message. Denise began to realize that she'd always been drawn to bluebirds, that the bird had consistently appeared in her life from the time she was a child. It wasn't until the bird came to her again at her darkest moment that she understood what he was offering."

"Which was?"

As Colt glanced back at her, Shay's gaze was direct.

"What was the bluebird's power and message?" she repeated. "Do you know?"

"Yes. The bluebird is symbolic for happiness within. He signifies a contentment and fulfillment that *is* happening or is about to happen."

Colt waited to see if the meaning sunk in. Although the bird had been Denise's totem, he suspected it had also made a connection with Shay.

It seemed her mind was working and she was putting two and two together. He made a turn onto Frank's street. Next time he looked at her, there were tears pooling in the corners of her eyes.

"The bluebird came to your wife to assure her," she said, apparently understanding. "To let her know it was okay to move on to the next world."

Believing that to have been the message of the bluebird all those years ago, Colt nodded. He pulled into Frank's drive.

When he cut off the motor, Shay reached for his hand. She was trembling.

Her voice was respectful when she asked, "Colt, do you think that was Denise's bluebird who came to me this morning?"

"I don't know," he answered with honesty. "It's a mighty odd coincidence. But then, there have been a lot of those lately."

Shay's eyes were bright with tears. He leaned forward and wiped one from her cheek. "No need to be sad, Shay. The bluebird totem is all about happiness. He chose you, as he chose Denise, to give you a message. There's a lot going on in your life right now. You must have many questions that don't seem to have answers right now, such as, why did you lose both your parents so close together? What drew you to Hill City, and why did you buy the saloon? Why are you seeing ghosts? Is it chance that you and I met?"

She sniffled and nodded. "What do you think the bluebird's message is for me?"

Colt took her hand and held it. "I think he wants you to know that it's okay to move past your grief and your fears. I also believe he wants you to listen to his song so you can find your own joy and open your heart. With your heart open, it'll be easier for someone close to you to fill that empty space inside."

She squeezed his hand. "Someone like you?"

The words that came out of his mouth flowed as smooth as honey. "Yes. Someone *exactly* like me."

When she lifted her gaze to him and smiled, he felt his own heart might burst from his chest with emotions he had kept locked away for so long.

"Do you think it's strange that the bluebird could be Denise's totem and mine, too?" she wanted to know.

"No. I'm starting to believe in a lot of things I never believed before. In fact, I think Denise may have had something to do with the bluebird visiting you this morning. She was a fine woman, and she didn't want me to go through life alone."

Shay smiled again, seeming relieved. Maybe she'd been thinking the same thing but hadn't wanted to suggest it.

"Even though the bluebird hasn't shown himself to you, perhaps the message is also for you, Colt," she said, looking hopeful.

"If I were a betting man, I'd say there's a good likelihood of that." He cupped her chin in his hand and kissed her softly on the lips, feeling the tides turning between them. They parted and he glanced through the windshield to Frank's house. The magical moment was destroyed when he saw a figure at the window.

"At least Opal could hide behind the curtains while she's spying on us," he growled.

TWENTY-THREE

"Who's Opal?" Shay asked, squeaking open the passenger door and following his line of vision to the front of the house.

"Frank's full-time nurse. She's standing right there in the window. Opal's a real trip. Ignore anything rude that might spew from her mouth. I don't think the woman can stop herself." As they walked up the sidewalk, he felt bad that Shay had hurt herself and was limping, but her spirits seemed to have lifted. He noticed her tears had dried. "Do you feel better?"

"Much."

Opal opened the door and greeted the two of them with a pleasant smile. "Come on in, Colt. It's nice to see you. Frank and I have been expecting you."

Colt narrowed his eyes at her. "You feeling okay, Opal? Are you running a fever?"

She laughed. "I'm not sick, silly. I'm as healthy as a horse, but thanks so much for asking. Who have we here?" Her curious gaze landed on Shay.

"This is Shay Brennan. She's the new owner of the Buckhorn Saloon I was telling you about. Shay, meet Opal Franklin."

"Pleasure to meet you," Opal said, extending a pudgy hand.

"Same here," Shay replied, shaking it. "I appreciate your letting us drop by today. How's Mr. Averill feeling? Is he up to having visitors?"

It was obvious she was anxious to meet Frank.

"He's awake and looking forward to meeting you, Miss Brennan."

"Please call me Shay. May I call you Opal?"

"Of course, honey. Come on back."

With Opal leading the way down the hall to Frank's room, Colt shook his head, wondering if aliens had abducted the real Opal and replaced her with a nicer version.

When they stepped into Frank's bedroom, his thin frame was propped against a stack of pillows, and his eyes looked clear.

"Come on in, Colt," Frank said in a stronger voice than Colt had heard in months. Without a moment's hesitation, Shay stepped up to one side of the bed and, in an unexpected gesture, took Frank's hand when he stretched it out. Colt sauntered to the other side.

"I'll leave y'all to your visit," Opal called from the doorway before tromping down the hallway.

Before Colt had a chance to introduce the two of them, Colt saw Frank's eyes grow large and his mouth drop open. In a matter of seconds, all the color began to drain from his face and he sat immobile, taut as if in shock.

"Frank, you okay?" Colt said, jiggling the man's arm. "You look as if you've seen a ghost." As soon as the words left his mouth, he realized his choice of phrasing might not have been the best.

Shay seemed not to notice his faux pas. She touched Frank's other arm. "Mr. Averill, are you all right?" Frank's face looked frozen in that strange expression. Shay looked over the top of him and said, "Colt, maybe you should get Opal. I think something's terribly wrong. He could be having a stroke."

"No." Frank's hand shot out and grabbed Colt's arm, and he suddenly came out of the trance—or whatever it'd been. With a firm voice, he said, "Don't need Opal. No stroke. I'm okay."

Colt released a sigh of relief and said, "You scared the hell out of me, Frank. You sure you're okay?"

He nodded, keeping his gaze on Shay. She placed a hand over her heart and sighed, too.

"What is it, Mr. Averill?" she asked quietly. "Are you confused? Do you feel ill? Please tell us what scared you a minute ago."

"I'm not scared," Frank said.

Colt noticed the color was slowly returning to his sunken cheeks.

"I was surprised. That's all. Still am, if truth be known."

"Surprised about what?" Colt asked.

"Her." Frank pointed a bony finger at Shay.

Colt and Shay exchanged uncomprehending glances over the bed.

"Do you mind explaining?" Colt said.

"Open that bottom drawer of the bureau," Frank commanded, pointing again. "There's a picture book I want you to get. And grab my eyeglasses from the top."

Colt did as Frank requested and laid the photo album in Frank's lap. With a shaky hand, Frank slid on his glasses and began flipping through the yellowed pages.

When Shay threw Colt another quizzical look, he shrugged.

"Here it is. Colt, take a look at this."

Colt pulled his own glasses from his shirt pocket and slipped them on. When Frank jabbed his pointer finger into a sepia-colored photograph, Colt lifted the album closer to his face and stared, feeling a jolt race down his spine. The resemblance was uncanny.

When he met Shay's gaze, she questioned him with her eyes but said nothing—waiting for him to explain.

"Who is this woman?" Colt asked Frank, whose intense gaze was riveted to Shay.

"My grandmother. Cynthia Averill."

Twenty-Four

Shay had to see why Frank was scrutinizing her and what had Colt's brows stitched together. She crossed to the other side of the bed and peered at the photo.

It was a professional photograph taken by the Spearfish Photography Studio in Hill City, circa 1887, according to the stamp on the bottom.

"These are your grandparents, Mr. Averill?" she asked, staring at the handsome couple.

"Dean and Cynthia," he answered. "And there's no need to call me Mr. Averill. I'm just plain Frank."

Shay smiled at him and then returned her gaze to the photo. Dean was standing with his hand on his wife's shoulder. He wore a suit and derby hat. Cynthia sat in a chair wearing a gown and a hat with feathers. Her hair was long, hanging down her neck in ringlets. Both were solemn, neither of them smiling for the camera.

"I found a photo of your grandfather," she excitedly told Frank, while retrieving from her purse the photocopy Doris had made from the book. "Look. He's wearing the same derby hat."

"Don't you see the resemblance?" Colt asked, abruptly stopping her.

"What do you mean?" She witnessed Colt and Frank exchange glances, but didn't know why. She had no idea what Colt was talking about.

"Cynthia Averill," he said, as if it were obvious. "You kind of look like her."

"Me?" Shay chuckled and took another, closer look. "You think I look like Frank's grandmother?"

"Yeah. I do."

"Why would you think that? I don't see it. The long hair maybe, but . . ."

Colt looked to Frank for confirmation. "You see it, Frank. Don't you? That's why you keep staring at Shay."

Frank blinked several times and his mouth folded downward. "I don't know. I'm an old man. I don't see so well anymore, even with these bifocals." He jerked off the glasses and stuck them into Colt's hand. "I get confused a lot these days."

"You're not confused about this," Colt insisted. "Look," he said, shoving the sleeve of his shirt up his arm. "The hairs are standing up on my arms. That must mean something."

"Don't be silly," Shay said, closing the photo album and placing it on top of the bureau. "Cynthia Averill was a beautiful woman. I can see why Dean married her. But I'm often mistaken for someone else. For years, people have come up to me and told me I look exactly like their sister. Or I remind them of a friend they knew years ago. It happens all the time. Guess I have one of those faces."

Colt shook his head. "No way. How can you not see the resemblance? With all that's going on, I'd think you'd find the similarity between the two of you unnerving. I do."

"They say everyone has a twin," Shay said, not understanding why Colt was getting riled up.

"But not everyone is visited by ghosts."

"Ghosts?" Frank had been silently observing her this whole time. He now stared at Colt for a moment and then looked at Shay again. "Are you seeing ghosts in the Buckhorn?" he asked.

She glanced at Colt, who nodded, giving her the go-ahead to tell him.

"Yes, I am. I don't want to upset you, but I'm hoping you can help me figure out who the spirits are. Colt tells me your father inherited the saloon from your grandfather, and then you took it over for a number of years."

"That's right. But, running a bar wasn't for me. I preferred hardware and tools. Got tired of dealing with drunks and troublemakers."

"Was that the real reason you got out of the business, Frank?" Colt asked. "Several times, I remember Granddaddy mentioning something about the ghosts that ran you out of the saloon. I never took his stories to heart . . . until now."

Frank's gaze pierced Colt like he was psychically willing him to shut up. Then his expression softened again when Shay leaned over and patted his hand. Inside, her heart was jumping because she knew Frank was hiding the truth.

"It would mean a lot to me to know if you had any of the same experiences I'm having now," she said quietly. "I feel like I'm being sent messages, but I don't know what they are or what they mean."

"Okay," Frank relented. "I'll talk about it." Jabbing a finger into Colt's arm, he said, "But you better not tell a soul about this conversation. I don't want to be a laughing stock."

"Promise," Colt said, drawing an invisible X over his chest.

He scooted two chairs up to Frank's bedside and he and Shay sat. She delved into Frank's clear eyes and took a deep breath before beginning her questioning.

"Frank, did you ever see the spirit of a young woman with blonde hair wound on top of her head? I think she may have been a saloon girl many years ago. She would have lived in your grandfather's time. Her name was Callie Hayes. Do you recognize that name?"

He shook his head. "Nope. Never heard of her and never seen her."

"What about Everett? Do you have any knowledge or recollection of a man by that name?"

Frank thought a moment. "Everett who?"

"I don't know his last name," she admitted. "But I believe he's the man who murdered this girl, Callie Hayes."

Frank flinched. "Murder? What's she talking about, Colt?"

Colt explained about the marks around the spirit's neck, how the woman had asked for Shay's help, and all the unusual things that had been occurring in the saloon, including the entity that had tried to throw her out the window.

"Oh, no."

Visibly distressed, Frank squeezed his eyes shut and clamped his mouth closed. Shay realized she'd gone too far with the questions. She believed he might have witnessed something evil inside the Buckhorn, too, but for whatever reason, Frank was now unwilling to discuss it.

Disappointed, but not wanting to cause the man further anguish, she assured, "That's okay, Frank. You don't have to talk about anything you don't want to. Maybe we can visit another time." Standing, she signaled to Colt it was time to leave.

"I'll stop by and see you tomorrow," Colt told Frank, gently clapping him on the shoulder.

"It was a pleasure to meet you," Shay said, squeezing his hand. "Thank you for talking with me today. I'm sorry if I upset you. I hope you feel better soon." As she strolled from the room, she looked over her shoulder to see he was fixing her with a poignant stare and realized he most likely knew his days were numbered.

After Opal had showed Colt and Shay to the door, she entered Frank's room to discover him in an agitated state. Rushing to his side, she said, "Frank, what's wrong? Are you having an attack?"

"No. Get me the picture," he wheezed. "You know which one."

Opal pulled open the bottom drawer of the same dresser where the photo album had been stored and retrieved a five-by-seven picture frame. Since she'd been working for him, he'd only asked her one other time to bring it out. The frame usually stayed hidden beneath old shirts Frank no longer wore. She handed it to him. "You haven't asked to see this in a while."

Opal fell silent as Frank studied the faded color photograph. When he finally spoke, his voice cracked. "Don't she look like the woman who was just here?"

Opal examined the photo and then patted Frank's arm. He was becoming more sentimental and befuddled as each day passed. She was afraid he wouldn't last much longer. To appease him, she said, "They're both real pretty gals, no doubt about it."

Frank laid the photo facedown on his chest and closed his eyes.

"Let's take your blood pressure," Opal suggested, reaching for the cuff. "Then I'll give you a pill so you can sleep."

She felt terrible he had no family to be with him in his final days. Colt was as close to family as Frank had left. Frank was a nice old man and she hated to see him fading. Unfortunately, watching patients die came with the territory. Still, it broke her heart.

TWENTY-FIVE

"Frank didn't give us much," Colt said, helping Shay into the truck. He jumped in on his side and backed up and headed for Main Street.

She sighed. "I get the feeling he had paranormal experiences in the saloon when he owned it, but I didn't want to push him. He looks so fragile."

She felt Colt's eyes on her. When she turned her head, he was smiling.

"You really didn't see the likeness between you and Cynthia Averill?" he asked.

It was impossible to deny that both Colt and Frank thought there was a similarity, but it was just one of those things. What she'd told them was true. All her life, people had mistaken her for someone else.

"I guess we look a little bit alike, if you consider us both being short and having long hair a resemblance," she said to end it. "The photo was grainy. Don't think too hard on it. You told me Frank has his senile moments."

"True." Colt reached over and grasped her hand.

The familiarity between them was growing more comfortable with each touch and kiss. His hand felt warm and comforting and strong.

"I think you need to forget about ghosts for a while," he suggested. "My brother's birthday is tomorrow and Mama asked me to invite you over to the house for supper and cake."

That caught her off guard. Apparently he hadn't told his mom that there was nothing between them. "That is so sweet of your mother to invite me. Does she think we're dating?"

A sheepish grin filled his face. "Yes. She's been trying to hook me up with ladies for a few years now. She just assumed . . ."

"You haven't told her you're not interested in a committed relationship?" Shay was confused. Why wouldn't his family know that, if he were so opposed to marrying again?

"She worries about me being alone. You know how mothers are."

Shay did know. Her mother had been a caring and loving woman, and Shay missed her every single day. Colt's mom seemed just as loving. She supposed it wouldn't hurt to accept her invitation. Some downtime with Colt's family might be what she needed to take her mind off of all that was going on.

"Do you want me to go?" she asked, not wanting him to feel pressured.

"Sure. I wouldn't have told you if I didn't."

"You don't think your brother will mind my being there?"

"Hell, no. The more the merrier."

"Thank you, Colt. It's been a long time since I've enjoyed a family celebration of any kind. And your family seems so nice. You're right. It'll be good to forget about ghosts for a day."

He squeezed her hand. "We're glad to have you. Especially me."

He flashed a dazzling smile that caused her insides to melt like hot butter. Despite the mixed messages she'd been getting from him since they'd met, she was having a hard time controlling the way she felt. She was so attracted to him, but still afraid of getting hurt. Could be he was acting one way, but felt another when it came down to brass tacks.

When he slammed the gearshift into park, she realized they

were already at the Buckhorn.

"That didn't take long to get back," she noted.

"We hit all the green lights this time."

They were still holding hands, their fingers twined. "Do you have any plans for tonight?" she asked, immediately wishing she'd left well enough alone.

"Yes, I do. I have a dinner meeting with some other Realtors."

"Oh."

"Why? What'd you have in mind?"

She had no idea what she'd had in mind, so she made something up. "I thought I could cook for you. Pay you back for the pizza. Maybe another night."

He scooted to the center of the seat and gazed into her eyes. "I could come over for dessert."

She shivered when he leaned in and grazed her neck with his lips. How did he know that was one of her sensitive spots?

"That would work," she breathed, tilting her neck and closing her eyes, relinquishing herself to the tingles that raced through her body as Colt lightly nibbled her neck. The musky scent of his aftershave drifted into her nostrils, causing her to feel lightheaded. She knew she should stop him, but it had been so long since a man had wanted her.

When his lips found hers and they melded, he put his arms around her and crushed her to his chest. The pounding of his beating heart matched hers in perfect rhythm as their tongues darted around in each other's mouths for a few seconds.

Finally pulling back, she rasped, "I guess I'd better let you go." If she didn't put an end to this, they'd end up lying on the seat making out in broad daylight. She wasn't interested in giving anyone in town a show, but the devilish twinkle in his eyes revealed he wouldn't care if that were to happen.

With ragged breathing and passion flashing in his eyes, he said, "I'll be over at eight o'clock. Sharp."

Shay couldn't speak. She could only smile as she pushed open the door and slid out of the seat. When he winked, she waved and stepped onto the sidewalk with her insides jumping. After he'd pulled away, she inhaled several deep breaths and wondered what trouble she'd just agreed to.

"Dessert. Nothing more," she murmured, trying to convince herself that was all there would be. "He's coming over for coffee and dessert."

Well aware of his double meaning when he'd said the word *dessert,* she was determined not to let him get the upper hand tonight. Although her foot was still sore, she decided to take her time and stroll to the corner grocery. She had nothing in her kitchen, and she fully intended to have something edible for him when he came over.

While browsing through the aisles, she had no idea of what to buy. Was Colt a cheesecake man? Did he like ice cream? Was he partial to pie? All men liked pie, but she'd never made a homemade one before. The freezer section of the small store had three types to choose from. She picked the cherry and bought a container of vanilla ice cream, too.

As she ambled home, she was more than aware of the fact that, besides not knowing what kind of sweets he liked, there were a million other things she didn't know about Colt. That was all the more reason for her to keep her emotions in check tonight. Falling for a man too soon had gotten her in trouble before.

Unlocking the door to the saloon, she stepped in and angled her head. All was silent for the moment. There was plenty of time to bake the pie, so after popping it and the ice cream into the freezer, she walked up the stairs, feeling light as cotton.

It was not easy to get a man like Colt out of her head. No matter how many logical protests she considered, there was no denying the connection she felt to him. If she was a believer in reincarnation, she would have thought they'd been lovers—or husband and wife—in another time and place.

Lovers. The word conjured up images best put into the locked corner of her mind. At thirty-three, she'd had her share, including the two men she'd been engaged to. But lovers came a dime a dozen. That was a lesson both men had taught her. They'd used her to get to her father's money. Being a man's lover no longer meant to her what it once did.

Colt was forty. He'd made it clear he had no intentions of marrying again. She had no intention of entering into a relationship in which she'd have to wonder if someone wanted her for who she was or for her bank account. That much they had in common—feeling the same way about relationships.

Shay flopped onto her bed, smiling with an epiphany. She and Colt were grown adults who were clearly physically attracted to each other. He was not hiding the fact that he wanted to have sex with her. Why should she be any different? Women had the same needs and desires as men. A couple didn't need to be in a relationship to enjoy sex. If sex was what he wanted, she would give it to him. Gary and Tom had proven that people could pair off the same as animals, driven by one purpose only—physical need.

Lots of people made love with no strings attached. Why couldn't she?

Twenty-Six

The sweet and tangy scent of warm cherry pie wafted out from the kitchen and up the stairs. It was seven o'clock. Colt wasn't due for another hour, so Shay ran a tub of water, added scented oil, and slipped out of her clothes. Her legs needed shaving and her hair washed. As she scrubbed all her bits and pieces with liquid soap and moved the razor under her armpits, her nerves began to dance.

Was she actually going to seduce Colt tonight? That had never been her style, to make the first move on a man. Maybe that was another reason Gary and Tom had both left her, she thought. *I wasn't sexy or seductive enough.*

Well, that was all going to change. Colt was going to be the lucky guy. She'd show him just what kind of a wildcat she could be, and give him one erotic night he'd never forget.

She sank lower into the tub. The hot water combined with the oil soothed her muscles and helped her relax. Before long, her eyes grew weary. She laid her head back and closed her eyes, letting sleep wash over her.

Shay woke with a start, struggling to breathe. Ice-cold hands gripped her throat, squeezing the air out of her lungs. Before she could catch a breath, someone pushed her face down into the water. She opened her eyes underwater and saw Callie leaning into the bathtub, holding her down, with her own face twisted in anguish.

From below the slick bubbles, Shay heard her grit out, "Ev . . . er . . . ett."

Nearly out of breath, Shay kicked her feet and water splashed over the sides as she jetted herself to the surface.

"No," she gurgled, trying to pry the hands from her throat. When her gaze connected directly with Callie's, the spirit vanished into thin air.

Sputtering and coughing, Shay gripped the side of the tub with one hand and massaged her neck with the other. She pulled the plug and climbed out of the tub and hurriedly dried off as her gaze constantly darted around the bathroom. A peek into her bedroom assured her Callie was not waiting to ensnare her again.

She'd just thrown on a robe and quickly toweled off her hair when she heard a knock at the front door. The bedside clock read eight o'clock. In bare feet, Shay limped down the stairs and flung open the door.

"Callie choked me," she cried to Colt.

He pushed his way inside. "What? When?"

"Just now. Do you see marks on my neck?" She stretched her neck out like a goose so he could inspect.

"No. Tell me what happened." He took her arm and led her further inside.

Shay explained. "I was taking a bath and I guess I fell asleep. I woke up and Callie was strangling me—and trying to drown me. Her face was angry and she spoke Everett's name again."

Sliding his hand under her wet hair, Colt examined her throat again and announced there were no bruises, no scratches or marks of any kind.

"Does she want to kill me?" Shay asked. "How can I help her if I'm dead?" Alarm turned to resentment. How dare this ghost continue to assault her! "I've been doing my best to figure out what she wants, and this is how she repays me?"

"That's a helluva way to convince you to help," Colt answered with sarcasm.

Shay felt more confused than ever. Had Callie been the one to choke Colt that night? She didn't think so. That had been a male. Why all the choking? Why was Callie angry with her? *Was* she angry? Or was she simply trying to send her another message?

"I don't think she really intended to hurt me," Shay decided after calming down.

"Darlin', I don't know what they call it where you come from, but around here we consider strangulation the act of a homicidal maniac. You should, too."

"I believe she's trying to tell me something."

"Then why doesn't she tell you already, instead of wrapping her damned dead hands around your neck?"

Shay felt his frustration, but her mind was functioning with more clarity now. "I don't know, but I need to learn more about Everett. He's the key. I'll go back to the historical society tomorrow and pick up where I left off reading the newspaper articles. Hopefully I'll find something that will confirm a murder did take place here."

"*If* there was a murder. You don't have proof of that yet."

"No, but I intend to find it."

Colt didn't argue with her. Seemed he wanted to end the conversation. As his gaze slid up and down her body, his mouth curved into a grin and she realized how she was dressed—in a short silk robe, naked underneath, with wet hair and bare feet. Her plan to seduce him wasn't going as expected, but he seemed willing to roll with whatever she had in mind.

"If you're trying to turn me on," he said, "you're doing an excellent job of it." She followed his wide gaze to the cleavage popping out of the folds of her robe.

This was the make it or break it moment. Colt looked ready

to sweep her into his arms and haul her upstairs like Rhett Butler. She could go with it and release her inner slut, as she'd convinced herself she would, or she could serve him pie and ice cream and then say good night and go to bed alone.

She cinched the belt around her waist tight and pulled the robe together. "I'm sorry, Colt," she began.

He chewed his lower lip and sighed—loudly. "I know what you're going to say. No need to apologize. It's been a long day for both of us. Try to get some rest tonight and I'll see you tomorrow evening."

Disappointment seeped from his voice, which made her feel bad, but not bad enough to stop him from leaving. It would have been a big mistake to sleep with him tonight. Call her old-fashioned, but she wasn't the kind of woman to jump into bed after a few dates. If he was the kind of man who liked that type of woman, they weren't right for each other.

Neither of them mentioned dessert.

"You still want me to go to your brother's birthday party with you?" she asked as he skulked to the door.

"Sure. Mama's counting on it."

Mama was counting on it, but what about him? She didn't want to ask. "Okay, then. Guess I'll still go."

He stepped outside and told her he'd pick her up at six o'clock tomorrow night. No kiss and no mention of getting together during the day tomorrow. He didn't even wave after he'd gotten into the truck. Just drove away.

She sneezed from her wet hair and glared at his taillights fading into the night. Maybe a one-night stand was what he'd been interested in after all.

She locked up, covered the pie with tinfoil, and struggled to tamp down the longing twisting in her heart as she climbed the stairs and crawled into bed alone.

TWENTY-SEVEN

After a restless night, Shay rose early the next morning and dressed, anxious to put the previous evening behind her and start a new day with a fresh attitude. She had no regrets when it came to her decision about Colt. She had to remain true to herself, and that meant holding out for true love, or steering clear of men altogether. Since she didn't believe in true love anymore, it was better to keep her distance from Colt—no matter how good-looking he was or how great he smelled, or how sweet he could be.

She'd go with Colt to his parents' house tonight, but once the party was over, she'd tell him they couldn't see each other anymore. She'd miss him, but the sadness of loss would pass. It had before. He wasn't interested in anything but a fun time, and being used wasn't her idea of fun. She'd been there, done that.

Today, the plan was to delve back into the binder of newspapers at the historical society. Callie's trouble obviously had to do with Everett, whoever he was. Being murdered seemed problematic enough, but there must be more, Shay thought. Callie had originally asked her for help. It was still to be seen what kind of help was needed. Everett was involved. That much Shay knew for sure.

Maybe Everett hadn't been caught and punished for his crime. Maybe Callie was seeking justice before she could move on to the next world. That had to be it. There seemed to be no other explanation.

Shay crossed through the saloon and heard the low murmurs of the invisible men bellied up to the bar and the slapping of cards and clinking of coins at the tables. The sensation of walking through a crowded room was becoming more familiar, but it still sent chills rippling through her body.

Doris was at the front desk when Shay stepped into the old schoolhouse.

"Good morning, Doris. Are you feeling better? Your husband told me you were down with a migraine the other day."

"Yes, I'm much better. Thanks for asking, dear."

"Do you still have that binder of newspapers under the counter? I haven't finished my research and I have some time to kill this morning."

"Of course." Doris pulled the binder up and flopped it onto the counter.

"Thank you." Shay hauled it to the back room and began flipping through the pages from the point where she'd left off before, but skimming the headlines only. This time she wouldn't read every column on each page. If a woman's trip to Deadwood had made front-page news, surely a young girl's murder would have. That's what she'd look for.

An hour and a half later, there it was in black and white, confirming what she had suspected. The date read September 25, 1885.

GIRL MURDERED BY TRANSIENT COWBOY

In the early morning hours of September 24 Sheriff John Manning was summoned to the Buckhorn Saloon by owner/ barkeep, Dean Averill, who informed him of two deaths that had occurred on the premises. According to Mr. Averill, Miss Callie Hayes was strangled to death in one of the upper-level rooms by a transient cowhand by the name of Everett Rawlins. Miss Hayes, aged twenty, had been employed as an entertainer at the Buckhorn. Mr. Rawlins was twenty-five years old, according to a birth record found amongst his belongings. He most recently worked at the Bar T Ranch, pursuant to foreman, Bernard Davies of the Bar T. Rawlins was found shot to death on the floor of the same upper-floor room.

When questioned by Sheriff Manning, Mr. Averill stated that another employee had heard people arguing. When Averill burst into the room to investigate, he discovered Rawlins accosting Miss Hayes. When Rawlins drew his gun, Averill shot in self-defense, thus ending Rawlins' life with one bullet to the heart. Unfortunately, Averill was moments too late to save Miss Hayes, as the young woman was already deceased.

Hayes and Rawlins were buried in the Black View Cemetery.

Shay closed the binder, having learned nothing she didn't already know or suspect—except that Everett Rawlins was definitely buried somewhere in the Black View Cemetery and Frank's grandfather had killed him for attacking Callie. That news was not altogether surprising since Dean had owned the place.

Poor Callie. Hers was too young a life to have been snuffed out by some violent cowboy. If only Dean had barged into that room a few moments earlier. Maybe Callie would have survived to become and wife and mother and live a long life.

Shay wondered if Frank knew this story. Surely he did. It was significant enough to have been passed down through the family history. If so, why hadn't Frank mentioned it yesterday? His mind was going, she reminded herself. He probably couldn't remember what he'd had for breakfast that morning.

Returning the binder, Shay said good-bye to Doris and stepped into the sunshine, pleased to have confirmed a few things, while knowing there were just as many questions still left unanswered.

As she walked back toward the Buckhorn, she heard someone

yell her name. Waving her arm from inside a blue Buick was Opal, Frank Averill's nurse. Shay waved back.

"Hold up," Opal called. She whipped her car into the nearest parking space. The car seemed to groan when she lifted her bulk out and slammed the door.

"Morning," Shay greeted. "Is it your day off?"

"No. I needed to run some errands and buy groceries, so a neighbor is keeping an eye on Frank."

"Is he doing any better?"

Opal shook her head. "He has some good moments, but his mind comes and goes. Sometimes he remembers things from the past when he can't even recall what he watched on TV an hour earlier. When you left the other day, he asked me to bring out a picture. It's an old one of his daughter. He just about started crying when he looked at it. It killed me."

"Oh, that's sad. Colt mentioned she died years ago. Do you know the story?"

"No. Frank never talks about her, but what I wanted to tell you is that he asked if I thought you looked like her."

Shay blinked, and the hairs on her neck stood on end. "That's strange. He showed Colt and me a picture of his grandmother, and although I don't agree, both of them think I look like *her*. We didn't see the picture of his daughter. What's your opinion? Do I look like the daughter?"

"I didn't see much of a resemblance at first, but I've sneaked a peek a couple of times since, and I believe Frank's memory is keener than we think. I can see why you remind him of her. He's taken with you."

"I remind him of his daughter?"

"Oh, yes. He's looking forward to your next visit. You're all he's talked about. See what I mean about him remembering certain things?"

Shay smiled, hiding the ache she felt in her chest. "That's

nice. Please tell him I'd love to visit again. I'll try to stop by soon."

"Okay." Opal saluted and left.

Once Opal was out of sight, Shay bent at the waist, bracing her hands on her knees, dragging in fresh air. She'd never fainted or hyperventilated before, but there was always a first time for everything. She'd kept it together while talking to Opal, but now the ache turned to a deep, agonizing burn. She squeezed her eyes shut, hissing against the need to let tears flow.

It wasn't enough that ghosts, and Colt, were messing with her life and her emotions. Now, a delusional old man believed she was his reincarnated grandmother or daughter. Enough was enough!

Twenty-Eight

Colt had barely been able to keep his mind on business today. Since leaving Shay last night, she'd been all he could think about. Thirty short minutes and he'd see her again.

After showering, he stood in front of the bathroom mirror with a towel wrapped around his middle and slapped aftershave on his face. The reflection staring back at him was that of a contented man.

In the past few years, no woman had come close to touching his heart. He'd built a fortress around it, positive that there was no one out there he'd want to share the rest of his life with. And then Shay Brennan had shown up, walked into his life, and the walls holding up that fort had begun to crack.

It didn't make sense to feel so connected to her after this short time, but it was as if they'd always been together and always would be. He felt as if they'd always known each other.

Colt slipped into jeans and buttoned a shirt. As he pulled on his boots, his gut began to spasm. Could he be falling in love with Shay? It had been so long since he'd allowed himself to be open to possibilities. Permission to feel something honest for a woman had been long in coming. It was not a feeling he intended to take for granted. Nothing had ever seemed more right since the day he'd asked Denise to marry him seventeen years ago.

Colt grabbed his keys and turned out the lights and locked the door. They hadn't known each other long at all, but it didn't matter what anyone thought. Love had pierced his heart and he ached to tell Shay.

She was standing outside the Buckhorn leaning against the hitching rail when he pulled up.

"Don't get out," she called, meeting him at the truck and yanking the door open.

Her long, shiny hair bounced on her shoulders and she looked beautiful in a blue sundress. A soft white sweater was draped over her shoulders and she held a small box wrapped in silver paper in her hand. After she slid onto the seat, Colt's chest tightened in response to being so near to her.

"You're as pretty as a picture," he said, kissing her cheek. "This is going to sound corny, but you take my breath away."

Shay smiled her appreciation, and her gaze traveled over him. "Thank you Colt. You look quite handsome yourself."

He'd take the compliment.

"I'm nervous," she confided, once he'd left the town limits and they were tooling down the highway.

"Why? You met my family already."

"For about ten minutes. I hope your brother won't mind me tagging along."

"Brady won't care. He's a laid-back guy. Mama wants to get to know you better. She thinks you're the sweetest thing to come along since sugar, and Daddy keeps commenting on how pretty you are."

The widening of Shay's eyes reflected a flash of surprise, probably that he and his folks had been talking about her, but she recovered well.

"Your family all seemed really nice."

She stared straight ahead, more closemouthed than usual, and fidgety. Her fingers drummed softly on the box in her lap. They'd parted last night with some tension between them, but he was over that and hoped she was, too. He wondered if there was something else wrong, or if the events of the previous evening were still bothering her. Ghosts were the last thing he was interested in discussing, however, so he made mention of the box instead.

"I had no idea what to get your brother for his birthday," she said, "but I didn't want to arrive empty-handed. It's a bolo tie with a sterling silver and turquoise slide. Do you think he'll like it?"

"He'll love it, but you didn't have to buy him anything."

"I know, but I wanted to. If you're invited to a party, you bring a gift. That's how I was raised."

"Well, he's going to appreciate it."

During the break in conversation, Colt pondered when the right time would be to tell her he was falling for her. The truck was definitely not the place. It would have to be later, after he'd driven her back home. He wanted to hold her in his arms and gaze into her sparkling eyes when he expressed his feelings. He felt like a teenager, the way he'd been rehearsing in his mind what he'd say.

"Are we going to the Double M Ranch?" she asked, peering out the window.

"No. The Double M is the family business. We're going to the house I grew up in."

"Oh!" She smiled. "So I get to see the room you slept in as a boy?"

"That's possible." The thought occurred to tease her about making out on his old twin bed, but considering her quiet mood, it didn't seem appropriate.

"Does your room still look like it did when you lived there?"

"It functions as a guest room now, but Mama has kept all my football and basketball trophies and sports memorabilia on the shelves. I'll warn you now. She's probably going to drag everything down and show them off."

"That's okay. I won't mind her telling stories about when you were a boy. You were a jock, huh?"

"You could say that." He wondered about the types of men she'd been involved with before but wasn't interested enough to ask.

A few miles out of town, he turned onto the paved road that led to the Morgan ranch. "About there," he said, pressing on the gas.

Shay turned her body to face him. "I forgot to ask, did you go see Frank today?"

"No. I had a closing and a couple of showings, and I ran out of time. My schedule might be less crowded tomorrow, so I'll try to swing by there. Speaking of Frank, did you get to the historical society like you'd planned?"

"Yes!" Her demeanor grew animated, which pleased him. "I found a newspaper article that confirmed Callie's death by strangulation. Everett Rawlins *was* the man who killed her. And get this. Dean Averill killed Rawlins."

"Huh?" He didn't want to talk about the Averills or that pesky dead girl in the saloon, but at least Shay had perked up, which set his mind more at ease. Maybe he hadn't done anything to upset her after all.

"The article said Frank's grandfather claimed it was self-defense. Rawlins was attacking Callie when Dean entered the room. When Rawlins pulled a gun, Dean shot him through the heart."

Colt parked in the driveway in front of the two-story farmhouse with green shutters and a brick chimney on the side.

"I never heard Frank mention that before," he said, cutting off the motor. "I'll have to ask him about it tomorrow." He jumped out and sauntered to her side and opened her door. He tried to sound nonchalant when he said, "If you're not busy, why don't you plan to come with me? Now that Frank's met

145

you once, maybe he'll feel more comfortable opening up. You might learn something new."

"As a matter of fact, I saw Opal in town today, and she said Frank would like me to come back." She accepted Colt's hand and stepped out of the truck. The touch of her hand in his sent electricity racing through his veins.

"You don't say?" That was convenient, he thought. *Thank you, Frank.* "It's a date then. Ready?" he asked, keeping a hold of her hand and hoping she didn't comment about calling tomorrow a date.

Taking a deep breath, she nodded.

"Oh, wait," he said. "Let me get *my* present for Brady." He released her hand and reached into the back of the truck and lifted out a box that fit snugly under his arm. When he reached for her hand again, she wrapped both her hands around her gift. It was a subtle move, but Colt got the distinct feeling she didn't want to hold his hand.

They strolled up the walk in silence, where Hannah was waiting at the front door.

Twenty-Nine

"Come on in," Hannah said, welcoming them into the foyer. She kissed Colt on the cheek and gave Shay a warm hug. "So glad you could join us, Shay."

"Thank you for inviting me."

Chet sauntered into the hallway, followed by Brady and a woman with curly dark hair. "Hello again," Chet said, offering his hand. Brady did the same and then introduced her to Dawn, his girlfriend.

"Nice to meet you," Shay said. Dawn looked and acted a lot younger than Brady, popping chewing gum in her mouth.

"Same here," the woman answered. "Hi ya, Colt."

"How you doing, Dawn?" he rhetorically asked.

"Happy birthday," Shay said, handing Brady her present.

His dark eyes lit up. "Thanks. I wasn't expecting anything."

"Can't have a birthday party without presents, can you?"

"Guess not."

She and Colt exchanged smiles and he shoved his box into Brady's chest.

"This one's from me. Happy birthday, kid."

"Thanks, bro."

"Let's go into the dining room," Hannah said, leading the way.

Gazing around at the home's modest but comfortable furnishings as they moved through the living room into the dining area, Shay said, "This house is very warm and inviting, Mrs.

Morgan. I can tell it was a good place for your sons to grow up in."

Hannah turned and grinned. "Thank you, Shay." Winking at Colt, she chuckled, "I think this one's a keeper."

When he turned and gave Shay a wink of his own, her heart skipped a beat. Seemed she'd earned a point with Colt's mother, but endearing Hannah to her would only make it more difficult to tell Colt they couldn't see each other anymore. Her stomach was already twisting in knots, dreading the conversation to come later.

"Y'all can have a seat," Hannah said. "Supper is ready to be served."

"It smells delicious, Mrs. Morgan."

"Every year Mama makes our favorite meal for our birthday," Brady said, dropping her and Colt's gifts beside two more presents setting on a buffet table.

"That's sweet," Shay replied, glancing at Colt and wondering what his favorite meal was.

Dawn said, "Brady's is barbecued ribs, biscuits with gravy, sweet corn, and baked apples with cinnamon and sugar. Have you ever heard of such a weird combination?" She elbowed him in the ribs and pulled out her own chair and took a seat at the dining table.

"It sounds delicious to me," Shay said, chuckling. "Of course, anything sounds good right now. I'm hungry." She knew she was commenting more than necessary, but she tended to chatter when she was nervous.

"For such a petite thing, Shay likes to eat," Colt announced, smiling. "She's not a nibbler."

"I'm glad to hear that," Hannah replied, inching into the dining room with bowls of food balanced on her arms like a professional waitress. "Because my life revolves around food. I don't feel needed if I'm not feeding people."

"Let me help you," Shay said, dashing over to take two teetering plates from the crooks of Hannah's arms.

"Thanks, dear." Hannah slid Dawn a look of displeasure. It was understated, but Shay noticed it. Dawn just sat there, not bothering to get up, cracking her gum. Hannah then counted out the dishes and said, "I'll bring the pitcher of tea in and we'll be ready to start."

"I can get it," Shay offered, starting for the kitchen.

"You're my guest," Hannah replied. "Go ahead and sit down. I'll be one minute more."

It was apparent that Hannah and Dawn were not close. Dawn hadn't offered to lend a hand, and she continued to pop her gum at the table until Brady told her to dispose of it.

Colt pulled out a chair for Shay, which garnered snickers from both Brady and Dawn.

"What are you laughing at? Have you forgotten the manners Mama taught us?" Colt said, staring at his brother. His tone was lighthearted, but Shay sensed the comment was meant to remind Brady about the way they'd been raised.

Brady wasn't that much younger than Colt, but her initial thought was that Colt seemed twice as mature.

"Maybe Dawn would like it if you pulled the chair out for her once in a while," he told his brother.

"Yeah, maybe I would," she agreed, smacking Brady's arm.

Hannah poured tea into each of the tall glasses and finally plopped onto one of the chairs and expelled a long sigh.

"It's about time you relax," Chet said, patting her hand. "She's worked hard getting the house ready and the boy's birthday supper cooked," he told all of them.

"Thank you, Mama," Brady said. "I appreciate it. It looks great."

"You're welcome, son. Happy birthday! Now, everyone dig in."

Conversation never lagged throughout the meal. Shay temporarily forgot about the discussion she planned to have later with Colt and joined in the laughter and jokes. It had been so long since she'd shared in that kind of family camaraderie. It did her heart good.

After supper, they gathered in the living room for Brady to open his gifts. He appeared to genuinely like the bolo tie she gave him. Either that or he was demonstrating the polite manners Colt had spoken of earlier.

From Hannah and Chet, he received some clothes and mud flaps for his truck, and Dawn had bought him a pair of maple drumsticks. When it was time to open Colt's gift, Brady shook it several times. It rattled.

"Sounds broken," he said, and everyone laughed.

Colt clasped his hands behind his neck and leaned back into the sofa cushions, grinning. "Just open it."

When Brady ripped off the paper and flipped up the box lid and looked inside, a wide smile spread across his face.

"What is it?" Dawn asked, peeking in.

Brady started lifting out the pieces of a toy train set and tracks, including fake trees, street lamps, buildings, cars and miniature people. Hannah clapped a hand over her mouth, and Chet laughed and nodded with satisfaction.

Shay knew there had to be a family story that went along with this gift. She and Dawn both stared at Brady, waiting for him to explain.

"When we were kids," he started, "I had a train set just like this. I got it for Christmas one year. Mama said I could play with it in the basement. So, Daddy fashioned a table out of plywood, and Colt helped me hook the cars together and we set up the village. The two of us spent hours in the basement running that train around the tracks."

Colt grinned, probably recalling the good memories.

"Why is Colt giving you a new train set now?" Dawn asked.

"Because my set got ruined."

Hannah broke in. "We had a big snowstorm that same winter. During the months of January, February and March, our county suffered the coldest temperatures on record in over a century. Many folks' pipes busted, as did ours. The basement flooded and froze everything, ruining so many items and keepsakes I'd stored down there."

"Including Brady's train set," Chet added.

Brady went on. "By the time the spring thaw came, it was too late for my train. The pieces were rusted. We had to throw everything out."

"Ah. That's sad," Dawn said. "Why didn't your mom and dad buy you a new train set?"

"We wanted to," Hannah answered quickly. "But Brady wouldn't have it. A lot of his friends lost more than toys that winter. Some of our neighbors lost their clothes and furniture from the flooding, and they had to start over again. Brady told his daddy and me that if his friends could do with hand-me-down clothes and shoes, he could do without a toy train."

Tears pooled in Hannah's eyes. "I was never more proud of my son as I was that day. And Colt, this was a thoughtful gift. What kindhearted boys I have."

The room fell silent for a moment. Shay felt happy tears form in the corners of her own eyes. Such a loving, caring family this was. Seeing the joy they shared made the loss of her mom and dad feel fresh.

Brady broke the quiet by saying, "Thanks, Colt. You want to help me set it up again? Mama probably won't mind moving some of her stuff out of the basement to make room."

The brothers laughed when Hannah shot them a *no you don't* look.

"It must feel awful crowded in this house. When are you going to buy your own place?" Colt asked him directly. "I've got a few on the market that have nice basements and extra rooms where you could set up the train, your drums, and still have space left over."

Hannah rolled her eyes and stood up. "Go ahead, Colt. Try and convince him to move out. It won't do any good. I'm going to get the cake and coffee ready."

Brady and Dawn exchanged glances and he cleared his throat. "Sit down, Mama. The cake can wait. Dawn and I have something to tell y'all." He grabbed Dawn's hand and took a deep breath. Hannah looked at Chet and retook her seat.

"We're getting married!" Dawn shouted.

"Isn't that something?" Chet said, slapping his knee. He and Colt stood and offered congratulations to the couple and shook their hands. Shay did the same and asked Dawn if they'd set a date yet.

"Yes. Two weeks from now."

"What? Why so soon?" Hannah's brow wrinkled.

Brady's cheeks flushed and his head dropped. He let Dawn answer. "I'm three months pregnant."

Hannah collapsed back into her chair and said, "Oh, Lord."

Thirty

Colt's cell phone blared. "Excuse me," he said, pulling it from his shirt pocket and stepping into the hallway. The timing couldn't have been better. He didn't want to hear more of Mama's reaction to Brady's news.

"Hello. Morgan Realty."

"Colt? This is Opal Franklin. Sorry to bother you."

"No bother, Opal. What's up? Is Frank okay?"

"That's why I'm calling you at this hour. You told me to call anytime."

"Yes, I did. It's all right. What's going on?"

"He's been agitated ever since you and your girlfriend left yesterday."

Colt let the girlfriend comment pass.

"Can you come over?" she asked.

"Right now?"

"Yeah." There was a pause before she said, "Frank is asking for you again, and for Shay, too."

"He's asking for Shay? By name?"

"Yeah. He's saying it over and over, and I caught him crying."

Frank was crying? Whatever was bothering him must be serious, Colt thought. "Sure, Opal. Shay happens to be with me. We can be there in about a half hour. It's my brother's birthday, but I think the party's about over anyway." He was thinking about the bombshell Brady and Dawn had just delivered to his folks.

Colt flipped the phone shut and rejoined everyone in the living room. His mama was calmly serving cake, with Shay following up with coffee.

"Is there a problem?" Shay whispered when he sidled up next to her. She must have noted the worried look on his face. He was concerned about Frank. He'd never seen a man of his granddaddy's generation cry before, or his father's, for that matter. Hell, the only time *he'd* ever cried as a full-grown man had been the day Denise received the diagnosis of terminal cancer.

Pushing that sad memory to the back of his mind, he said, "That was Opal. Looks like we're going to be seeing Frank sooner than we expected."

Explaining to his family that he needed to go see Frank, he and Shay wished Brady happy birthday again, as well as congratulations to him and Dawn on their upcoming nuptials.

As Colt kissed his mama good-bye at the door, he whispered in her ear, "Brady's a grown man, Mama. You may not be crazy about his bride-to-be, and they're doing things in the wrong order, according to you, but at least he'll finally be out of your house."

She rolled her eyes. "Don't count on that. When you were taking your phone call, he asked your daddy and me if they could live with us for a few months after the wedding, while they save up for a place of their own."

Colt shook his head, but was not really surprised.

Hannah hugged Shay and said, "Honey, do this old woman a favor. If you and my son become serious, will you please do things the right way? Marriage first, and then a baby?"

Colt groaned. "Mama. Come on, now." His mother had never been one to censor her words. He kissed her cheek again and placed his hand at Shay's back and gently pushed her out the door before Hannah could say more. "See you later, Granny," he teased.

"That was an interesting evening," Shay said, once they were in the truck and on the road. "Particularly the ending."

"My brother may be thirty-five years old, but Mama's old-fashioned. Sorry if she embarrassed you back there."

"I wasn't embarrassed. Your family is great, especially your mother. She's a lot like you. She shoots from the hip, says what's on her mind."

Colt slid a grin her way. If only Shay knew what was on his mind right now. A visit to Frank wasn't what he'd planned for tonight. But it was only a quarter past eight. The night was young.

When Opal ushered them into Frank's bedroom, he was holding a picture frame, staring intently at it—so intently, Colt noticed, that he didn't even notice them until they were standing at his bedside.

"Howdy, Colt. Why are you here?"

Colt took note of Frank's eyes. Despite them being bloodshot, he appeared lucid. Colt looked at Opal, who shrugged.

"I told you I'd stop by today, Frank. I'm sorry it's late, but this was my first chance to get over here. Shay came along, too. Opal said you were asking about her today. Do you remember her from yesterday?"

Frank's gaze stuck on Shay. "Of course I remember you. You remind me of my grandma, Cynthia."

Shay smiled politely. "You and Colt seem to think there's a resemblance."

Frank's gaze swung to the picture in his hand. "You look like this girl, too."

"What have you got there?" Colt asked, feeling his pulse speed up.

Frank handed him the picture frame, and the hairs on the back of Colt's neck stood at attention. At the exact moment, streaks of lightning lit up the sky, followed by a boom of thunder. Colt's head jerked to the window. A storm hadn't been predicted for tonight, but the air suddenly buzzed with static electricity.

When the lights dimmed and then flashed off and back on again, Opal said, "I'll go check the circuit breaker and grab some candles in case the power goes out."

Colt hadn't even realized she'd still been standing in the doorway.

He gazed at the photo and felt his gut twist. "Who is this, Frank?"

Frank appeared captivated by Shay. "Where've you been all these years, girl?" he asked her. His voice sounded dreamlike and Colt realized he was hallucinating.

Shay glanced at Colt and stretched out her hand. "Can I see that photo, please?"

He handed it to her over Frank's prone body and jiggled Frank's arm. "Who's the girl in the picture?" he said again.

The old man's lips curved upward. "That's Alicia. Don't you remember her, Colt?"

"This is your daughter?" Colt blurted.

Shay peered at the photo and muttered, "What the hell?" Apparently she saw what Colt saw, because her face grew ashen, and he could have picked her chin up off the floor.

"I . . . I don't understand," she said, sinking into the chair next to the bed. Colt strode to her side and placed his hand on her shoulder and felt her shaking.

Frank's face was glowing like a light bulb when he crooned, "I'm glad you came home, Alicia. I've missed you so."

156

THIRTY-ONE

I've got to get out of here.

Shay thought she was going to vomit. The hard chair tipped over as she jumped up and pushed by Colt. Staggering to the door, she bumped into Opal, sending candles and matches clattering to the floor.

"I'm sorry," she mumbled.

"Hold up, Shay." Colt was at her side within seconds, with his arm snaked around her waist.

"What's going on?" Opal asked.

"She needs some air. We'll be back in a few minutes." Colt escorted Shay outside where they sat on the front steps and she gulped in fresh, cool air.

"Do you feel like you're going to faint?" he asked. "If so, put your head between your legs."

She shook her head. "I've never fainted in my life. I don't think I'm going to now. I just need to catch my breath." She inhaled and exhaled a few times.

No words were spoken between the two of them while she gathered her wits about her. Staring into the sky, she pondered what had just happened. The freak lightning storm had passed, and twinkling white stars now blanketed the expansive sky, causing her to think about heaven, which made her think about her parents again. Her heart lurched and she tried, but was unable to hold back tears.

This was all too much. Why were these things happening to her?

When Colt wrapped his arm around her and pulled her close, she surrendered, crying, and letting him shoulder the burden of her uncertainty and fear for a few moments.

Once she'd sewed her emotions back together, she wiped her eyes and said, "The girl in that picture looks like me, Colt. Or I look like her. Either way, we could be sisters. What does it mean?"

"I'm as confused as you are. I thought you resembled Frank's grandmother but . . ."

Seemed he was at a loss for words.

"Frank thinks I'm his daughter. It's obvious he's losing his mind. We both know this is just another bizarre twist amongst a bunch of coincidences."

"Do we? Is it a coincidence?"

Her mouth dropped open to think he believed this was something more. "Of course that's what it is. I told you, I have a common face."

"Nothing about you is common," he said, unsmiling. "This is becoming complicated by the day. What have the ghosts in the Buckhorn got to do with Frank's grandmother and daughter? Anything?" He paused a moment. "As soon as you moved into the saloon, you claim that dead girl paid you a visit. Now, Frank shows us photos of his grandma and his daughter, both of whom look enough like you to be your sisters."

"Yes, but neither of them are. That's ridiculous." She rolled her eyes, starting to feel annoyed. "And, what do you mean I *claim* Callie paid me a visit? You told me you believed me. She tried to strangle me twice. I know you saw her, too. That night in my window."

"I never said that."

Shay didn't want to argue. She saw his mind working, figuring out the math that divided the three women.

"Even if there was some reasonable explanation, which there isn't, Alicia couldn't be my sister," she stated. "The years don't work out. Besides, I've never been to South Dakota in my life until this trip. I have no ties here. I think we should both calm down. Frank's wild imaginings have caused us to think things that can't be possible."

"What kind of things?" Colt asked.

"I don't know. Nothing. Never mind." She rubbed her temple. "I'm getting a headache."

Colt didn't let up. "Frank and Alicia might be related to you somehow," he suggested. "Your parents never mentioned having family out here in the Black Hills?"

"No," she barked. "My dad's ancestors were all Midwesterners. Mom came from the East Coast. She and Dad met while in college in Illinois. I had one aunt and uncle back in Maryland, but they both passed away years ago. There's no one left on Dad's side. That's how I inherited his fortune. Don't you think he or Mom would have told me if we had any relatives out here? Why would they keep that a secret?" Her irritation was quickly reaching its peak.

"Families sometime keep secrets for any number of reasons."

Shay turned toward him and narrowed her eyes. "Are you inferring my parents were liars?"

"I'm not saying that—"

"My mom and dad had nothing to hide," she retorted. "I would have known if we had people out here."

"Sure." He clamped his lips together, apparently knowing when to shut up, but his gaze remained fixed on her.

Questions nagged at her, hinting there was more. Was she willing to delve deeper to discover answers to those questions? It felt like someone was beating her in the head with a hammer.

"I need to go home, Colt."

He rose from the step. "Sure. Let me tell Opal and Frank we're leaving."

"I'll meet you in the truck." She didn't have the energy, or courage, to go back in and face Frank again.

A few minutes later, Colt slid into the passenger seat and told her Frank was already asleep. "Opal's going to keep an eagle eye on him the next couple of days." He started up the engine.

The ride back to the saloon was a quiet one. When Colt walked her to the door, he smiled and said, "We can talk more about this tomorrow when you're feeling better."

This isn't how she'd wanted to end it with Colt, but there was no use in putting the inevitable off. "I don't want to talk about it. I don't want to think about what any of it means." When he reached to stroke her hair, she stopped his hand midair and backed up. His smiled faded.

"Have I done something to upset you, Shay? You've acted . . . different all evening."

Her gaze fell to the ground before meeting his. "I don't think we should see each other anymore."

"Why? I thought we were getting along so well."

Her heart was beating out of her chest. "We were. That's part of the problem."

"I don't understand."

There was no point in trying to explain how she was falling in love with him and was afraid of getting hurt. He wasn't interested in a long-term commitment, and she wasn't interested in sport sex. They were not in sync.

She set her jaw. "You don't believe I've seen and been assaulted by Callie and Everett," she used as an excuse. "I need someone in my corner. That's why I've decided to call Brenda Preston."

Colt groaned. "Shay, don't do that. I know that woman. She's a nut, pure and simple. You're not going to find the answers you're looking for by getting mixed up with her."

"I'll decide that for myself." Head aching and heart breaking, she didn't want to discuss anything more. "I'm sorry, Colt. Good-bye."

With him still standing at the door, Shay closed it and turned the latch—locking him out of her life.

This sure wasn't the ending Colt had expected tonight. He stomped up his front steps and slammed the door and tramped to his bedroom. Tore his clothes off, tossed them in the corner, and crawled into bed in his skivvies, jerking the sheet up to his chin.

There'd been something strange in the air tonight: Brady announcing his upcoming marriage and pending fatherhood, Frank showing them that damn picture of his daughter, lightning flashing across a still sky, and Shay deciding to call Brenda Preston. Oh, and Shay telling him to take a hike.

Dammit! Had there been a full moon out tonight to cause the world to go psycho?

The only two things he was sure of right now was that Brenda was nothing but trouble, and the woman he wanted didn't want him.

So much for pleasant dreams.

Thirty-Two

"Yeah," answered a voice groggy with sleep.

"Hello? Is this Brenda Preston?" Shay sat on a stool at the bar staring into the mirror at her reflection as she held the cell phone to her ear. It was nine o'clock in the morning, but it sounded like she'd roused the woman.

"Who's calling?"

"Ms. Preston, my name is Shay Brennan. I got your business card from Doris Rockwood at the historical society."

"Did you say Shay Brennan?"

"Yes."

Brenda yawned into the phone. "I heard about you. You purchased the Buckhorn Saloon."

"That's right. Mrs. Rockwood told me you're a psychic medium, and I have a . . . a situation. I'd like to speak to you about some paranormal things that have been going on in the saloon."

When she received no response, Shay thought maybe Brenda had hung up the phone or fallen back asleep. "Ms. Preston, are you still there?"

"I'm here. You say you need my help?"

"Yes. Are you free to see me today or tomorrow? I'm anxious to find some resolution to my problems."

"Would you like to know how much I charge for a consultation?"

"I'll pay your fee, whatever it is."

After another moment of silence on the other end of the phone, Brenda said, "We're talking about spirits, right?"

"Yes. There are two who are causing me problems."

"I see. It'll be one hundred dollars for an initial consultation. I'll be glad to meet you today. What time is convenient?"

Shay didn't balk. "My schedule is open. You name the time."

"Ten-thirty?"

"Fine. We'll meet here at the Buckhorn. Thank you. I'll see you then."

Relief flooded Shay's body when she flipped the phone shut. She felt a little silly calling on a psychic, but she didn't know where else to turn. She wanted some answers. Surely a person who saw dead people would be able to provide her with those answers. Anyway, what could it hurt? If Brenda Preston was a fake, as Colt had suggested, Shay would find out soon enough. All it would cost her would be a hundred bucks. That was a drop in the bucket.

She swung off the barstool and sauntered into the kitchen for a second cup of coffee while thinking about the events that had occurred last night. The entire evening had exhausted her. The hardest part had been telling Colt good-bye. Although she already missed him, she knew calling off their relationship was for the best. The highly charged sensual dream she'd had about him last night hadn't helped, however. For a split second, she thought of calling him and telling him she'd made a terrible mistake saying good-bye.

Shay flipped the phone open again and punched in his number. Before he could answer or it went to voice mail, she pushed the *off* button.

What am I doing? I was the one to end it, and for good reason. I have to be strong and forget about him.

Colt and his dad sat at the kitchen table drinking coffee and eating sausages and eggs that Hannah had cooked. She buzzed around the kitchen wiping down the counter and putting things into the refrigerator. She seemed to still be fuming over the announcement Brady and Dawn had made last night.

"You would have thought the two of them had more sense," she groused. "Hasn't either of them ever heard of birth control?"

"Please, Hannah. Not while I'm eating breakfast," Chet complained lightheartedly.

"Maybe they wanted to get pregnant," Colt said, adding fuel to the fire. He winked at his dad, knowing that would get his mama going.

Hannah spun and pointed her spatula at him. "That girl probably did it on purpose. She thinks Brady's got money. You know her family. They come from nothing."

"Oh, Hannah," Chet said, biting into his sausage link. "Don't talk bad about the girl. She can't help how she was raised. She's going to be the mother of our grandchild. I think it'd be best if we support her and Brady. Maybe some of our values and ways of doing things will rub off on her."

Colt stared at his father. He'd never heard his daddy string that many words together at one time in his entire life, unless they pertained to ranching or music. And he'd sure as hell never heard him express an opposing opinion from Mama's.

With her back to them, Hannah ran water into the sink for washing dishes. She was quiet for a minute, as though she were thinking over what Chet had said.

"I suppose you're right," she finally said, turning to face them again. "It could be worse, I guess. At least they're getting married. She'll probably start to show soon, but if any of my friends say anything, I'll tell them to stick their comments where the sun doesn't shine."

Colt and Chet laughed.

"It sure was nice to see your lady friend again last night,

honey," Hannah said, changing the subject. "I like her. She's a sweet gal."

"Yes, she is," Colt replied. "But, she's not my lady friend. We're not seeing each other anymore."

"Why?" Hannah frowned. "What'd you do?"

"I didn't do anything," Colt said, rising and placing his clean plate in the sink. "She blindsided me. Told me it was over practically before it's begun. I thought we were getting along just fine."

"Hmmm." Hannah turned back to the sink and scrubbed his dish with a soapy rag, apparently not going to pry. "Sorry to hear that," she offered. "It sure is nice to have you here for breakfast. Wish you'd come more often. I miss cooking for you." She rinsed the dish. "Why aren't you in the office yet?"

"I don't have any appointments until later. And I wanted to ask the two of you some questions about Frank."

"What kinds of questions?" Chet asked.

"Do either of you know what happened to his daughter, Alicia? I remember Granddaddy mentioning she'd died a long time ago, but do you recall any more details?"

"You know more about that family than I do, Chet," Hannah said, running a sponge over the stovetop.

After Chet forked the last of the eggs into his mouth, he pushed back his plate and patted his stomach. "That was a wonderful breakfast, Hannah. Thank you."

"You're welcome, dear."

"Well, Daddy? What do you know about Alicia?"

"Why are you asking, son?"

The whole thing about ghosts appearing to Shay would take too long to explain. But his folks would understand his curiosity regarding the photograph of Frank's daughter that looked like her. Even though Shay wanted nothing more to do with him, his newfound interest in the Averill family had been piqued.

After describing to Chet what had happened at Frank's, his father said, "Alicia Averill ran away when she was about twenty years old. She met a much older man, someone from out of town, at the café where she worked. When Frank found out, he threatened the guy. Leave Alicia alone or he'd kill him. Next thing Frank knew, Alicia was gone. She'd apparently left town with the man. Frank and Bonnie received one letter from Alicia a few months later, but they had no idea how to find her. The postmark was illegible. Next time they got word, about seven months later, Alicia was dead. She'd died in a car accident. It tore them both up, as you can imagine."

Colt shook his head. For the second time in a matter of moments, his daddy had expounded on a subject not related to music or ranching. "Did Frank blame himself for her death?"

"I expect so."

"You say Shay looks like Frank's daughter?" Hannah asked, stopping her work and joining them at the table.

"Yep. The likeness is uncanny. We also saw an old photograph of his grandmother Averill. There's a resemblance there, too."

Hannah's eyes grew large. "What does it mean?"

"I have no idea, but I appreciate you talking to me about the Averills, Daddy." He stood up and jiggled his belt buckle while expelling a deep breath. "Let's keep this conversation to ourselves for the time being, if you don't mind."

"Of course, son."

"Mama, thank you for breakfast." He kissed her on the cheek and shook his father's hand then lifted his Stetson off the seat of another chair and slid it on his head.

"I'll see y'all later."

As he headed for the front door, Hannah followed and swung him around by the shoulder. "How did you respond when Shay told you she no longer wanted to see you?"

Colt shook his head. "There wasn't much I could say. She

166

has her reasons, I guess, and I have to respect that."

"Hogwash," Hannah snapped. She wagged her finger in his nose. "You like that girl. I can see it written all over your face. I haven't seen you this jolly in years."

"Happiness is fleeting, Mama. I learned that a long time ago."

She punched his arm.

"Ow! What'd you do that for?"

"For once in your life, Colton Morgan, stop being a good ol' boy and don't let this woman slip away. If you want her, go after her! You can't let her call all the shots."

"It's not that easy."

"The hell it isn't."

Colt's eyes bulged. He'd never heard his God-fearing mama curse before.

"How do you think I got your *good ol' boy* father to marry me? I went after him, that's how."

When Colt saw his dad appear in the door behind his mom and shrug and nod, he had to laugh.

Hannah whispered in his ear. "If you love her, son, you've got to fight for her. You'll regret it if you don't. Remember, a day without love is like a day without sunshine."

He cocked his head, having heard a familiar saying. "I think that's a commercial about orange juice."

Hannah shoved him out the door. "Whatever."

THIRTY-THREE

Brenda didn't look like a person who saw dead people. Shay wasn't sure what she'd expected; maybe a hippie wearing a flowing skirt, peasant blouse, silver bangles and flowers in her hair. Or a Goth dressed all in black. But Brenda Preston was nothing like either of those. She was a tall brunette with a short, stylish haircut and was dressed in jeans and a crisp white blouse and heels. From the way Colt had spoken of her, Shay thought she'd be a space cadet, too. Pleasant and professional, Brenda was not at all how Colt had made her out to be.

They shook hands. "Come in, Ms. Preston. Thank you for coming."

"I don't mind if you call me Brenda. May I call you Shay?" Her smile was open and friendly.

"Sure." Shay welcomed her inside, liking her immediately. "Won't you have a seat?" After offering her a chair at one of the gambling tables, she asked if she'd like coffee or tea.

"No, I'm fine." Brenda's gaze traveled around the big room. "Believe it or not, I've never been in this building before."

Shay pulled out her chair and sat. "There hasn't been anyone living here for years. The previous owner closed the saloon a long time ago."

"That would be Mr. Averill."

"Yes. He's elderly now and quite ill."

"So I've heard." Brenda gazed up at the ceiling and over to the staircase. "There's a lot of activity in here."

Shay didn't reply. Brenda suddenly placed her palms flat on the table and closed her eyes. Shay wanted to ask if she was already connecting with a spirit, but was afraid of interrupting her trance, or whatever she was experiencing. She herself didn't feel any presence nearby at the moment.

When Brenda opened her eyes, she said, "There are many souls here. They continue to linger because this is where they are most comfortable. It's like home to them."

Shay nodded. "I often hear men playing cards in this room. Seems they're still enjoying poker games and smoking their cigars. It can be unnerving, but I'm not afraid of those ghosts."

Brenda smiled. "No need to be. They have no intent to harm. They simply don't know they're dead. They should be guided into the light."

"Can you guide them?"

"Yes, but not today. We'll hold a special ceremony another time. It's the others you're concerned with. Am I correct?" Without waiting for an answer, Brenda's gaze drifted to the staircase. Shay held her breath. Although she had previously mentioned two troublesome spirits, she hadn't referenced Callie or Everett, specifically. It was her way of testing Brenda and her abilities.

"There's a spirit upstairs," Brenda stated.

Again, Shay didn't respond, but felt a tingle race across her shoulders. When Brenda stood up and propelled herself toward the stairs, Shay scooted her chair out and followed.

Brenda stopped at the piano and smiled. Speaking to someone invisible, she said, "Yes, you're a lucky man to be surrounded by so many pretty girls."

She turned to Shay. "The piano player says he has the best job in town because the girls sit next to him on the bench when they sing."

Shay glanced at the piano and remembered the photo of the

saloon girls gathered around it. She didn't recall seeing a man in any of the pictures she'd found, but that probably only meant there wasn't a picture of him in those particular books.

"Would you like to go upstairs?" she asked Brenda.

"Yes."

Shay led her to the top of the stairs and then stopped and waited to see which room Brenda was drawn to. Without hesitation, she stepped into Shay's bedroom and stood at the foot of the iron bed. With her heart lodged in her throat, Shay waited with baited breath to hear what Brenda was going to say next.

"Have you seen the physical manifestation of the woman who haunts this room?" she asked Shay. Her eyes were closed again.

Shay's tongue was tied for a moment. Brenda really did have a gift.

"Yes," she answered. "She's shown herself to me three times." She didn't know how much information she should share and decided to let Brenda ask specific questions.

"She's blonde with blue eyes."

"That's right." Shay grew excited but didn't allow her stoic veneer to crack.

Brenda turned and pointed to the fireplace. "She was there. I can feel her residual energy. She's hiding now. Come out," she requested softly. "I'd like to speak to you. We are not here to do any harm."

Shay looked around the room but didn't see Callie anywhere. She didn't feel her either. If Brenda claimed Callie was in the room, even for a minute, why didn't Shay see her or feel her like before?

"This woman keeps a secret," Brenda went on.

"Do you know her name?" Shay asked, testing again.

Brenda took a deep breath and opened her eyes. "I believe her name is Elizabeth. Yes, it's definitely Elizabeth."

Disappointed, Shay softly sighed. Maybe Colt was right.

Maybe Brenda was a fake. To say Callie had blonde hair and blue eyes was probably a lucky guess. But she hadn't even gotten the first letter in her name correct.

A door slamming downstairs jerked Shay from her wandering thoughts.

The two women looked at each other, and then Brenda bolted out of the room and flew down the stairs. Shay followed, nearly tripping down the steps. Brenda came to an abrupt halt at the basement door.

"Someone is down there."

Recalling how the entity had terrified her that day in the basement, Shay quietly said, "Yes. He's the bad one."

"I'm going down." Brenda reached for the doorknob.

"No." Shay's hand shot out and covered hers. "He's violent and powerful. He has tried to hurt me."

"I'm not afraid," Brenda said, wrenching the door open. As soon as she took a step forward, a strong gale-force wind whooshed up the stairs and knocked them both backward. Shay flew into the back wall, and Brenda fell to the floor. The familiar rotten smell swirled and clung to her nostrils.

Very clearly and loudly, a deep voice commanded, "Leave!" and the basement door banged shut, and he was gone.

Shaken but not injured, Shay offered her hand to Brenda and helped her stand. "Are you okay? You took a hard fall."

Nodding, Brenda rubbed her hip after Shay got her to her feet. "I didn't fall. I was pushed."

"Did you see the entity's face?" Shay asked.

"No. Did you?"

Shay shook her head. "I haven't seen it even once."

"I felt his strength and his anger," Brenda said.

No kidding, Shay thought. She'd felt Everett's anger on several occasions, but she'd never heard him speak until now. "Did you hear anything?" she asked tentatively, wondering if

Brenda had heard the voice, or if Shay had only imagined it.

"He wants you to leave," Brenda stated.

"His name is Everett and I think he killed the girl upstairs," Shay blurted, immediately wishing she had kept her mouth shut. She should have waited for Brenda to provide that information.

"Everett? Do you know his last name?"

With the cat out of the bag, Shay went ahead and told her more. "Yes. It's Rawlins. I read about him in an old newspaper article. It's all there about how he murdered Cal—one of the saloon girls—and was then shot by the owner of this establishment, Dean Averill."

Brenda threw her a sideways glance, but thankfully didn't question her further. Maybe she hadn't caught Shay's slip of the tongue. Since Brenda had gotten Callie's name wrong, Shay didn't want to give away any hints in case Brenda later retracted what she'd already told her about the girl.

"I don't think the spirit in the basement is Everett Rawlins," Brenda said, walking back into the main room and lifting her purse from the table.

"If it's not Everett, then who is it?" Shay asked, narrowing her eyes. She didn't know whether to believe Brenda's hunch or not.

"I don't have a firm handle on that yet, but . . . hold on. I'm receiving a message right now, and it's coming from a cowboy. I think it is Rawlins." She closed her eyes and flung the back of her hand to her forehead in dramatic fashion. Shay watched Brenda's chest rise and fall as she inhaled deep, cleansing breaths.

"What kind of message are you getting?" Shay's muscles twitched, still hoping Brenda was not a fake and could help somehow.

"He's trying to tell me something, but it's hard to understand.

His words are garbled. I'm seeing blood. Blood is filling his mouth, making it difficult for him to speak."

Shay gulped, picturing that vivid picture.

"I can tell you he's not here in the Buckhorn," Brenda continued. "Mr. Rawlins' spirit is stuck somewhere. He's not far from here, but something, or someone, is holding him back."

"Do you mean he's in limbo?" Shay asked. "Is he between heaven and hell?"

Brenda's eyes popped open and her voice grew lively. "Shay, the newspaper article you read said he'd been shot. The townsfolk must have buried him. Do you have any idea where his grave is located?"

"I've already looked for it in the Black View Cemetery with no luck. That's the only public cemetery in town, I was told. I don't suppose the town would have buried him on the church grounds, seeing how he was a murderer. Do you?"

Touching her arm, Brenda said, "Rawlins is guiding me to his grave. He wants us to find it. We should go now."

Shay remembered the last time she was in the graveyard. She wasn't anxious to return, but her confidence in Brenda was starting to rise. She wanted answers to the haunting and perhaps Brenda was the one to provide them after all.

"Let me grab my purse."

Thirty-Four

Brenda drove. When they parked at the bottom of the hill at the cemetery, she slipped off her heels and exchanged them for a pair of tennis shoes that were lying on top of a folded pile of clothes in the backseat.

"I always keep a change of clothes in my car for an impromptu outing such as this," she explained, plunging her feet into the sneakers and then slamming the car door.

Shay stood by the car, waiting for Brenda to make the first move. She looked up. There wasn't a cloud in the sky. It was just as peaceful as it had been the other day, before the storm hit and all hell had broken loose.

Brenda seemed to know where she was going because she trudged forward and began climbing the hill with quick steps in a definite direction.

"Is Everett speaking to you now?" Shay asked, hobbling and puffing to keep up. Her foot was still a bit sore from the fall she'd taken when she was here last.

"Not in words. His energy is guiding me."

As they crossed in front of Denise Morgan's headstone, Shay glanced around, wondering if she'd see the bluebird again. There was no sign of him today, or his chirping. She was surprised when Brenda paused in front of the stone.

"You must know Colt Morgan," she said. "He was the listing agent for the Buckhorn."

"Yes. He handled the sale of the saloon."

Brenda smiled. "I heard he's been handling more than real-estate transactions lately."

Shay felt the hairs on her arms prickle. "I don't know what you mean." She didn't like the insinuation, nor did she care for the smug look on Brenda's face.

"This is a small place, and Colt's a well-known single man. When he starts dating the new girl in town, word spreads like wildfire."

"You've been misinformed. We're not dating."

"Oh. I'm sorry. That was what I heard. In that case, there won't be any conflict of interest, which is good."

"What conflict of interest would there be?" Shay didn't comprehend what Brenda was getting at.

"He and I went out for a while. We were close. I wouldn't want there to be any awkwardness between you and me because of my relationship with Colt."

Shay's stomach gripped as if she'd been struck a blow. Colt and Brenda had dated? Why hadn't he told her? No wonder he'd been against her calling Brenda for help. He didn't want her to find out about their relationship. He'd called Brenda a nut so Shay wouldn't call and find out about the two of them. When had they dated, and for how long? Just how close had they been?

Shay's gaze traveled up and down Brenda's slender frame as questions mounted in her mind, with the foremost being, had Colt slept with her?

She squeezed her fists at her side. Even though she'd been the one to end it, she couldn't stand the thought of him with anyone else.

With jealous heat scorching through her veins, she wanted to change the subject before Brenda offered more about her relationship with Colt than Shay was prepared to hear.

"Are you still receiving a message from Everett?" she asked, trying to keep her voice from trembling.

A noise coming from the old section of the graveyard caught the attention of them both.

"This way," Brenda called, as she dashed toward the far corner of the cemetery. Not far from Callie's grave, she stopped and placed her finger to her lips to warn Shay to keep quiet. All was hushed except for the rustling of insects in the grass.

Shay glanced toward Callie's grave site. It appeared undisturbed from the last time she was here. Her neck pivoted and she bit back a squeal when she felt Brenda's fingernails digging into her arm.

"Over there," Brenda whispered, pointing.

Standing next to a simple wooden marker was a man. Shay knew he'd once been human, but was no longer of this earthly plane. Wearing typical cowboy garb, he could have been any cowhand, except for his ashen face, the hole that had ripped his shirt apart near his heart, and the blood dripping from the corners of his mouth.

Shay struggled to hold in a scream. Absolutely certain the apparition with stubbly cheeks and dark eyes was Everett Rawlins, her gaze flew to Brenda, who seemed to have suddenly delved into a trance.

"Brenda! What's wrong? Are you okay?"

Her eyes were glazed and she was staring straight ahead, unmoving.

"Wake up," Shay urged, jiggling her arm. Brenda remained motionless.

When the man took a step forward, Shay felt her body turn cold as ice and she yelled, "Stay back!" She glanced at Brenda again, who was in a definite stupor. Heart hammering as Everett approached, Shay screamed, "I know who you are and what you did to Callie! And what you tried to do to me, too!"

Unbelievably, at the mention of Callie's name, the man's

countenance seemed to change. She could swear his face went from dead and blank to his eyes flickering. Just as quickly, his mouth drooped, like he was sad. His lips began to form words, but unfortunately his words were illegible.

Feeling a magnetic pull that she was defenseless to stop, Shay's legs spontaneously began to move. Turning her head, she saw Brenda was still rooted to her spot, seemingly unaware of what was transpiring around her.

As if a rope was tied around her waist and being drawn with invisible hands, Shay was tugged toward Everett. She should have feared for her life, but a sense of calm washed over her instead. She was about ten feet away when he looked down at the wooden marker, gazed sideways to where Callie lay buried, and then met Shay's gaze once more before fading away.

With her heart in her throat, Shay fell to her knees and read aloud the words on the marker. "Everett Rawlins. Died eighteen eighty-five." That was it. No other inscription.

Something didn't feel right. Why had his face changed when she called out Callie's name? And why had he gazed with longing toward Callie's grave? Did ghosts have feelings? Did he regret murdering the young woman? Did he wish to be forgiven? Was that what he'd been trying to tell her just now?

Another feeling drew her gaze to the untended mound of grass at the base of his marker. Poking up through the tall blades was a ring. She scooped up the tarnished band that hung from a thin chain and studied it. Was this what Everett had been looking at when his gaze had dropped to the ground before he vanished? Was this the reason he had guided Brenda here? So they could find the ring?

What did it mean?

"Shay!"

She spun to find Brenda had awakened from the trance and was staggering toward her.

With more pieces being added to the puzzle at every turn, and unsure whether she trusted Brenda or not, Shay shoved the chain in her pocket and scrambled to her feet.

"Are you all right?" she asked, placing her hands on Brenda's shoulders.

Wobbling like she was drunk, Brenda answered, "I feel exhausted. That has never happened to me before. The last thing I remember was seeing a man right here where we're standing and then, boom. I must have blacked out. Did you see him? Was the man Everett?"

Once again doubting Brenda's true abilities and intentions, Shay decided to keep her experience with Everett to herself for the time being. She couldn't explain Brenda's trance, but right now she didn't care if she'd been faking or not. She needed time to think.

"It was only a shadow," she reported. "But this is Everett Rawlins' grave. You found it." She tapped on the wooden marker. "There doesn't appear to be anything of significance here, however. I think we've been led on a wild-goose chase. Let's go back to town. You look pale."

She was anxious to be rid of Brenda and ponder over Everett, Callie, and the ring.

When they reached the car, Brenda still felt fatigued and asked Shay to drive back. At the Buckhorn, Shay pulled two fifty-dollar bills from her wallet and handed them to Brenda before stepping out of the car.

"Thank you for coming today. I appreciate your help in locating Everett's burial site. I hope you'll feel better soon."

Accepting the cash as she scooted into the driver's seat, and still looking confused, Brenda said, "I'll be happy to come over and conduct the ceremony to guide those other spirits into the light. Just give me a call and we'll arrange a time."

"I will."

"Shay," Brenda said through the open window, "I'm sorry I wasn't able to give you more information about Elizabeth and Rawlins. I'd be glad to try to contact them again. I want to help."

"I'll call you," Shay said, before stepping onto the curb. She wasn't entirely sure she'd be calling her back. As Brenda's car pulled away and moved down the street, Shay's cell phone rang.

"Hello."

"Hi, Shay. It's Colt."

Her knees grew weak at hearing his voice, and then she remembered what Brenda had told her about the two of them dating.

"I know what you told me last night, but I need to see you," he said. "All I want is a few minutes of your time. I have something very important to tell you."

She considered it. "Okay. I have something to tell you, too. Are you in your office?"

"Yes."

"I'll be there in five minutes."

THIRTY-FIVE

Colt rose from his desk when Shay stepped through the door. As always, one of her smiles was all it took to snatch his breath away. "Thanks for coming over."

"You're welcome." Her gaze landed on the unoccupied chair scooted up to the front desk. "Where's your secretary?"

"Out to lunch."

After a pause, she said, "I'm beginning to wonder if you really have a secretary."

He chuckled. "I do."

"Is she young and pretty?"

Not understanding and tilting his head, he said, "Why do you ask?"

"With only the two of you in the office, I guess you and her must be pretty close."

"What kind of question is that?" he asked. "And what relevance does it have to anything?" Shay had a strange look on her face.

"How many women do you get close to, Colt? I'm curious. Do they all know you're not interested in a committed relationship when you start seeing them?"

"What the hell?" He stepped back with his mouth hanging open, not believing what he was hearing. This didn't seem like the Shay he knew. The jealous attitude seemed out of character. Or maybe not. He'd only known her a short time, he reminded himself.

She didn't skip a beat. "I met Brenda Preston and she doesn't act nuts to me. Oh, and by the way, I know about you and her." Her arms crossed in front of her breasts, and her mouth drew into a tight line.

"Hold on," he said, understanding now. "What did that woman tell you?"

"Why don't you tell me? Let's see if your stories jive."

Clearing his throat, he said, "There's nothing to tell, except that we went out a couple of times. It was a long time ago and we only went on two dates, if you'd even call them dates. *Two,*" he emphasized, holding up two fingers. "I've known Brenda since we were kids in school, but I was never interested in her. Not in the way you're insinuating."

"Which way is that?"

He knew what was bugging her. "In a physical way," he stressed.

"If that's true, then what made you become *interested* enough to date her?"

"I didn't." He shook his head again and clarified calmly. "It was a couple of years ago, when I was still going out to bars. We were at the same dive one night, and we sat at a booth together and she told me she'd just broken up with some guy. After a few laughs and reminiscing about high school, we agreed to meet for a drink the next night, as friends. A week later, she invited me to a party. I knew the host, so I accepted. At the end of that evening, Brenda let me know she was interested in being more than friends. But she wasn't my type. A relationship would have gone nowhere and I told her so. By then, I wasn't into dating just for the hell of it. She didn't like my honesty, apparently, and she screamed a few choice words and keyed my truck before storming off. That was the same night I gave up on dating."

After finishing his story, Shay's shoulders sagged and she uncrossed her arms.

181

"So you never slept with her?" Her voice came out small, like a child's.

A hearty laugh erupted from deep within his belly. She was jealous! *Thank you, God, for small miracles.*

"Lord, no, darlin'. I swear what I've told you about Brenda is the truth and nothing but the truth." He put his hand up as if he were giving an oath in front of a judge.

She still didn't seem totally convinced.

"Why did you tell me she's a nut? I expected to meet someone who smelled of incense and chanted in tongues. She acts pretty normal to me."

"I shouldn't have called her that," he admitted. "I was basing the term on what happened between us last time I saw her. She had no right to key my truck. And I never heard talk in school about her being a psychic, so I figured it was a hoax she'd dreamed up to dupe folks out of their money. I don't know if she's had a real job in years. I didn't want you to get hurt or waste your money on what might turn out to be a bunch of baloney."

When Shay let her arms drop to her sides and her lips curved into a small smile, he moved forward and placed his hands upon her waist and drew her close. He knew she'd been under a lot of stress lately. He wouldn't hold this little outburst against her. He was glad when she sank her head onto his chest.

"I'm sorry," she whispered. "I had no right to come here and accuse you of things—"

"You're forgiven," he interjected. Her eyes glistened when he sat her back. "For the record, I haven't slept with a woman in over two years."

That little tidbit rocked her. "Colt, I had no idea . . ."

"Of course you didn't," he said. "That's not something a man goes around broadcasting to the world. I don't kiss and tell, especially when there's nothing to tell." He chuckled, hoping to ease any anxiety between them.

"I'm sorry I said those things," she apologized again. "I shouldn't have jumped to conclusions or let my imagination run wild—especially after what I said to you last night."

"Are you referring to when you cut me loose?"

She nodded, and he couldn't help but grin. "I like that you're jealous."

"I'm not . . ."

His arms wound around her like thread on a spool, and he felt the blood in his veins heating as his heart pumped double-time. He'd been waiting to tell her how he felt. Now seemed like the perfect time.

"Shay, I don't mind that you're a little jealous, because that would mean you care about me the same way I care for you."

She gazed at him with eyes shining brighter than the noonday sun.

He tipped her chin up with his finger, and they gazed into each other's eyes.

"I know we've only known each other a short time, but . . ."

The bell over the front door tinkled as it flung open and his fifty-something secretary, Norma, breezed in. Obviously startled, Shay broke from his embrace and twirled.

"Oh! Did I interrupt something?" Norma said, dumping her purse on her desk and giving Colt a knowing grin.

Shay's cheeks flushed pink and she looked like she wanted to crawl under the desk.

"Shay, this is my secretary, Norma Rudd. Norma, meet Shay Brennan, the new owner of the Buckhorn."

Norma reached out to shake Shay's hand. "I typed up the paperwork for the sale. It's nice to finally meet you, Ms. Brennan."

"Thank you. It's a pleasure to meet you, too."

Just then, Shay's cell phone jangled. "Excuse me. I'll take this outside." She trotted to the door like a pony ready to break into a lope.

Colt watched her hips sway as she exited the office with the phone to her ear. Dammit. Would luck ever be with him?

"Pardon me, Norma," he said, tromping past her to peek out the window.

"Better hurry if you want to catch her. I don't know what you just said or did, but she looked ready to bolt," Norma teased.

Shay was flipping her cell phone shut as he stepped outside and closed the door behind him.

"Good news, or bad?" he asked, noting the confused expression on her face.

"You decide," she said. "That was Brenda. You won't believe what she just told me."

THIRTY-SIX

Shay started by giving Colt the *Reader's Digest* version of the time she'd spent with Brenda, both in the saloon and in the graveyard. She also removed the chain and old ring from her pocket and enlightened him on how she'd found it cradled in the grass at the foot of Everett's tombstone while Brenda was in the trance.

As he examined the ring, rolling it between the pads of his fingers, he said, "This is real interesting, but it sounds like I was right about Brenda. The name Elizabeth doesn't even come close to Callie. You have to be disappointed."

"I was thinking about that when she and I parted a while ago. It crossed my mind that perhaps Brenda had seen *another* spirit in my bedroom, one called Elizabeth, and that's how she came up with that name."

"Unlikely." Colt didn't seem impressed.

"I confess it was a stretch, but I wanted to believe Brenda and was hoping she could help. She *did* sense the card-playing ghosts, and we both experienced the evil basement guy. And she led us to Everett's grave."

"But you said she blanked out once you got there. Her psychic abilities didn't guide her to this ring either. This seems like a significant clue she shouldn't have missed." He handed the gold band back.

"True. She said nothing like that blackout had ever happened

185

to her before, so I'll give her the benefit of the doubt on that one."

"So, now where do you turn if you're done with her?"

Shay shook her head. "That's just it. I don't think I'm done with her. Just now on the phone, she told me that shortly after she left the Buckhorn, something drew her back. She turned her car around and found herself standing on the sidewalk below my bedroom window. When she looked up, Callie was staring down at her. Colt, that's how Brenda referred to the woman. *Callie.* Brenda said the young woman's name popped into her mind, as clearly as if the spirit had spoken to her. Brenda wanted me to know her first name is Callie. Callie *Elizabeth* Hayes."

She waited, hoping his reaction would be the same as hers, which was one of excitement and renewed trust in Brenda's abilities. Although Colt wasn't commenting negatively, he was as easy to see through as cellophane wrapping. Doubt was written all over his face. Or was it something else?

"What is it?" she asked. "Do you still think I shouldn't work with Brenda anymore?"

"It's your decision," Colt assured. Snaking a protective arm around her waist, he guided her around the corner into an alley, where he surprised her by gently backing her against the wall. With his hands on either side of her face, he leaned in and kissed her. It was a deep kiss that sent a shudder thundering through her body as his lips molded to hers.

When the kiss broke, she was unable to utter a word, and she simply stared into his emerald pools, mesmerized by her reflection in them, and the way his touch had sent her spinning into another world.

"Shay, I'm falling in love with you," he blurted. "I know you probably think it's too soon to feel that way, but it is what it is."

"I . . . ah . . ." Her breath locked deep inside her throat, and it felt like a grenade had gone off in her stomach. Colt had such a hopeful, eager expression on his face. "Ah . . ." Not knowing what to do or say, Shay wriggled free and turned her back to him.

Although she was falling for him, too, they barely knew each other. While her heart told her one thing, her head told her another. It wasn't safe to trust her heart.

As she stood wringing her hands, she could feel his eyes boring into her back. No doubt he was waiting for a response. He'd just told her he loved her and was probably hoping to hear the same thing in return.

When she swung around to face him again, he'd shoved his fists into his jeans pockets and the eager expression on his handsome face had been replaced by disappointed longing.

"Colt," she murmured.

"I figured it was too soon," he mumbled. "But I'm honest to a fault. Remember?"

She nodded.

"The last thing I want to do is put you on the spot. I understand you can't make your heart feel something it doesn't."

"It's not that."

His finger touched her lips to shush her. "You don't have to say a word."

"But I want to. I've never met anyone like you before, Colt," she whispered.

"You never will again."

She wanted to believe him, but she'd trusted before and had ended up brokenhearted.

Her mind replayed the moments she and Colt had spent together. Neither Gary nor Tom was Colt. He was ten times the man either of them had been. She'd come west to start fresh, and starting over was all about risk-taking. She'd taken a risk buying the saloon and putting down roots in Hill City. Why couldn't she acquiesce to these feral sensations and take one more chance at love?

Without another word, Colt stepped out of the alley and turned the corner, ripping her from her mixed-up thoughts. She followed him back to the office wishing she had the courage to return his affection the way he deserved.

"Call Brenda back," he said, at the door. "I think she may be able to help with those ghosts after all."

"Are you sure?"

"It's not for me to judge her—or you. It's your life. Do what you want." His gaze held steady, and he looked like he wanted to say more, but he kept his mouth shut and placed his hand on the doorknob.

Her heart sank, feeling as heavy as lead. Colt was dismissing her the way she'd dismissed him before.

"I have more information on Frank's daughter, Alicia, if you're interested," he said while easing the door open.

"I am." Smiling, she hoped he would reconsider being friends.

"My dad gave me some insight on what happened to her. It was a typical Romeo and Juliet story, only Alicia's Romeo had been quite a bit older than her, and Frank disapproved. Alicia ran away with the man after Frank threatened the guy. Frank and his wife only heard from her once after she left. A letter came, but they had no idea where she'd gone. The postmarked had been illegible. Next time they got any word was seven months later, and she was dead. She'd died in a car accident."

The shock stung like a slap in the face. "That's terrible. Do you know who sent the letter to Frank and his wife informing them of Alicia's death?"

"I didn't think to ask Dad that. He probably doesn't know. Could that be important?"

"Maybe. I'd like to ask Frank some specific questions about his daughter when I see him next, if he's up to talking about her."

Colt nodded. "Good luck. I need to get inside and back to work."

She didn't want to say good-bye yet. "I'll call Brenda," she said, stalling. "I'll show her the ring I found and see what else she can come up with about Callie. I still need to know why she has asked for my help."

"Sure. Hope you solve your mystery, Shay."

"Thanks."

Colt stepped through the door, leaving her standing on the sidewalk alone, sad and confused.

Walking toward the Buckhorn, she wondered why relationships had to be so complicated. Why couldn't she let go of the past and trust that Colt wouldn't hurt her? With her parents gone, she had no one on this earth to love anymore. By some miracle, she'd come to Hill City and met Colt, and he had fallen in love with her. She should be ecstatic—and she was.

It had been so hard to keep her emotions in check when he'd confessed his feelings. True love and happiness were what she yearned for, but she wasn't sure those things existed anymore. Colt might think he loved her today, but love didn't matter if their goals in life were not the same.

Was meeting Colt her destiny? Or was he another cruel joke fate had chosen to play on her?

When she reached the saloon, Shay stopped dead in her tracks. Sitting on the hitching post in front was a bluebird. Its beady eyes latched onto her like a laser beam, and their gazes remained locked until he started chirping his song.

"Is it you?" she whispered, sensing he was the very same bird who'd come to her in the cemetery.

Remembering what Colt had told her about the power behind the bluebird's message, she quietly recalled his words.

The bluebird comes to show you about happiness within. He signifies contentment and fulfillment that is happening or about to hap-

pen. Listen to the song of the bluebird in order to find your own joy with an awakened confidence and internal peace.

The appearance of the bluebird, twice, had not been a coincidence. It symbolized fulfillment and internal peace, according to Native American legend. If she believed that lives from the past deserved respect and eternal happiness, certainly her own life deserved the same. How could she ignore this sign? With her heart soaring, Shay spoke to the bird, not caring if anyone on the street heard her and thought her crazy.

"Thank you, bluebird, for coming to me with your song. I understand, and I won't take your message for granted."

His chirping halted and the bird flapped his wings and disappeared.

With the blood rushing to her head, Shay unlocked the saloon door, closing it behind her. Colt was not like any man she'd ever known. Since she'd met him, she'd felt more alive than she had in years. He was in love with her. She was falling for him, too. What kind of fool would she be to let him go?

THIRTY-SEVEN

Hand trembling, Shay punched in Colt's number on her cell phone. After four rings, it went to voice mail. Let down, she flipped the phone shut without leaving a message. The blare of her phone ringing seconds later caused her to jump. The number flashing at her was Colt's.

Managing the thrill that threatened to creep into her voice, she answered, "Hello, Colt."

"You rang?"

"Uh. Yes." He obviously saw the missed call.

"That's a coincidence, because I was just going to call you."

"You were?" She couldn't imagine why, but was ecstatic, since she'd had a change of heart. Maybe he was calling to ask her to reconsider their friendship.

"I just hung up from Opal. Frank would like to see you."

"Oh." That's not what she'd expected or hoped to hear, but she kept her tone lighthearted. "I'd be glad to stop by. When is a good time?"

"Any time you're free."

He didn't sound the same. His answers were short and to the point.

"I could go over this evening," she said.

"I'll give you the number. You can call Opal and let her know."

Shay hated this. She wanted to go back to the way they had been. "Colt, what would you think about going over with me? I was hoping we could talk some more. I don't like the way we ended today."

The silence on the other end of the line was deafening. The thumping of her heart inside her chest felt like beats of a tom-tom as she waited for his answer.

"Okay. I can do that."

The sense of relief had never felt so strong before. "Thank you," she said. "I can drive. Is seven all right for me to pick you up?"

"Sure. See you then."

When Colt glided into the passenger seat, Shay assaulted him with a long apology that came straight from her heart. "I'm so sorry for the way I've been acting," she began. "Everything has happened so fast between us. I got scared. I haven't had the best luck with men. I've been engaged twice. Both men betrayed me, which has made me afraid to give my heart to someone again. And with my parents dying so close to one another— well, I just can't bear another loss."

She hadn't meant to blabber or become emotional, but couldn't keep the tears from squeezing from her eyes.

Despite the shocking revelation that hearing she'd been engaged twice must have been, Colt smiled and scooted over and wiped the tears with his finger.

"Can you forgive me?" she asked.

He trailed his finger down her wet cheek. "You don't need forgiveness, darlin'. You've done nothing wrong. I've been moving too fast. For that I apologize."

She hiccupped. "Thank you. I do like you, Colt. Can we take this one day at a time? See where it goes?"

"Sure." He palmed her cheek.

As she drove to Frank's, she felt a burdensome weight lifting off her shoulders.

Opal greeted them at the front door. "Go on in. Frank is

waiting for you. I'll be in the living room if you need anything."

"Evening, Frank," Colt said, striding to his bedside.

"Howdy, Colt. Hello, Miss Brennan."

He was sitting up in the hospital bed with several pillows cushioning his thin back. Shay was grateful to see his eyes looked clear and bright, and he'd remembered her and her name without being reminded. Last time she'd been here, he'd called her his daughter's name. Hopefully, she'd be able to learn a lot more about Frank's family tonight, since he did appear lucid and ready to talk.

"Please, Frank. You can call me Shay."

"Okay." He cleared his throat. "I want to tell you about Alicia."

Shay met Colt's gaze across the bed. They pulled chairs up to the bed and listened as Frank told a couple of stories about his daughter when she was a girl growing up.

"My poor girl," he said after a long pause, in which he'd closed his eyes and Shay thought he'd gone to sleep. "I killed my own child."

Her gaze flew to Colt. What was Frank talking about?

Colt laid his hand on Frank's arm. "Frank, you didn't kill Alicia. Why would you say such a thing?"

The old man's wrinkled face bunched up. "I killed her as sure as if I'd used a gun on her. I drove her away and she died." He hung his head and shook it back and forth slowly.

"Dad told me Alicia died in a car accident. Is that what happened?" Colt asked.

After a few moments, Frank admitted such. "Yes, but she never would have run off to Chicago in the first place if I hadn't told that man to get out of town. I should have known she'd follow him. Alicia had a wild, stubborn streak in her a mile long. Guess she got that from me."

Shay's ears pricked at the mention of Chicago. "Frank, how

did you know Alicia had been living in Chicago? Who told you that?"

He peered at her with longing in his eyes. "You look so much like her," he said. "How can that be? My eyes are going, but I haven't lost my mind completely."

She took his hand and held it. "I don't know. It's something I can't explain." There was no point in denying that she did resemble Alicia, but she was interested in hearing more about the girl's connection to Chicago. "Do you remember how you found out Alicia was in Chicago?"

His head moved up and down. "It was in the letter Bonnie and I got from the police chief."

Shay's pulse sped up.

"Did you keep that letter?" Colt asked him.

"Yes. Bonnie threw it in the trash, once she'd read how our only child had died. She said she couldn't bear to have it in the house."

"But you kept it," Shay stated.

"Yes." He pointed to his dresser. "I keep the letter in a box in the top drawer. It and the first one Alicia sent us. It's all I have left of her, besides her picture."

Standing nearest to the dresser, Colt pulled open the drawer and removed a rectangular tin box from beneath some socks and underwear. "Do you mind if Shay and I read the letter?" he asked Frank.

With a wave of his hand, Frank said, "Go ahead."

Moving to her side, Colt unfolded the paper and the two of them read it silently to themselves. The words were typed on stationary with the police department's name and address on top. It was brief and basically stated that Alicia Averill had been the victim of a hit-and-run accident, which had not been solved as of the date of the letter. The police chief, whose name was Trevor McGinty, expressed his sincere condolences.

"Frank, why did the police chief send a letter? Why didn't someone call to tell you the news? *Did* they call?" Colt wanted to know.

Shay was glad he'd asked, because she'd just been wondering the same thing.

"They probably tried, but we had no phone at the time. It was on the blink. They must have found our address in Alicia's belongings. Bonnie and I made arrangements to drive to Chicago as soon as we got the letter, but we were too late once we arrived."

"Too late for what?" Shay asked.

A tear spilled down his cheek. "Too late to bury our child. They'd already done it for us. It about killed my Bonnie, not being able to kiss our baby good-bye."

"Who buried her, Frank?" Colt asked. "The City of Chicago?"

"No. The police chief told us Alicia's funeral had been paid for by people who wished to remain anonymous. They were Good Samaritans, or some such nonsense. I never heard of other folks burying someone else's child." His mouth turned down.

Shay wondered if the anonymous people had been related to the person who'd hit Alicia and they'd paid for a funeral out of guilt, but she didn't want to say that in front of Frank.

"The chief told us they were just some folks who did this sort of thing when the need arose. They had a little money and took it upon themselves to see to it that every John or Jane Doe received a proper burial."

"But Alicia had family," Shay said. "She wasn't a Jane Doe."

Frank shook his head. "No, she wasn't."

After a moment of contemplation, Shay said, "Did you and Bonnie visit Alicia's grave?"

"Yes. The stone was nice. Simple. We only saw it that one time. Never went back. It's a long way to travel."

He paused to take a deep breath before going on. It was obvious he'd been holding onto his pain and keeping the story to himself for so many years, and now it was flowing out of him like a river.

"Bonnie and I came home together, but things were never the same. If I hadn't threatened that man, Alicia never would have left with him, Bonnie claimed. It was my fault Alicia was killed. Bonnie told me so, time and time again. She never let me forget it. She blamed me for the loss of our daughter until the day she died."

Shay's heart broke in half. The story was so tragic all the way around. Poor Frank. His only child had been killed and laid to rest in a cemetery so far away. He'd borne the brunt of his wife's suffering, as well as keeping his own agony hidden from friends and community for so long. She wanted to comfort him, to assure him he'd see his daughter again, in the next world. But she didn't think it would be appropriate to speak of such personal matters with a near stranger, even if she did look like his deceased child.

"I'm sorry," was all she could say as she wiped the traces of her own salt tears from her cheek.

Shay heard Opal's heavy steps enter the room. "Visiting hours are over," she announced, as if they were in a hospital. "It's Frank's bedtime. Time for you two to go."

"Don't get your bowels in an uproar," Colt said, frowning at Opal. "I guess Frank can tell us when he's ready for bed."

Shay saw Colt nonchalantly shove the letter into his back pocket.

"I *am* a bit tired now," Frank said.

"We'll go," Shay announced, tucking the covers up to this neck. "Thank you for telling us about Alicia. I know it wasn't easy for you to talk about her . . . and her death."

"Take it easy," Colt said. "I'll be back to see you soon." He patted Frank's shoulder.

"Easy? How else would I take it, Colt? I'm stuck in this god-damned bed all day and night." A hint of a smile crossed the old man's lips and then he closed his eyes.

Colt bent and kissed him on the cheek, which took Shay's breath away. What a sweet gesture. And Frank wasn't even his own flesh and blood. She offered Colt a tender smile. Little actions like that were what reaffirmed that he was a man any woman would be proud to be loved by.

Once they were back in her car driving down the road, Colt asked if she was okay.

Shay nodded, aware that she'd been lost in thought.

"You look like you're a million miles away."

"Do you think it's simply another coincidence that Alicia Averill died and is buried in Chicago?"

"What do you mean?"

"We look enough alike to be related, and I was raised in Illinois, in a suburb outside of Chicago. Don't you find that strange?"

"Well . . ."

"And who were those anonymous people anyway?" she interrupted. "The ones who generously paid for a funeral and a headstone for Alicia? Do you believe what the police chief told Frank? If Chief McGinty found Frank and Bonnie's address in Alicia's belongings, he knew she came from Hill City. Why didn't he go to greater lengths to contact them before Alicia was put in the ground? He could have called Hill City's police department and had them get word to Frank if Frank's phone was out. Why didn't that happen?"

Shay glanced over and could tell Colt's mind was working with questions, too.

"Something isn't right," she said. "I'm going to do some investigating. Frank deserves to know the truth."

"The truth about what?"

Shay pulled into Colt's driveway and shifted into park. "About why Alicia was interred before he and Bonnie could get to Chicago. That seems unethical to me. It rings of a cover-up."

Colt shifted in his seat to face her. "Who would want to cover up Alicia's death?"

"I don't know, but I'm sure going to try to find out. For Frank's sake."

"You like the old man," Colt said, grasping her hand.

"Yes, I do. He's suffered so much. He deserves to know the truth, whatever that might be."

"I'll help if I can."

"You will?"

"Yes. Whatever you need, you can count on me."

"Thank you, Colt."

When he leaned in and placed a soft kiss on her lips, she didn't resist this time.

THIRTY-EIGHT

Colt sat at his desk the next morning with the letter addressed to Frank and Bonnie Averill lying open in front of him. Something about Frank's story had been nagging at him. Mostly he'd been thinking about the city in which Alicia apparently died, and the year she was killed. The date on the letter was 1977, thirty-three years ago. Shay had been born thirty-three years ago and raised in Illinois. Was it another twist of fate?

He picked up the phone and punched in the number for the Chicago police department that was printed at the top of the stationery.

Chances were, Chief McGinty was long retired, but maybe someone would know how to get in touch with him. Colt had a few questions that he suspected only the chief could answer.

A deep, raspy female voice answered. "Chicago PD. How can I help you?"

"Chief McGinty, please."

"The chief's name is Halloran, sir. You want me to connect you to his office?"

"No," Colt said. "I'm trying to reach Trevor McGinty."

There was a pause on the other end of the line. "There's no Trevor McGinty here, sir. We have a Detective Terry McGinty. Want me to ring his desk?"

"Yes. Thank you."

Colt tapped the tip of a pencil on the desktop as he waited for the call to go through. Terry, no doubt, was related to Trevor.

Colt wondered if he'd cooperate and tell him how he could reach his father, or grandfather, or whoever the chief was to him.

"Officer Howard."

Colt stopped tapping. "I'm trying to reach Detective Terry McGinty. Someone at the front desk was connecting me."

"Hold on." Colt heard the man shout, "McGinty! Pick up the phone."

There was a lot of background noise, voices, and then a click. Had he been disconnected? *Hell.* He was about to hang up and call back when a voice said, "Terry McGinty."

Straightening his back, Colt replied, "Hello, Detective. My name is Colt Morgan and I'm calling from Hill City, South Dakota."

"Yeah? What can I do for you?"

"I'm in possession of a letter written by Police Chief Trevor McGinty back in nineteen seventy-seven. I'm trying to reach the chief to ask him some questions about a case he worked that year involving the daughter of a friend of mine. Are you related to him, by any chance?"

"Trevor's my uncle. What'd you say your name was again?"

"Colton Morgan." He felt his gut jump. Maybe he was closer than he imagined to helping Shay get to the bottom of the mystery surrounding Alicia Averill and learn how, or if, there was some connection to her and the Averills.

"It's very important that I speak to Chief McGinty," he said, keeping his voice calm and controlled. "Do you know how I might be able to get in touch with him?"

"I'm sorry, Mr. Morgan, but that's not possible, because my uncle's been dead for ten years."

The air whooshed from Colt's lungs. *Damn.* The secret involving Alicia had probably been buried with McGinty.

"Sorry I couldn't be of more help," the detective said.

Colt thought fast. "Maybe you still can be of help, Detective. Would you have access to the files your uncle worked on thirty-three years ago?"

The man chuckled. "No, sir. Those would be stored in a warehouse downtown. That was way before computers, you know. It'd take a miracle to dig through all the records, let alone find the boxes holding the file for the particular case you're inquiring about. I'm sorry, but it would be almost impossible to locate, even if we had the manpower to conduct a search for you, which we don't."

Sighing, Colt was about to thank the detective and acquiesce to the fact that they might never know the true circumstances surrounding Alicia Averill's life and death in Chicago, when an idea struck him. He might be grasping at straws, but he couldn't give up without trying all avenues. A strong feeling hinted that Shay settling in South Dakota had been more than happenstance.

"Detective, my friend was told, back in nineteen seventy-seven, by your uncle, that there were some people who often paid for funerals of deceased individuals who were in unfortunate circumstances—those without family to pay for their funeral. Would anyone in the department or your family know anything about that?"

McGinty said, "Hmmm. It's odd that you should mention that."

"Odd? Why?"

"I recently heard my aunt talking about a couple who have been doing that very thing for many years here in Chicago. I was at a birthday party for my cousin's kid, when I heard her discussing some newspaper article with relatives."

Colt's leg started to jump. "Your aunt?"

"Uncle Trevor's widow. Aunt CeCe."

"What, specifically, did your aunt say about this couple? Do you remember?"

"Sure. She said it was a shame that the husband and wife had both passed. That the community was certainly going to miss them. They'd done so much for the homeless and the unfortunate through the years."

Both had passed. That was another disappointing blow. Colt had thought he'd be able to contact them and ask more questions. He held his head in his hands. How would he ever learn why Alicia Averill had been buried so fast, before her parents had even been contacted about her death? None of this set right with him.

He pumped his fist in an attempt to relieve nervous tension. He was almost afraid to ask the next question. It might not matter anyway, but he needed the satisfaction of an answer.

"Detective McGinty, did your aunt mention the name of these civic-oriented people, by any chance?"

"She might have, but I left the room while the conversation was still going on. I'd only gone into the house to get more beer."

Pounding his fist on the desk, Colt swore under his breath. *Dammit!* Why couldn't anything be easy? There had to be another way to find out who those Good Samaritans were. His mind was racing.

"Mr. Morgan."

Having forgotten he was still hanging on the phone, Colt heard McGinty in his ear and wondered if he'd heard him cuss.

"Sorry, Detective. I was distracted for a moment."

"No problem. Look. If it's that important to you, I can call up my aunt and ask her the names of those people. Give me your phone number and I'll call you back."

That was easy. Why hadn't he thought of that? Colt gave him his cell phone number and thanked the detective.

"I'll be in touch soon," McGinty promised.

"This is going to be a big help. I appreciate it."

As soon as Colt hung up, he dialed Shay, but after five rings, the phone went to voice mail. He left a message, glanced at his watch, and locked up the office to head to an appointment.

THIRTY-NINE

Shay had just finished her coffee when someone pounded on the front door. Who'd be calling so early? The visitor on the other side of the door was completely unexpected. Shay felt her mouth drop open when she flung the door open.

"Dawn! It's nice to see you again."

Brady's fiancée didn't look happy. In fact, her eyes were puffy and red, like she'd been crying.

"Hi, Shay. Hope you don't mind that I stopped by."

"Of course I don't. Please come in." She welcomed Dawn inside and asked if she cared for a glass of water or juice, knowing caffeine wasn't good for a baby.

"I sure could use a beer," Dawn said.

Shay wondered if she was joking and was relieved when Dawn patted her stomach and said, "I'm just teasing. I know I can't drink with the baby coming, especially at this hour of the morning, but I really *could* use a beer."

"Couldn't we all?" Shay joked. "Please have a seat," she said, scooting out a chair.

"Thanks." Dawn sniffled and sat. "You're probably wondering why I'm here."

"Well, you look to be upset. Do you want to talk?"

"Yeah. I guess I do. I liked you right off when we met at Brady's birthday party. You're so different from me. You're from the big city and have traveled all over. The farthest I've been is to Deadwood." She looked around the room. "You bought this saloon on your own? I could never do something like that."

Shay wasn't sure what to say, so she said nothing—just smiled.

"It's cool you're dating Colt. He's a good guy."

"We're not exactly dating," Shay said, not feeling the need to explain further. She could tell Dawn was stalling.

Shay hadn't spent enough time with the woman to develop much of an opinion of her, but she didn't want to hurt her feelings. She had only learned a few things about Dawn's life the night of the party. She remembered thinking that Dawn hadn't seemed interested in making a new friend, and she also hadn't acted concerned about making a good impression on Mr. and Mrs. Morgan. She'd barely strayed from Brady's side all evening and cracked her gum like a rude teenager. But right now, she looked so young and sad and in need of a friend that Shay couldn't refuse the girl's reaching out.

"Did you and Brady get into an argument?" she dared to ask.

Dawn shook her head. "No. Brady's so cool. We hardly ever fight. He's laid back about most things."

"I got that impression." If it wasn't because of trouble with Brady, then why was Dawn here?

"I came to you, Shay, because you were nice to me the other night. I only have a couple of good friends and they've never had this problem. Not to say that you have," she added quickly. "I don't mean to imply . . ."

Dawn's shoulders sagged, and Shay became even more curious. She looked so lonely, so lost, staring at Shay with round, wet doe eyes.

"That's all right," Shay said, patting her hand. "Why don't you tell me what's wrong, and I'll try my best to give you advice, if I'm able."

Dawn lowered her gaze. "It's about the baby."

Shay inhaled slowly and a terrible thought occurred to her. *Oh, no. Please don't tell me this isn't Brady's baby.*

Dawn's eyes filled with tears. "This baby is . . . is . . ."

Shay had just said she'd help, but why did the girl have to come to her with this information? She had enough of her own troubles to worry about. She grabbed Dawn's hand and blurted, "People make mistakes, honey. If Brady's willing to raise the child as his own, that's all that matters. No one else needs to know. I'll keep your secret."

Dawn sniffed again and tilted her head. "What do you mean, you'll keep my secret? What are you talking about, Shay?"

"Uh. Aren't you trying to tell me that Brady isn't the father of your baby?"

"*What?*" Dawn's eyes bulged. "What gave you *that* idea? I'm upset because I don't think I can have this baby."

"Pardon me?"

"I don't know how to be a good mother. And I don't like getting fat either. Look!" She lifted her top to show how the button on her jeans was popping open. "I'm going to have to start wearing maternity clothes any day now. I'm going to get as big as a barn!"

As Dawn began to sob, Shay stared, both relieved and confused. She suspected Dawn was less worried about getting big and more concerned about what kind of a parent she was going to be. And why wouldn't she be worried? It was a huge responsibility to bring life into the world. Giving birth was only where it began. Raising a child to become a good human being was the hard part.

Shay could picture Colt as a father. He came from good stock. He'd teach his children the important things in life and give them plenty of love. Shay's parents had been great role models, too, which is why she wanted children. Her mind wandered, moving forward into the future, imagining herself with Colt and their little family, living a fairytale life.

Dawn's hand jiggling her arm brought her back to reality.

"Did you hear what I said?" Dawn asked. "I'm scared."

Shay smiled. "You've got yourself a good man in Brady. His parents seem to have done a good job raising him, so I think he'll make a fine dad. The two of you can figure things out together. And I wouldn't worry about the baby weight," she added. "Your body is going to change, but you'll change with it. I've never been pregnant, but I imagine the love for your child will grow along with your belly."

She slipped out of her chair and knelt to be at eye level with Dawn and wiped the tears from her cheek, like a mother or sister would. "When your baby's born, you'll hold him or her in your arms, and your life will be different from that moment on. You'll be a family, you and Brady and your baby. You'll look into your baby's eyes and the instinct to protect and care for him will be as natural as breathing. The love you'll feel will be like nothing you've ever experienced before. That love is what will make you a wonderful mother."

Dawn's lips curved into a weak smile. "You really think I'll be a good mother? I don't know anything about mothering. My own mama wasn't much of one."

Shay placed her hand on Dawn's arm, realizing this was her true fear. "Hannah's a good woman. If you ask, I know you'll be able to count on her for help."

After some contemplation, Dawn scooted back from the table and stood. "You think? I wasn't sure Miss Hannah even liked me much."

"Of course she does. I know she's looking forward to being a grandma. You might want to get to know her better. This baby can bring you two closer."

"What about you?" Dawn asked. "Will you help me, too? You seem to know a lot about babies."

Dawn seemed like a good kid. She just needed the right guidance in making that giant leap from carefree girl to responsible adult. Shay could be her friend, even if she wasn't involved with Colt or his family.

"Yes," she answered in sincerity. "I'm not going anywhere. I'll be here for you if you need me."

She walked Dawn to the door.

"Thank you, Shay. You made me feel a whole lot better." With eyes glistening, Dawn gave her a big hug and then waved good-bye. "Maybe I'll see you later."

Shay returned the wave and closed the door. She'd heard her cell phone ring as Dawn was leaving, so she jogged upstairs and saw that she had a voice message from Colt. They'd kissed good night last night, and he'd told her he'd help gather more information about Alicia Averill, but nothing had been resolved as to whether they were going to pursue a real relationship or not.

When she called him back, it went straight to his voice mail, so she left a message saying, "Guess we're playing phone tag. It's your turn."

She rinsed the coffeepot while thinking about the things she'd told Dawn about having a baby and raising a child. She herself had been lucky, having been blessed with loving parents. They'd instilled in her good values and self-worth, and had given her the building blocks for one day being a successful mother. But, she feared the lies and injustice she'd suffered at the hands of both Gary and Tom might have jaded her. A woman couldn't be a wife if she didn't trust her husband.

Her stomach flipped when she considered the possibility of sharing a life with Colt. He'd told her he was falling in love, but where did marriage and family fit into that? Did he want children? She'd never want to have to talk a man into having kids. And she certainly had no intention of pushing a man into marriage.

Shay sighed. He'd already told her he wanted nothing

permanent. Permanent, to her, meant forever—a marriage, a home, and eventually a family. If they couldn't even agree on the kind of relationship each wanted, it was doomed before it had barely begun.

FORTY

Colt and Shay finally caught up with each other on the phone later in the day. Sitting in his truck outside the Buckhorn now, as the sun was melting behind the hills, he prepared himself for breaking the news to her.

Terry McGinty had phoned him back early afternoon. After processing the information given to him by the detective via his aunt, Colt had called Shay and asked if he could come over tonight, to which she'd hesitantly agreed. He hadn't mentioned why, and she hadn't asked. He suspected she'd been wondering.

They hadn't talked much last night, like he'd hoped. She'd apologized for blowing him off, but she hadn't reciprocated his feelings in words. Maybe she'd been hurt so badly in the past that she couldn't recover. Hearing she'd been engaged twice had given him second thoughts. Maybe she wasn't the marrying kind after all.

Or maybe she simply wasn't interested in marrying *him*. If that were the case, he'd turn her loose and move on. After all, he wasn't getting any younger. There were other fish in the sea.

Hell. He didn't really mean that. Something implied Shay could be the real thing, but how had she managed to come close to the altar with not one, but *two* other men? That didn't bode well for him. She'd mentioned betrayal, but perhaps she had been more to blame than she wanted to admit.

Despite the mixed-up way he felt, he thought it his obligation as a friend to tell her what he'd found out. He slammed the truck door shut and sauntered to the saloon. She opened the front door before he'd even knocked, and his heart jumped in his chest, the way it always did when he saw her. It didn't matter whether she was dressed in a sexy outfit or in casual jeans and a T-shirt, like she was now. Every time he laid eyes on her, he wanted to plant a big kiss on her.

Tantalizing smells drifted out from the kitchen, and he noticed she had on quilted oven mitts.

"Something smells good."

"It's a casserole my mom used to make. Have you eaten yet? I'd love for you to join me."

"Well . . ."

"Come on in. Take a load off." She showed him to the bar and then entered the kitchen, squeaked open the oven door, and returned carrying the hot dish. A bowl of salad was already on the counter. As she set two plates down, she asked, "Do you want a beer?"

He scooted his stool up to the bar, suddenly famished, and a little surprised at her light and welcoming mood, but pleased that she was happy. "Think I'll have iced tea tonight, if you have it."

When she sat two glasses and the tea pitcher on the bar, he filled their glasses and they began to eat.

"Thanks for supper. It's delicious."

"I appreciate the compliment. I like to cook. My mom taught me. After being on the road for so long, I'm glad to be getting back to it."

After a few moments of awkward silence, Colt said, "You're probably wondering why I wanted to see you."

She smiled. "I knew you'd tell me when you were ready."

There was no point in wasting time with small talk. He put down his fork and looked her in the eye. "I called the Chicago police department today to speak to Chief McGinty. I wanted to see if he could clear up some of the loose holes regarding Frank's daughter."

The disappointment in her face was understated, but not lost on him. Apparently she thought he'd come over to talk about something else.

"Did you speak to him?" she asked, noticeably distracted.

"No. He died ten years back. But his nephew, Terry, is a detective and we had an interesting conversation."

"What did he say?"

Colt's throat felt raw. He took a long swig of tea and then filled her in on their discussion, up to the part that had to do with the mysterious good citizens who'd paid for Alicia's funeral.

"Don't keep me waiting," Shay urged. She'd pushed her plate back and leaned toward him, now rapt with attention. "What did McGinty's widow tell her nephew about them?"

Colt exhaled deeply then said, "Their names were Alex and Grace Brennan."

He watched her face pale. Placing his hand over hers, he said, "Were Alex and Grace your parents, Shay?"

"Yes, but . . . I don't understand. Are you saying my parents were the anonymous patrons all those years? They're the ones who arranged funerals for people who were homeless or alone in the world? Including Alicia Averill? Even though she had a family?" she added quickly.

"Yes. According to the chief's widow, they've done that sort of thing for over thirty years. Terry McGinty told me his aunt was certain of their identity because your dad and her husband had been friends. They'd known each other since they were boys in school together."

Shay shook her head. "How could that be? I've never heard of Trevor McGinty until today when we read the letter from him to Frank. Maybe the woman was mistaken about the friendship. Or the name."

"Maybe," Colt said, knowing there was no mistake. He could see in Shay's expression that she had doubts about the information.

"I can understand my mom and dad doing that sort of thing—paying for someone's funeral who couldn't afford it. They gave to several charities and donated money to the hospital, library, and other nonprofit organizations. But, why would they keep that a secret from me? That would be a service to be proud of."

Colt wanted to assure her there was probably nothing surreptitious about what her parents had done. "Giving to charities is one thing," he suggested, "but picking out headstones and paying for funerals, well, that's very personal. I can see why they wouldn't have wanted to advertise something like that. Although their generosity was commendable, they probably wanted to keep their actions quiet to avoid embarrassment for anyone, just in case a family member or friend stepped forward later. Like Frank and Bonnie. Besides, maybe they thought it wasn't classy to toot their own horn."

"You're probably right," she agreed. "But it's still a very strange coincidence that my parents were connected to Alicia Averill in nineteen seventy-seven. Now, here I am in South Dakota, discussing details of Alicia's life with her father." She shook her head.

That was the part that was bothering Colt, too, but he refrained from expressing his thoughts out loud.

Shay was quiet while they finished their meal. He knew she probably had more questions, and he wished he had answers for her that made sense. There were none at the moment, but he had a feeling they'd only touched the surface.

"Who was the one person closest to your parents?" he asked, helping her clear the bar once they'd ended the meal.

"That would be their attorney, Lee Stansbury. He and Dad were college roommates. He handled all their business and personal affairs from the time they were married."

"You know this guy, right?"

"Of course I do. Lee is my godfather."

"Great. Tomorrow, you're going to call your godfather and ask him to fill you in on Alicia Averill. If you have to, play the sympathy card. He won't hold out on his goddaughter, will he?"

She didn't know. "What kinds of questions should I ask?"

"Whatever will get him to tell you the truth about whether your folks knew Alicia, or if this is all just a big twist of fate."

Although Shay was desperately trying to remain calm, cool and collected, Colt could tell the news came as a terrible shock. He wanted to reach out and hug her, but it didn't seem appropriate. She might think he was taking advantage of her in a moment of weakness. If she wanted comfort, she would ask for it—but she didn't. Actions spoke louder than words, his mama had taught him.

"I'd better be going," he said, walking toward the door, realizing there was no reason to hang around if she didn't want him there. "Thanks again for supper."

"Sure." Her earlier cheerful mood had gone south.

Damn. He hated to see her sad. "Call me if you want, after you've spoken to the lawyer. I'll be interested in hearing what he has to say."

That seemed to perk her up a bit. "Okay. Thanks for making the call to Chicago today. I appreciate your help."

"No problem. I said I would. Good night, Shay."

He didn't know why, but her face fell again. "Good night."

As he strolled to his truck parked at the curb, he felt her hot gaze on his back. Turning around would only strengthen his desire to kiss her confusion away. And kissing her again was not a good idea. There were only so many cold showers a man could take before he shriveled like a prune.

As he jerked open the truck door, a movement caught in the corner of his eye. Glancing up at Shay's window, he thought he saw a shimmer of white play across the glass, and then realized it must have been the streetlight reflecting off the windowpane. Just like before.

Colt climbed into the truck, wishing he'd never brought Shay the news about her parents. He should have minded his own business. What if she couldn't handle more secrets, particularly when those secrets involved her own family?

FORTY-ONE

It was after nine when Shay rose the next morning. For the first time in a long time, she'd cried herself to sleep last night. Now her eyes were puffy and red, and she felt physically drained.

Some of the tears had been shed for her parents, and some for the doubt Colt had instilled in her about them, but the majority of tears had been spilled specifically for him.

Even though he'd kindly offered his assistance in hunting down information about Alicia, it was obvious his feelings for her had cooled. He hadn't even tried to kiss her good-bye last night. What a fool she'd been to push him away in the first place—and not to tell him how she felt.

A strange dream about her parents had kept her tossing and turning all night, too. She had to get to the bottom of this before she exploded. She dialed Lee's number.

"Lee Stansbury's office. How may I help you?"

Shay recognized the voice. "Karen, this is Shay Brennan."

"Shay! How nice to hear from you. It's been a long time. How are you doing?"

"I'm well, thank you."

"Glad to hear it. Where are you now? Lee mentioned you left Chicago and have been doing some traveling."

"That's right. I'm in South Dakota, in a charming little town called Hill City. Have you heard of it?"

"I've heard of Deadwood, because of the HBO show."

"Hill City's not far down the road. The strangest thing has

happened, Karen. I've met a man in town who has an unusual connection to my parents. I'd like to speak to Lee and see if he knows anything about this family. Is he available?"

"Sure. Hold on and I'll connect you. It's great talking to you again, Shay."

"Same here."

She listened to elevator music while waiting to be connected. When Karen came back on the line, her voice sounded different—nervous and overly apologetic. "I'm sorry, Shay. I was mistaken. Lee isn't in his office. Would you like to leave a message?"

"When will he be back?"

"I . . . I don't know. Would you like me to put you into his voice mail?" she asked quickly.

"No. When he returns, will you give him my number and ask him to call me as soon as possible? It's very important that I speak to him."

"I'll be glad to. What's the number?"

Shay gave Karen her cell phone number and hung up, feeling a prickly sensation dance across her neck. Why had Karen sounded odd when she'd returned to the line? Maybe someone had interrupted her and said something rude. Lee had a partner who didn't censor his thoughts often enough.

Oh, well. Hopefully Lee would call back soon.

There was no smell of cigar smoke or any of the other sounds associated with the ghosts this morning as Shay strolled down the stairs. Just because she didn't sense them didn't mean they weren't hanging around somewhere.

Wanting to get Colt off her mind, Shay decided to call Brenda. She'd meant to get back in touch with her before now, but one thing after another had happened to postpone another meeting. Luckily, Brenda was home when she called.

The first thing Shay mentioned was the ring on the chain.

"You say you found it at the foot of Everett Rawlins' headstone?" Brenda asked.

"Yes. I'm sorry I kept it a secret from you. I wasn't convinced you were legitimate at the time, so I made a snap decision not to mention it right then. I was a skeptic because you'd gotten Callie's name wrong and then you went into that trance at the graveyard. I wasn't sure if you were faking. Also . . ."

"What?"

"To be honest, I wasn't sure I could work with you after you told me of your former relationship with Colt Morgan."

Brenda laughed. "I thought maybe that's why you hadn't called me back. I'm sorry if I led you to believe there had been more between us. Nothing happened with Colt and me, but not for my lack of trying. I wanted to sleep with him, but he wouldn't have me." She laughed again. "You have my blessing. Based on the auras surrounding both of you, I think you two would make a great couple."

"Well, thanks." There was no point in saying more, but it did make Shay feel better to hear Brenda admit she and Colt hadn't been lovers.

"What changed your mind about me?" Brenda asked.

"I was impressed when you sensed the ghosts in the saloon, and of course, we both had the experience at the basement door. I almost became a believer when you went straight to Everett's grave. But the thing that finally convinced me was when you called back that day and told me Callie's full name. It was then I was sure you do have a gift. I'm sorry."

Brenda chuckled. "It's all right, Shay. I don't blame you for testing me. I get that a lot from people. There are a lot of fakes out there, so it's good to be cautious. The truth is I've seen spirits since I was a little girl. They used to scare me so bad, and I didn't understand why I was seeing them when no one else did. It was difficult for me to keep friends when I was in school because I was always worried if they found out about me, they'd think I was insane, or a witch or something. Which is exactly what happened the couple of times I did share my secret with someone. As a result, I became isolated. It's tough maintaining relationships when people think you're crazy."

Colt had been one of those people who'd called Brenda a nut without knowing and understanding what she'd been through her whole life.

Brenda continued. "It wasn't until I became an adult that I learned to put away my fears and use my gift for good. I can't change the way I am or what I see, so now I just try to help those I can, however I can."

"Thanks for sharing your story with me," Shay said. "I'm one of those who need your help, and I hope we can be friends when this is over."

"I'd like that, too. Tell me what your goals are for this case."

"I want to know why Callie has shown herself to me and what kind of help she needs. Second, I need to discover who owned this ring and what it symbolizes. Third, I want to know the identity of the bad ghost—whether it's Everett or not—and get rid of him. Finally, I'd like for you to cross over the spirits still hanging around the saloon."

"That's a long laundry list," Brenda said.

"Are you up to it?"

"You bet. You name the night. Spirit activity tends to be stronger in dead time."

"Dead time?"

"From midnight on. The spirits prefer coming out in the dark."

"Of course they do. I should have known that. I've seen enough spooky movies," Shay chuckled. "What will we need?"

"Just a couple of small flashlights, which I'll bring."

"You received a psychic message from Everett, guiding you to his grave. Is that always the way it works for you?" Shay asked.

"Normally I request the spirits to show themselves to me. If they're cooperative, I see them and can hear them speaking, as if they were alive and holding a conversation. Sometimes I see visions. The best way I can describe what happens in that case is it's like a movie running in front of my eyes. I see the spirits acting out an experience they had, and I can also feel what they feel when the scene is being played out. Does that make sense?"

Shay said it did. "I'm not psychic, but Callie has spoken to me. I've seen her body and her blue eyes. I've felt her hands around my neck. And the other one felt one-hundred-percent real when he lifted me in the air and tried to throw me out my bedroom window. Plus, I saw Everett in the graveyard. How do you explain that I've been able to see those things? I'm not psychic."

"Everyone has psychic power within them, Shay. Not everyone recognizes that power or has an occasion to use it. Sometimes a person's abilities can lie dormant until something occurs that opens a door into the world of the paranormal."

"Such as?"

"A traumatic experience, a significant life change, or a death. I don't know much about you or your life, but it's obvious you are a sensitive."

Shay had never told anyone before, but there had been some prophetic dreams that had come true when she was a teenager, and a few times she'd awoken from sleep, feeling like someone was standing at the end of her bed watching her. She hadn't told her parents. She just pretended nothing had happened and tried to forget about the incidents, hoping she wasn't nuts.

Could the death of her parents and the decision to stay in South Dakota have been the catalysts for the supernatural things she was going through now? It was an intriguing thought.

"Call me to set up a date and time," Brenda said. "And one

more thing. It can get hairy when I call up bad spirits. I want you to remember, whatever happens, spirits are just that. They're dead people. This entity, whoever he is, is not alive, and he won't be able to hurt us."

Right, Shay thought, as she recalled again being picked up off the floor and clutching the curtains for dear life. "I'll call you soon."

FORTY-TWO

Shay had just traipsed to the second floor to apply her makeup when her cell phone rang. Expecting it to be Colt after seeing his number pop up on the screen, she was surprised to hear a female voice on the other end.

"Shay, this is Hannah Morgan."

"Hannah! Good morning. It's nice to hear from you." It *was* nice to talk to her, but a chill immediately ran through Shay's body. Why was Colt's mother calling her, from his phone?

"I'm calling from Colt's cell phone," Hannah said, reading her mind. "I found your number in his contact list."

Shay knew Hannah to be a direct woman, but she hadn't even said hello. That didn't seem like her. And her voice sounded thick, choked. Shay knew something was wrong. "Hannah, what is it?"

"It's Colt. He's been in an accident."

Shay's heart skipped. "What happened? Where is he? Is he okay?" The questions flew out of her mouth like bullets shot from a gun.

"He's in the emergency room at Regional Hospital. Do you know where the hospital is?"

"No. Please give me directions." Shay ran to her bedroom and dumped her purse onto the bed and scribbled directions on the back of a blank check. "What happened to him? Is he all right?" she asked again.

"We'll explain when you get here," Hannah replied. "Hurry, Shay."

She jerked on the jeans and the shirt she'd worn the previous night, grabbed her purse, and dashed out the door.

When she entered the emergency-room waiting area, she glimpsed around and found Hannah and Chet huddled in the corner. Chet stood up and offered her his chair when she approached.

"How is he? Have you seen him?" Shay asked.

"He's with the doctor," Chet answered. Even under the harsh fluorescent lights, Shay noticed Colt's dad was still a handsome man for his age. She nodded and gazed into Hannah's eyes. There were no traces of tears, so Colt's injuries couldn't have been too bad. But, on second thought, Hannah was a strong, stoic woman. Maybe she didn't cry.

"Please, tell me what happened," Shay said. Her stomach was in a knot. It had been twisting with worry all the way here.

Hannah explained. "Colt was showing a farm, first thing this morning. He and his client were in the barn inspecting the horse stalls when some loose boards fell from the second-story rafters. Colt was hit in the head and on the arm."

Shay gasped. "Is he conscious?"

"Now he is. The client wasn't hurt. He called nine-one-one and told the paramedics that Colt was knocked out cold for a couple of minutes. They did a PET-scan on his head as soon as the ambulance brought him here. He has a concussion, but the doctor says it's mild, thank God. His left arm is fractured. The doctor is doing a nonsurgical treatment on him right now called reduction, where he moves pieces of bone back into the correct position. It doesn't require any anesthesia and will take less recovery time than traditional surgery."

Gulping back the tears that stung her eyes, Shay bit her lip and nodded.

Hannah patted her hand. "He's going to be okay," she said. "It could have been so much worse. The doctor said his arm should heal fine within a few weeks."

"Good thing our boy has a hard head," Chet added. "You'll find that out soon enough, I suppose." He winked at Shay.

The two of them were being so kind, setting her at ease when they must have been just as afraid as she. Plus, Colt must not have mentioned their "breakup."

"Thank you for calling to let me know," Shay finally managed to say. "Will we be able to see him?"

"Yes," Hannah said. "He doesn't need to spend the night. The procedure shouldn't take too long. Have you got time to sit and wait with us?"

"Sure. I have nowhere to be. I'd like to stay."

"Good. We can get to know each other better. Find a chair, Chet," Hannah said to her husband, nodding to the empty seat on the other side of her. "Shay and I are going to have a little girl talk. Here's something for you to read." She shoved a *People* magazine in his hands.

"That's better," Hannah said, returning her attention to Shay. "He was making me nervous, hovering like a helicopter." She chuckled. "Now, tell me, Shay. What is it about my son that has you in such a dither?"

Feeling her face flush, Shay smiled and began, "Mrs. Morgan . . ."

"No need to try and fool me. It's obvious you care for him. When you look at Colt, you have the same expression on your face that my mama told me *I* had on *mine,* when Chet first started courting me."

"That was about fifty years ago," Chet said, leaning in front of Hannah. "It was love at first sight. For me, anyway."

"You're eavesdropping," Hannah chided, lightheartedly.

"Can't help it. I'm sitting right here."

"Don't you want to read about *People's* sexiest man on earth?" she teased.

His face grew red and he mumbled, "Aren't there any farm magazines in here?"

"So, what is it?" Hannah urged, turning back to Shay. "Is it Colt's handsome good looks? Or that sweet smile of his? Maybe it's his sparkling eyes and witty sense of humor. Do tell."

Shay didn't get a chance to answer because the automatic doors opened and Brady burst in, gazing around. Chet whistled and raised his hand in the air to get his attention.

"What's going on?" Brady asked, squatting in front of his parents. When he noticed Shay, they exchanged hellos.

Hannah gave him the same information she'd given Shay, and Brady breathed a sigh of relief.

"You want to wait with us until he comes out of surgery?" Hannah asked.

"Nah. It sounds like he's gonna make it. I've got to get back to work. Tell him I came by, though."

"Will do," Chet said. "You can talk to him later."

"Okay. Shay, can I speak to you a minute before I go?" Brady asked.

"Sure." She excused herself and they stepped a few feet away so they could talk in private.

Brady lowered his voice. "I'm glad to find you here. Dawn told me she went to see you yesterday. I want to thank you for talking with her. She felt a lot better after your visit."

"It was my pleasure. She's a nice young woman. I hope we'll get to spend more time together."

"I expect you will." He winked. "I think my big brother's smitten."

Shay felt her face grow warm again. Did all the Morgans have the habit of saying whatever came into their mind?

"Hey, I've gotta go. I'm on the time clock. But, it was good to see you again. Let's go out sometime when Colt's up to it. The four of us can double-date. Grab a pizza or something."

She didn't know whether she'd ever have another date with Colt at all, let alone double with his brother, so she simply nodded. He said good-bye and then kissed his mother's cheek and shook his father's hand before departing, which Shay found sweet. It was another sign that this family was close and loving.

"Mr. and Mrs. Morgan!" A nurse called out their names. She held a clipboard in her hand.

"Right here," Hannah called, while pulling Chet up by the arm.

"You can come back now."

Hannah gathered up her purse. "Come on. Let's go see our boy. You come too, Shay."

FORTY-THREE

Colt was sitting up in a hospital bed, with his arm in a cast and his head bandaged. Tears burnt Shay's eyes again when she saw him, but she had to hold herself together in front of his parents. When his gaze landed on her, she could tell he was stunned to see her.

"Shay. What are you doing here?"

"Your mother called, and I rushed right over."

"I thought you might want her here," Hannah said.

Colt held out his right hand and Shay stepped forward and grasped it. He squeezed and said, "I'm glad you came."

"How are you feeling, son?" Chet asked.

"A little loopy."

"We've given him pain medicine," the nurse said. "The doctor has already talked to him and I've gone over his discharge instructions. I've got the release papers here. One signature, Mr. Morgan, and you'll be free to go."

Colt signed his name. "Good thing my left arm is the busted one. Don't think I could learn to be ambidextrous at this age."

The nurse indicated it was time for him to get into the wheelchair.

"I don't need that," he said.

"Hospital rules, Mr. Morgan. Have a seat and I'll give you a lift to the front door."

"This is silly. I can walk," Colt repeated.

When he hopped off the bed, he lost his balance and tipped

to the side, but his father caught him and helped him into the wheelchair.

"See, smarty pants," Hannah said. "Listen to the nurse or you'll bust your other arm."

Once they reached the parking lot, Hannah said, "Do you want to go home with us, Colt? With that concussion, someone should watch you tonight. Your daddy needs to be at the ranch, but I can stay with you."

"I'll take care of him," Shay piped up. Three pairs of eyes gazed at her. Colt grinned.

"All right," Hannah smiled. "Thank you, Shay. That's much appreciated."

"Do you mind staying at my house?" Colt asked Shay.

"No. I expect you'll be more comfortable there."

"Daddy," Colt said, "my truck is still out at the Hull farm. Could you and Mama pick it up and drive it to my place?"

"Sure, son. Be glad to."

Colt reached into his back pocket and tossed Chet the keys.

"Let me help you into Shay's car," Chet said, "and then we'll be off."

Once he was ensconced in her vehicle, the four of them said their good-byes, with Chet and Hannah saying they'd be over with the truck soon.

Later in the day, Shay had a pot of beef stew simmering on the stove and biscuits in the oven, ready for Colt as soon as he woke up from a nap, which she suspected would be any time. The pain medication had made him drowsy and he'd been sleeping most of the day. In that time, his folks had brought his truck home, and Norma, his secretary, had called to say she'd rescheduled his appointments.

Since his house was already neat as a pin, there hadn't been any tidying up for Shay to do. She'd gone into the bedroom and checked on him several times, covered him with a blanket when she saw him shiver in his sleep, and then watched some television to kill time. She'd also phoned Lee Stansbury's office again, but no one had answered, so she'd left another message.

Mostly, Shay had reflected on the way she'd reacted and felt when Hannah had called to tell her Colt had been in the accident. Her heart had dropped to the pit of her stomach.

While driving to the hospital, she'd imagined never seeing him again, and that thought had reduced her to a shivering mess. When she saw him in the room bandaged and with his arm in a cast, she'd wanted to hug and kiss him and never stop. And she'd jumped at the chance to come back here and take care of him. Thank God Hannah had called. Shay felt like she had a second chance with Colt.

She was sitting at the kitchen island daydreaming with eyes closed and chin in her hands when he sauntered in, sniffing the air. "Smells great. What did you fix? I'm starving."

Jumping up from the stool, Shay smiled and pulled out a stool for him. "Beef stew. Did you sleep well?"

"I never take naps during the day, but those pills knocked me right out, I guess."

"I'm sure you needed the rest." She ladled stew into two bowls and removed the biscuits from the warming oven.

"You made biscuits, too?" He licked his lips.

"Don't get overly excited," she warned. "They're not homemade like your mom makes. I found a box of quick bread mix in your pantry."

"Works for me," he grinned, grabbing a biscuit off the baking sheet and biting it in half.

Shay laughed. "Let me butter a couple for you. Do you want honey on them?"

"Okay. I'm so hungry I could eat a bear. I didn't want to waste any time with butter and honey." He swallowed a spoon of stew. "Hmmm. That hits the spot. Thank you, Shay."

"You're welcome."

In short time, he'd finished the early supper and she cleared the dishes and joined him on the couch in the living room. "How's your head?" she asked, settling next to him.

"Not bad. My arm's throbbing some."

"Want me to get you more pain pills?"

"Not yet. I don't like taking medication unless I absolutely have to."

"I understand," she said, "but this is probably one of those times." She started to rise from the couch to get the pills, but he pulled her back down with his good hand.

"Sit here with me. I'll take more before bed tonight."

"Okay."

They were quiet for a few moments. She felt comfortable with the silence that united, rather than separated, them.

With her heart racing, Shay finally said, "Colt, when your mom called me today . . . I was so scared. I thought . . ."

"What?" His intense gaze pierced her. "What did you think? Tell me."

"I didn't know what had happened to you, but I thought I'd lost you. I imagined the worst. The idea of being without you . . . well . . ." She lowered her gaze to her lap. "When I was driving to the hospital, I asked God not to take you, to give us another chance. You could be the man I've been waiting for. I wanted the opportunity to tell you that."

Relief at finally opening up and speaking the truth flooded her body as if a dam had broken.

Colt tipped her chin up and traced his finger over her lips. "What about your past?"

"What are you referring to?"

"The two men you were engaged to. What happened?"

She explained how they had both used her to get to her

father's money. Fortunately, she'd seen through each man's facade before it had been too late, but the incidents had still left her heart with a gaping hole. And the death of her parents had opened the wound even further.

"What will it take for you to trust again?" Colt asked, stroking her face.

"Patience. Kindness. Time."

"I can give you all that, and more."

Her stomach flipped as his gaze delved into hers. Her resistance was growing weak, but there were still important questions left unanswered.

"You told me you don't want anything permanent," she said. "Is that because you'd feel disloyal to your wife?"

"I worked through that feeling years ago," he said.

She angled her head. "Do you think you'll never be able to love another woman the way you loved her?"

"No. I have a lot of love to give to the right woman."

"Then help me to understand, Colt, because someday I want to be married and have a family. To me, that means a committed relationship. It's senseless to waste your time or mine if that's not something you want."

When he didn't answer, she pressed. "Do you want children?"

"I don't know," he said.

Her heart dropped to the bottom of her stomach.

"I always wanted kids, but I'm forty years old now. Even if I could magically have a kid right now, I'd be close to sixty when he graduated high school. Everyone would think I was his grandpa, not his dad."

She wanted to reinforce that he was healthy and in great shape. There was no reason why he couldn't be a vibrant father at his age and for many years to come. But what was the use? She'd received the answer she sought, and the rip in her heart grew larger.

FORTY-FOUR

The sun streamed into the windows the next morning, awakening Colt and setting his bedroom afire with light. Though he felt stiff from apparently lying in one position all night, the pain pills had done their job again. He'd slept like a baby. He smelled eggs frying and heard bacon sizzling.

"Good morning," Shay said, appearing and leaning against the bedroom door jam. "Are you hungry? I have breakfast waiting."

Her smile was friendly, but not as warm as usual. After their conversation yesterday, she'd grown more distant as the evening went on. By bedtime, she hadn't been rude, but she hadn't been speaking much either. She'd acted like a nurse-for-hire, attending to his needs, instead of a girlfriend or love interest.

He knew he'd disappointed her when they'd talked about children, but he'd had to be honest with her and himself. That was a subject neither could dance around, so he was glad it had come out. The fact was, he *did* want to be a father—cherished the idea—but he would never want his kids to be embarrassed by an old dad.

Even though the evening hadn't turned out the way Colt had liked, he was just glad Shay was talking to him this morning. Maybe he could set things right with her again.

"Thanks," he said, getting a hand from her out of bed.

After a breakfast including small talk about nothing important, Shay prepared a sponge bath for him, but declined to bathe him herself. Then they confronted the problem of dressing him with the arm cast.

"I guess we're going to have to cut my shirts," Colt said.

"No need for that. A T-shirt will slip over that cast easily," she said, asking where he kept his T-shirts. He pointed to a dresser drawer. When she grabbed one, he slipped his left arm with the cast in the sleeve first. She then held the neck open while he stuck his head through. "That technique should work with your button-up shirts, too," she said.

"Only if you help," he replied, daring to slide the fingers of his good hand around her waist.

She stepped away from his touch and went into the master bathroom to squeeze toothpaste onto his brush.

"I can put toothpaste on my toothbrush," he grumbled, seeing she was going to be a hard nut to crack.

"I'm sure you can. You can probably do everything on your own." She handed him the paste and brush and left the room. He sighed, knowing he'd ticked her off again.

When he stepped into the living room, she was on her cell phone.

"I'm calling my godfather again," she whispered, with her hand over the mouthpiece. "I haven't heard back, which isn't like him. Any time I've ever called in the past, he's always gotten right back to me. I hope he's not sick and Karen's not telling me."

Colt sat in the chair across from Shay and she put the phone on speaker. A female voice came on the line.

"Good morning. Lee Stansbury's office."

"Good morning, Karen. This is Shay Brennan calling again."

"Oh. Hello, Shay." Karen's voice immediately went flat.

"Lee hasn't returned my call yet. Is he in?"

"Uh. Let me check."

"Something is not right," Shay whispered. "Karen has never

sounded so distant and impolite." Karen returned to the line in a few seconds, saying Lee was unavailable.

It was obvious by the turn of her mouth that Shay's patience had run thin. "Please interrupt him and tell him no excuses this time. I need to speak to him *now.*"

Lee must have understood the seriousness of her demand to talk to him, because he came on the line within moments.

"Hello, Shay. How are you, dear? It's been a while."

When she switched the phone off speaker and hesitated before answering, Colt got the hint and exited the room.

"I'm well, Lee." There was no point in chitchat. Now that she'd finally reached him, she felt an urgent need to discuss Alicia Averill and her parents. "I've called twice," she pointed out. "Did you receive my messages?"

"Yes. I apologize for not returning your calls. I've been in court."

Karen hadn't mentioned that before and Shay didn't believe it.

"No matter," she said, letting it go and moving on to the reason for the call. "I'm in Hill City, South Dakota, and I've met a man by the name of Frank Averill. Does that name mean anything to you?"

"Averill? No. Should it?"

"Yes. My parents paid for the funeral and headstone of Frank Averill's daughter, Alicia, in Chicago, in nineteen seventy-seven. I'm sure you were aware of that."

She could practically hear the shoe drop on the other end of the line.

"There's no use denying it," she continued, as her hands started to tremble. "My parents didn't make a move, financial or otherwise, without you knowing about it."

She could feel the anger rising in her like a kettle set to boil. Lee was hiding something. She felt it in her bones.

"Averill," he mulled. "Seems I do recall the name, now that you've refreshed my memory."

"Let me refresh it even more. I've learned that my parents paid for many funerals throughout the years, which was something I was totally unaware of until recently. Do you have any idea why they'd hide that from me?"

"I don't know, Shay. Parents don't always tell their children everything."

"True, but they didn't start that practice until nineteen seventy-seven. Alicia Averill was the first. What I don't understand is, why her? Alicia had parents. There was no reason for strangers to have buried her. Why did my parents think they had the right to take it upon themselves to bury someone else's child without their permission? Without them even knowing what was going on?"

Colt obviously heard her raised voice and sensed her agitation, because he reentered the room and mouthed the words, "Stay calm."

She nodded and took a deep breath before going on. "Lee, I need to know how my parents knew Alicia Averill. I don't want lies. I have to know the truth."

A long silence followed. Shay could hear him breathing, so she knew he was still there.

"I have a right to know," she prodded. Remembering Colt's suggestion from the other day about using the sympathy card, she added, "You're my godfather. You've always been there for me when I needed you. I need you now. My parents are gone. You're the only one I can turn to. This is very important. You have to tell me what you know."

"How did you run across Frank Averill?" he asked.

"That doesn't matter. The fact is, I did meet him, and somehow he and I are connected. My folks are gone. Chief

McGinty is dead. You're probably the only person who knows the truth."

"McGinty? How do you know about him?" Lee said. He sounded distressed.

Shay ignored his question. "How did my parents know Alicia Averill?" she repeated.

"Alex and Grace are gone," Lee stated. "There's no good that can come from opening up a can of old worms. *Why* do you want to know about Alicia Averill?"

Shay gritted her answer through pursed lips while pumping her fist in frustration. "Because I look just like her, Lee. We could be sisters. My parents buried her the same year I was born. That's more than chance. I'm a grown woman and I deserve to know what was going on back then."

After another long pause, he sighed. "I have to go, Shay. I'll call you back soon."

"No! Don't hang up!"

The phone went dead and she flipped her cell phone shut and threw it on the floor. She could have spat nails, she was so angry.

"The jerk hung up on you?" Colt asked.

"Yes. He was so close to telling me! What kind of secret could hold so much power over him all these years later?"

"I don't know. What were his last words before he hung up?"

"He said he'd call me back soon."

"Okay. Maybe he just needs a little time to get his thoughts together, or to check his facts before he goes off half-cocked."

Tears were stinging the backs of her eyes. "You really think so?"

"What I think doesn't matter much. I'm sure the guy will call back when he's ready."

"I don't know if I have the patience to wait. What if it takes him another day or two?"

"Then you wait a day or two," Colt said. "Good things come to those who wait. Or so I've heard."

She recalled asking him to give her patience, only yesterday. Their gazes locked. He was absolutely right.

FORTY-FIVE

"I want to go to my office," Colt said, jerking his truck keys off the foyer table.

"You don't think you're driving, do you?" Shay leaped up from the couch.

He acted like he hadn't heard her and moved to the door.

"Did the doctor say you could?"

"Dammit," he complained. "He *did* suggest I stay out from behind the wheel since my truck is a stick. But I don't want to be chauffeured wherever I need to go. And I can't sit around here. I'll go stir-crazy."

"It's only for three weeks. Besides, if it's not against the law, I'm pretty sure you'll get behind the wheel way before that. Why do you have to go to the office today? You should rest some more."

"I'm tired of resting. I need to get out of this house."

She sensed he needed to get away from her, too, but that wasn't happening. He could wreck his truck with his arm in the cast. "I'll drive you," she said, grabbing her purse from the kitchen.

Mumbling under his breath, Colt acquiesced and locked the door behind them then marched down the steps to Shay's car.

When they entered his office in short time, Norma was working at her desk for a change. They greeted each other and she was inspecting Colt's arm cast when Shay's cell phone rang.

"Excuse me." Shay stepped away from the conversation. "Hello."

"Shay, this is Lee."

She felt her eyes widen. "Lee!"

"I want to apologize for hanging up so quickly this morning."

Tingles raced across her nape and down her back. "It's all right. I appreciate your calling back so fast. You must know how anxious I am to hear what you have to say. You *do* have something to tell me, don't you?"

"Yes. I do." After a moment's vacillation he said, "There's something you need to read. Do you have a computer? I can scan this and e-mail it to you, or if you have access to a fax machine, I can send it that way."

She looked at Colt, who must have heard her mention Lee's name, because he was watching her, listening to her end of the dialogue. "Hold on, Lee." She put her hand over the mouthpiece and asked, "Do you have a fax machine?"

Norma wrote the number on a slip of paper and handed it to her. Shay read it off to Lee.

"I'll fax this right now," he said. "After you read it, feel free to call me back if you have any questions. I'll keep my line open, and I'll tell you anything more you want to know."

With heart beating fast, Shay said, "What exactly is it you're faxing me?"

"It's a letter written by your mother."

When the piercing screech of the fax machine sounded, Norma excused herself, saying she had some errands to run.

"I can leave, too, if you want privacy," Colt said.

"No. I'd like you to stay. You're invested in learning the truth, too. I wouldn't have contacted Lee if it weren't for you."

"Okay." He wheeled out the chair from behind his desk and took a seat. Shay stood over the fax machine watching the pages slip out. Her hands vibrated when she picked them up.

"I'm not sure I want to read this after all," she admitted, recognizing the familiar slanted handwriting that had been her mother's. She felt her lip quivering as she glanced at Colt.

"Do you want to know the truth, no matter how difficult it may be to hear?" he asked.

"Yes."

"Then go ahead. Read the letter. I'm here for moral support."

Shay sat in the chair in front of Colt's desk, took a deep breath, and read the letter out loud.

First, I want to say that I have written this letter without the knowledge of my husband, Alex Brennan, and delivered it into the trustworthy hands of our longtime friend and attorney, Lee Stansbury, for safekeeping. I have never once gone against Alex in all the years we've been married, but I do so now, because I am dying, and I feel an urgent need to cleanse my soul for the sins I have committed. I cannot go to my grave without exposing the secret Alex and I, as well as others, have kept for over thirty years.

"Oh, my gosh," Shay said, frowning. "What does this mean?"

"Read on," Colt prodded.

Shay continued.

When I have spoken to my husband on this subject many times before, he has maintained that it is best for "the past to remain in the past." But I cannot keep it there any longer. I will not rest in peace until I have unburdened myself by telling the truth. Therefore, I have given the only copy of this letter to Lee and sworn him to secrecy. He has agreed to hold the letter until I have gone and Alex has also passed away. At that time, if the need should arise and Lee sees fit to share this information with our daughter, Shay, or any member of Alicia Averill's immedi-

ate family, I have given him permission to do so.

Shay glanced at Colt, to which he nodded for her to go on.

For Mr. and Mrs. Averill, I ask forgiveness from you, the two people whose lives were forever altered because of the actions we took and the lies we told.

For my daughter, Shay. If you are reading this letter, please know that your father and I have loved you with every breath we had, loved you more than life itself. You have made us proud and given us such joy. Please forgive us. We did what we did because of you.

Let me get on with it. My life and Alex's changed forever on the day we met Alicia Averill. We became acquainted with her through a friend of ours who worked at a local shelter. Alicia was a young, pregnant girl from South Dakota, who had apparently run away from home with an older man. He brought her to Chicago and promptly abandoned her, as is the case in so many similar situations. Alicia needed a job and a place to stay. My friend at the shelter thought of Alex and me because we had just lost our longtime housekeeper who married and moved out of state with her new husband.

I immediately liked Alicia when we met, and my heart went out to her for the predicament she'd found herself in. Normally, I'd request references and forms of identification and so forth before bringing someone into our home to live. But there was something about Alicia that made me forget my common sense. I knew she was a good girl who had simply made a mistake. After what she'd gone through, she needed people who would care for her and treat her well. I wanted to help, so I hired her on the spot.

Some months later, once she became comfortable with me, I asked about her family. All she would tell me was that she could never go home pregnant, or with a baby she'd had out of wedlock. Her parents had no idea she was pregnant, and she was too ashamed to tell them. She didn't want to let them down. I tried several times after that conversation to get her to call home, but she never would. Finally, I let it go. She was, after all, a legal adult who was free to make her own decisions.

It was always my sincere hope that once Alicia gave birth, she would contact her family and perhaps even move back to South Dakota, where her parents could help her raise the baby. When I suggested that once, she emphatically told me she'd never burden them, and that she planned to raise the baby on her own. She asked if she could continue living with Alex and me, working for us after the baby was born. She was a hard worker, trustworthy, and we'd become close to her, so, what was I to do? She would never name the baby's father, and he appeared to be completely out of the picture. I didn't want her and the baby on the streets. Of course, I agreed.

One night, Alicia woke me up. She was in labor, but something was not right. She was bleeding. Everything happened so fast. Before I could phone our doctor or call for an ambulance, she gave birth, with my assistance, to a precious, perfect baby girl. The happy moment turned tragic, however, when our poor, darling Alicia hemorrhaged and died moments later.

I cannot begin to describe the sorrow I felt when I held that baby girl in my arms. Her mother was dead and the precious little babe was all alone in the world. Well, not entirely alone, of course. She had grandparents somewhere far away in South Dakota, people who had no idea she even existed. She also had Alex and me.

We had tried to have a baby for many years, with no success. All I'd ever wanted was to be a mother. Alex knew that. When we were younger and all our friends were starting their families, I would cry myself to sleep at night while asking God why He didn't see fit to give Alex and me a child. By the time Alicia came into our lives, I was forty years old, and we had given up hope of ever becoming parents. And then this little miracle, this bundle of love, dropped right into our laps.

Alex loved me with all his heart and soul. He must have seen that the light that had gone out of my eyes so many years earlier miraculously returned when I held the baby and cooed to her, because he immediately devised a plan. He called his good friend, Trevor McGinty, who was police chief, and the two of them concocted a story about Alicia having been killed in a car accident. Trevor put his career on the line by writing up a fraudulent police report. Alex then paid an undertaker by the name of Smith to prepare a death certificate so that no doctors or hospitals had to be involved. Through Mr. Smith, Alex and I arranged to have Alicia buried and a tombstone placed at her grave. Her funeral was conducted quickly and without suspicion. Trevor contacted Mr. and Mrs. Averill about the death of their daughter. We never met them. Trevor told them we were Good Samaritans who wished to remain anonymous. Shortly after Alicia was buried, Alex contacted our dear friend, Lee Stansbury, who drew up fake adoption papers and prepared a birth certificate listing Alex and me as parents to our baby girl, Shay.

The plan never would have worked if Alex and I hadn't implicitly trusted Trevor and Lee, and if those two men hadn't risked everything in the name of friendship. Trevor has since passed away. Lee, I pray, will not be punished for our travesties. If possible, perhaps no one will ever need to know of his involvement.

Alex and I did our very best to raise Shay to be a productive citizen and a loving human being. And she has not disappointed us. I am her mother and always will be. But it's time she knows she had another mother—a woman who would have cared for her and loved her as much as I have. Maybe now that

Alex and I are gone, Shay will be able to find her other family, the Averills, if she chooses to seek them out, and they will accept her with open arms and shower her with the same love her father and I did. She deserves that. As do they.

I regret having kept this secret from the Averills all these years, but I have never regretted being my daughter's mother. Not once. Not ever.

May God forgive me.

Grace Brennan

Shay stared at the letter for a long time. When tears began to roll down her cheeks, Colt rose from his chair and knelt in front of her on his knees. He placed his hand on her leg and squeezed. "Now, it all makes sense," he said. "Fate *did* bring you here."

"I'm Frank's granddaughter," she whispered. "I'm an Averill."

Colt smiled. "So you are. You're a South Dakotan, like me."

After several more moments of silence and trying to comprehend it all, Shay said, "We have to tell him."

"We can go see him whenever you want."

Standing up, she folded the letter carefully into thirds and said, "Now."

FORTY-SIX

Frank didn't appear astonished, the way Shay had expected when she told him the news. With Colt by her side, she'd read the letter to Frank, pausing periodically to check his reaction and to make sure the revelation was not too much for his heart to take.

Today, as it turned out, was one of his better days. He smiled and reached for her hand. "I felt a connection the first day Colt brought you here," he said. "You looked like my Grandma Cynthia, but I didn't need my bifocals to see you were the spitting image of Alicia. Colt saw it, too, didn't you?"

"Yes. I didn't know how to explain it, but I saw the resemblance right off."

"Funny how I didn't," Shay said.

"Your mind probably wouldn't let you," Colt suggested. "In a million years, you never would have fathomed you had a family connection here in Hill City. Or with Frank."

Learning her parents' secret had been like getting hit by a Mack truck. It was going to take time to heal from the impact and accept the notion that the two people who had provided her with all she'd ever wanted and loved her so deeply could have been capable of deceiving Frank and his wife for their own selfish purposes. Shay wasn't sure she'd ever be able to think of her mom and dad in the same way again, and it made her heartsick.

Alicia was her birth mother, but Alex and Grace were the

only parents she'd ever known. She wondered how different her life would have been had Alicia lived. Would Alicia have returned to Hill City? Would Shay have grown up here and been close to Frank and Bonnie? Would she and Colt have met earlier in life?

Shay's heart ached for the two families she'd lost.

And who *was* the man who had fathered her and then abandoned Alicia?

"Frank, do you remember anything about the man Alicia—my mother—ran away with?"

"Does it make you feel good to call her that?" he asked, smiling. "She *was* your mother."

Shay now knew the truth, but it didn't make things easier. She was more perplexed than ever. She didn't want to hurt Frank, but she also didn't want to betray the memory of Grace, the only mother she'd known. So she smiled and said, "Yes. It's good to know the truth." Then she repeated, "Do you remember what the man's name was, or what he looked like? Anything about him?"

"Don't think I was ever told his name. He was too old for my Alicia, I remember that much. I wanted to kick him from here to Sunday when I found out he'd been sneaking behind our backs with our little girl."

Shay sighed, realizing she'd probably never know anything about her birth father. Did it matter anyway? A couple of hours ago, she'd been Shay Brennan, daughter of Alex and Grace Brennan of Chicago. Now she was . . . who? Was she a Brennan or an Averill?

She looked at Colt. He was staring at her in that deep, intense way, as if he was reading her mind. When he winked, she realized the question was irrelevant. She was her own person, and it didn't matter what her name was. What she did with her life was what counted.

Frank pointed to the framed photo of Alicia sitting on his

dresser. "Colt, can you get that for me?"

He handed the frame to Frank, who handed it to Shay. "I've been looking at her picture for thirty-three years. It's your turn now."

Shay gazed at the face staring back at her. She didn't know how she'd not seen the likeness before. It was as if she were looking at her reflection in a mirror. The shape and hue of her eyes, the color and thickness of hair, the pouty mouth . . . they were the same.

"Thank you," she said, hugging the frame to her chest. "I'll treasure it always."

Frank nodded and looked pleased. He breathed a sigh of relief and looked happier and more at peace than she'd seen him since they'd met. She kissed his cheek and promised him she'd come by tomorrow.

As Shay and Colt strolled to the car, he stopped her and said, "I have something to tell you."

"Can it wait? Opal is watching us from the window." A smile crossed Shay's lips. Although in some ways her life had just become more complex, her body felt as light as air. A big secret had been exposed, and she hadn't fallen apart. It was not the end of the world. Her parents and her godfather had deceived her, but it wasn't as if they'd committed a crime against Alicia. In fact, her mom and dad had done all they could to help her birth mother. They'd given her daughter a loving home and financially set her up for life. How could Shay be angry with them?

She and Colt slid into the car seat. "Opal can't see us now. What was it you wanted to say?" she asked, starting the engine.

Just then, her cell phone rang. "Excuse me, Colt."

He laid his back against the seat and blew air out of his mouth, like a horse.

With a sideways glance at him, she said, "Hello. Oh, hi,

Brenda. Yes, I was going to get back to you. I've been pre-occupied with another matter but it's just been resolved, so I'm ready to get together with you. Tonight? That will be great. Okay. I'll see you shortly before midnight. Bye-bye."

She flipped her cell phone shut and smiled. "That was Brenda."

"I heard. What's happening at midnight tonight?"

"She's coming to the saloon where she'll be sending the ghosts into the light, and hopefully putting an end to the haunting. I pray it works. I need to get back to a normal life."

She backed out of the driveway and drove to his house. When she parked in the drive, she asked, "What was it you wanted to say at Frank's? You kept getting interrupted."

Colt twisted his body to face her. His face was open and warm. He took her hand and held it. "Shay, I know we've been having our ups and downs the past couple of days, but through it all, my feelings for you haven't changed—and they're not going to change. I love you, and I want you to know that I'm always going to be here for you. I would never hurt you. Once I make a promise, I keep it. I'm a man of my word. I will be patient. I will treat you with the utmost kindness and respect. And, I will give you all the time you need to fall in love as deeply with me as I am with you." He scooted as close as possible without bumping his cast. "I only want your happiness."

When he cradled her face in one palm and kissed her tenderly, she squeezed her eyes shut to keep the tears from spilling down her cheeks. Too overwhelmed to speak, she melted into his shoulder and let him hold her.

FORTY-SEVEN

At fifteen minutes before midnight, Shay shut off all the lights except for the ones in the main room, and waited for Brenda.

She began hearing murmurs and the slapping down of cards right before Brenda arrived. Even the piano plinked out a few notes, which spooked her.

"The cigar smell is strong in here," Brenda said, upon entering and removing her sweater. She handed Shay a flashlight and they clicked them on. "You can switch the main lights off. The spirits are restless tonight, so we won't keep them waiting."

Shay flipped the switch, and the room went dark as a tomb.

Brenda pointed her flashlight beam across the room and started for the staircase. "We'll guide these souls into the light later. I can feel Callie's spirit. She's in your bedroom waiting for us."

A shiver danced up and down Shay's spine. It had been several days since Callie had shown herself or communicated with her in any way. Brenda sounded sure she was there. Shay's legs vibrated as she climbed the stairs and led Brenda into her bedroom.

Brenda stood in the middle of the room and incanted, "Callie Elizabeth Hayes. I feel your presence. Please show yourself to us. We want to talk. We're here to help you."

Creaking stairs caused Shay to jump. She turned and waved her flashlight into the hallway, seeing nothing. When she turned around again, a gray mist was beginning to form in front of the fireplace. Slowly, the mist took the shape of a woman. Shay held her breath. Callie's blue eyes penetrated her as the rest of her body materialized.

"That's her," Shay whispered to Brenda.

"I've never before seen a full body apparition that looked so much like a living person," Brenda whispered back.

Callie's arms stretched out and she continued gazing at Shay. "Help . . . me," she begged. It was the same beckoning, the same sad pleading Shay had heard before.

"That's why we're here," Brenda assured. "What do you need from us? Tell us how we can help."

Shay suddenly remembered the tarnished band on the chain and removed it from her pocket and held it in front of her.

"Do you recognize this ring, Callie? Do you know who it belonged to?"

Callie's eyes grew wide and she moaned, "Ev . . . er . . . ett."

Shay and Brenda exchanged glances.

A loud *bam* coming from downstairs sent a jolt straight through Shay's body. "What was that?"

"It sounded like a door slamming open."

Shay knew which door it was. "It's the basement door. He's coming!" Her heart thundered so hard and fast, she thought it was going to rip through her chest. She grabbed Brenda's arm, and the two of them scurried toward the windows as heavy, ominous footsteps pounded up the staircase.

Suddenly, the bedroom door slammed shut. Shay felt her hand open and her fingers spread apart. She was unable to keep her grip on the chain as it began to float on the air toward Callie.

"Wh . . . what's happening, Brenda?" she stammered.

"Remember how I told you I sometimes see scenarios play out like a movie?"

Shay nodded.

"I think we're about to see the events that took place in this room one hundred and twenty-five years ago. Together, our psychic power is strong. We're causing this to happen."

Shay worked to still the racing rhythm of her heart and the trembling of her legs as Callie reached for the dangling ring and slipped the chain over her neck. The moment the ring rested against Callie's skin, a bright light flashed outside the window. Callie smiled, holding the ring between her fingers, admiring it, the way any woman would proudly regard a cherished gift.

Shay realized Callie had returned to 1885 in her memories, which projected themselves into the room in present day.

"She's reliving a happy moment in her life," Brenda whispered.

Callie no longer gazed at Shay. She waltzed around the room, holding her white slip in her fingertips, looking like an elegant lady dancing at a ball. Shay could even hear her humming softly.

Not daring to breathe, let alone make a sound, Shay realized Brenda was as still as a mouse next to her.

When a knock sounded on the wooden door frame, Shay's breath stuck in her throat. She watched Callie float to the door and fling it open. When Dean Averill pushed his way in, Shay bit back a gasp. She recognized him from the old photo she'd had copied from the book at the historical society, and from Frank's photo of his grandparents.

She could see Frank in Dean's features, but there was no time to ponder the family connection further. Something was terribly wrong. A rotten smell engulfed the room. It was the same sickening odor Shay had smelled before. Her heart stopped.

Dean's eyes were hard, as cold and black as BBs, and his mouth turned in a snarl. He shut the door behind him and began to unbuckle his belt.

Callie backed up, shaking her head vehemently. She whirled

to run, but shook her head as she realized there was no escaping the room.

Dean stalked toward her like a tiger and gripped her around the shoulders and forced a kiss on her. When Callie struggled away and spat on him, he violently slapped her across the face, sending her flying across the floor. She stumbled into the fireplace and reached for the poker. A tussle ensued as she tried to hit Dean with the poker, but she was overwhelmed by his strength and he batted the poker out of her hand. He grabbed her brutally around her waist. As he hauled her to the bed, she kicked and screamed, "Help me!"

Dean shoved her onto the bed so that her legs were dangling above the floor and she got another slap for screaming.

"Shut up, whore! My wife's with child and you're going to give me what I need. Right now!"

Dean unbuttoned his pants with one hand and roughly pushed Callie's slip to her hips and she began sobbing.

"Do something!" Shay pleaded with Brenda, eyes wide with terror. "He's going to rape her!"

"I can't do anything," Brenda replied. "Neither of us can. We're watching this as it happened that day in eighteen eighty-five. We can't change the course of history."

Dean grunted as he struggled to get his pants down while Callie fought like a cougar, scratching at him with her nails.

"Help me!" she screamed again.

Shay closed her eyes. "I can't bear to watch this."

At the sound of more footsteps thumping up the staircase, Shay's gaze snapped to the door as it catapulted open.

When Everett Rawlins entered, his eyes popped open and he growled with rage.

Shay felt weak, like she might faint. She clutched Brenda's hand and they stood motionless together, pressed against the wall between the two windows. Even Brenda was trembling.

In one split second, Shay realized Everett did not look the way he had in the cemetery. Also a full body apparition, his mouth was not dripping blood nor was his shirt ripped open. He'd not been shot yet!

She also realized, sadly, that Dean, not Everett, was the entity who had been tormenting her all this time. Her stomach churned at the realization that she was related to this evil man.

She watched Everett grab Dean by the scruff of the neck and drag him off Callie. He swung him around. Everett was taller than Dean by a good six inches. Dean didn't know what had hit him when Everett retracted his arm and punched him, shattering his nose and sending him sprawling onto the floor.

"Ev . . . er . . . ett," Callie whimpered.

He lifted her from the bed and cradled her in his arms, saying, "Sweetheart, did he hurt you?"

"Not yet," Dean thundered from the floor.

Instinct caused Shay to scream. "Everett, watch out!"

Everett turned and pushed Callie out of the way, but was unable to save his own life. The blast from Dean's pistol sent a bullet whizzing through the air straight into Everett's heart. With a heavy thud, he fell to the floor, dead.

Crying, Callie ran for the door, but Dean was too quick. He was up on his feet blocking it, with blood flowing from his nose.

"I can't have you telling the sheriff what happened here. Nor my wife," he spat out, as he wrapped his hands around her neck.

"Stop!" Shay shouted, knowing it wouldn't change what was destined to happen. Wringing her hands and barely breathing, she watched Dean Averill choke the life out of Callie and then toss her onto the bed like a rag doll.

FORTY-EIGHT

Shay watched, still shaking, as Dean sat on the bed and ran a hand through his disheveled hair, seemingly in a world of the past, and unaware that she and Brenda were nearby and had seen everything.

Now she understood why Callie had been asking for her help—to see that Everett's name was cleared of her murder and that justice was served. Everett had been her lover, and Dean Averill the murderer of them both.

Shay remembered the old newspaper article she'd read. The sheriff had found Callie and Everett dead, and Dean with a bloodied nose. Obviously, Dean had contrived a story making him appear the hero, and Everett Rawlins had gone to his grave labeled a rapist and a killer.

Shay wept for Everett and Callie, who had been in love. It was all crystal clear. Apparently Callie had been unable to move on until the truth was revealed. The only question remaining was why she had tried to strangle Shay.

"What do we do now?" Shay whispered to Brenda.

At the sound of her voice, Dean lifted his head and turned. Dark eyes drilled her, and the room grew so cold, she shivered. "Brenda? What's happening? I thought he couldn't see us."

"Stay calm," Brenda advised, as Dean slowly stood. A low growl erupted from his throat.

Brenda took a step forward and called out to him in a strong, powerful voice. "Dean Averill, you have no power here. You are dead and cannot hurt Callie or Shay any longer. We want you gone. You are not welcome in this place. Go to hell where you belong!"

Moving at the speed of lightning, Dean grabbed Brenda by the throat with elongated fingers. Shay screamed as he hauled Brenda into the air with what seemed like superhuman strength. Brenda's feet kicked and she gasped for air.

"Let go of her!" Shay shrieked, striking at him with fists that went straight through him.

What was she to do? She knew what this demon was capable of, dead or not. How was she going to save Brenda? She threw her arms around Brenda's waist and pulled on her, but Dean's strength was too potent.

"Leave us alone!" she screamed, repeating Brenda's incantations. "Go to hell!"

Suddenly flames exploded from across the room. Shay jerked her head and saw Callie hovering next to the fireplace. Dean's dark gaze flew to her, too. Remarkably, he released Brenda and she fell to the floor, wheezing for air, but conscious. The orange flames shot out of the fireplace and licked the sky. Groaning, Dean hid his face.

Shay helped Brenda scramble to the corner as Everett rose from the floor. In the same lightning speed that Dean had latched onto Brenda's throat, Everett rushed Dean and pushed him toward the fire.

"No!" Dean cried. "No fire!"

Callie's eyes penetrated him like swords as she plunged her hand into the flames and scooped up a ball of blazing heat and hurled it at him.

The ball exploded and a raging inferno engulfed Dean in a spinning vortex. Covering her ears to drown out his animalistic screams, Shay watched as the tornado of fire disappeared into the floor with a big whoosh.

The long silence that followed was eerie. Shay and Brenda were still huddled together on the floor in the corner. Brenda pointed to the doorway. "Look over there." Standing outside in the hall were more than a dozen men. Shay knew they were the cardplayers, drinkers and gamblers who had been her invisible companions.

Shay helped Brenda to her feet.

Callie and Everett stood near the fireplace, arms wound around each other, with their bodies growing lighter in hue and density. Shay moved toward Callie.

"Is that why you came to me? Is this what you wanted? For Everett's name to be cleared and for the real murderer to be known?"

Callie nodded and smiled at Everett.

"Are you ready to go into the light now?" Brenda asked, joining Shay at her side.

Again, Callie nodded, as did Everett.

"I'll help you to cross, too," Brenda said, acknowledging the men in the hall. "It's time for you all to move on."

"Wait," Shay said. "I need to know one thing before they go. Callie, why did you choke me that first night and then again in the bathtub? It felt like you were trying to kill me." She rubbed her neck, recalling the sensation that had felt very real.

"Cyn . . . th . . . ia," Callie said.

Shay remembered the photo of Frank's grandmother—the woman Frank and Colt thought she resembled. "Cynthia Averill?"

Nodding, Callie repeated, "I . . . thought . . . you . . . were her."

Shay believed she understood. She looked so much like Dean's wife that Callie must have been confused about the time period and wanted to take out her anger on Cynthia for what Dean had done.

"It's all right," Shay assured her. "I promise to make the truth known about what really happened to you both that day."

"Thank . . . you," Callie smiled.

In what seemed like the best special effects Shay had ever seen, the ceiling opened just then, showering them all with blinding white light, and Brenda said, "It's time for you to cross over. Go now, and rest in peace."

Shay was a silent witness as the spirits stepped into the light and faded away one by one. But when Callie and Everett turned and waved, bringing up the end of the procession, it took great effort to keep her tears from flowing. She was happy the lovers would be together now, for all eternity.

After closing her eyes and quietly saying a prayer for their journey to be a safe one, she looked up and the ceiling had closed again.

Brenda sighed. "It's done, Shay. They're all gone. How do you feel?"

"Good. I feel very good. Are you okay?"

Brenda touched her neck. "Yes. That was one of the strongest entities I've ever had to confront. It's hard to imagine what drives people, now or then, to commit heinous crimes, isn't it? I guess we'll never know why Dean Averill's heart was tainted."

Speaking of Frank's grandfather—her great-grandfather—that way made Shay's own heart heavy. The old man had no idea of the grievous sins his kin had committed. And he never would. She'd keep her promise to Callie and Everett about setting the record straight, but not before Frank passed.

As she walked Brenda downstairs and paid her, she noticed there was a different feeling in the saloon. It felt lighter, peaceful, and finally at rest. "Thank you, Brenda. I don't know what I would have done without you."

"Thank *you*, Shay, for trusting me. I look forward to getting to know you better. Let's have lunch sometime soon."

"I'd like that."

Brenda stepped outside. "Sleep well. It's all over now."

Forty-Nine

"Hi, darlin'."

Colt's voice sounded as smooth as honey, which sent tingles across Shay's neck and straight into her heart. "Did I wake you?" she asked, pacing the floor with the phone to her ear. After what she'd just gone through, there was no way she could simply crawl into bed and fall asleep.

"No. I've been watching TV, waiting for your call. I couldn't sleep, wondering if you were okay. Did everything go as planned?"

She was so glad he'd asked. "Better than I expected," she replied. "Brenda did it. All the ghosts are gone, Colt. And I learned the truth about what happened to Callie. You won't believe it when I tell you."

"Yes, I will," he said. "I'll believe anything you say."

A long pause hung between them. Shay held her breath. Her lungs were about to burst with expectation and renewed hope and joy for the future.

"Do you want me to come over?" he tentatively asked. "I'd be glad to listen if you feel like talking."

She released her breath and said, "Yes. I'd like that very much. See you soon. And Colt, bring your toothbrush."

When she opened the door he stepped through and held up his toothbrush. She smiled and kissed him.

"What's that for?" he asked, once they'd parted.

"For being you. For being so patient and sweet and for giving me time." She ran her hand through his hair and stared into his sparkling green eyes.

He cocked his head. "Is something happening here?"

"Would you mind if it was?"

"Not at all."

They kissed again.

Colt stepped back and gnawed on his lower lip, looking unsure. "Shay, I . . ."

"Ssshhh." She placed her finger on his lips. "I love you, Colt."

His eyes lit up. "Are you sure?"

She nodded. "More sure than of anything else in my life."

He cupped her face with his hand and kissed her with such vigor she could feel her toes curling. With no words spoken, he kicked the door shut, turned the lock, and wrapped his good arm around her waist.

As they sauntered up the staircase, she planted tiny kisses all over his neck. He smelled so good—spicy and masculine—and his arm felt so strong and protective around her. Her heart was beating a hundred miles a minute.

There was no hesitation once they'd entered her bedroom. She slipped his T-shirt over his head, taking care with his arm, and tossed it on the floor. When she unbuckled his belt and unzipped his jeans, she felt his erection pressing against her hand. He shimmied out of the jeans and yanked his stretchy underwear down.

Shay's breath hitched as he expertly unbuttoned her shirt with one hand and unhooked her bra. When it slipped off her shoulders and she wiggled it free of her arms, her exposed breasts felt ripe and beautiful. Colt wasted no time laying her on the bed and exploring them with his hand and tongue.

As his mouth found hers again, his free hand fumbled with the snaps on her jeans. Lifting her pelvis, she assisted by squirming out of them, and his hand grasped her panties and he peeled them off.

Melting beneath his roving fingers, Shay's breathing came fast. He stopped kissing her just long enough to gaze into her eyes. Feeling her hot skin beneath his fingertips and the moistness between her legs, Colt must have realized she was not wasting any more precious time; she was ready for him. He offered her a slow, sexy smile.

His gaze pored over her body, scrutinizing her from top to bottom, as he ran his fingers over her breasts, down her belly and over her hips. After a lengthy and tender study of her body, Colt knelt on his knees between her legs.

Aroused and erect, he plowed a hand through his hair and grinned. Built like Adonis, Shay loved that he was a confident man, proud of his physique.

When he slid next to her on his side, his mouth covered one breast, and she closed her eyes and stroked his neck with her fingernails. After giving the other breast the same attention, Colt's lips trailed down her ribcage to her belly, causing her to quiver and arch into his touch.

Every nerve ending screamed, desiring release, as his hands, mouth and tongue danced and played over her body. The tension built to a crescendo as Shay moved and shuddered under his touch.

Colt finally eased on top of her and captured her mouth once more as he pressed his weight on her. With her hands clasped around his neck, she acquiesced to his prying tongue, feeling contentment as his muscular body formed to hers.

Lying between her thighs, he reached underneath with his good hand and grasped her bottom. Pulling her into him, he lowered himself and began to thrust. Every muscle in Shay's body pulsated as she lifted her pelvis to take him all in, and the rhythm built until their bodies were in complete sync with one another.

When she could hold out no longer, he filled her with his heat, and her body shattered in a million pieces. Her climax was made even sweeter by realizing his release arrived at the same time.

They stayed molded for a while, slick with perspiration, their breathing ragged. Wild and powerful as an unstoppable storm, their lovemaking had also been beautiful and spiritual, as their bodies had united as one.

When at last he rolled off her, she dropped her head onto his chest and listened to the erratic skipping of his heart. As if he couldn't get enough of her, his free hand gently fondled her breast for a while and then rested on her belly. He seemed in no hurry to separate himself from her.

After a few minutes, they rolled to face each other and their legs entwined.

"Do you want to hear about the exorcism that took place here tonight?" she asked.

With his eyes shut, Colt kissed her softly once and pulled her close, as if he never wanted to let go. "There'll be time for that tomorrow. Right now I just want to hold you."

Satisfied and content, Shay tucked her hand under her cheek and closed her eyes, too.

It was pitch black when she bolted awake. The bedside clock staring her in the eyes flashed three A.M. Feeling Colt spooning her with his casted arm resting on her, and his face buried in her neck, was a reminder of what life could be like from here on.

FIFTY

Shay's warm body was curled next to Colt when he woke hours later. He turned his head to stare at her beautiful face. Had last night been a drug-induced dream? Or had she really told him she loved him? Smiling, he knew it hadn't been the painkillers.

Soft breath escaped through her lips. Her eyelashes fluttered and a tiny smile danced on her mouth. Who or what was she dreaming about? Him, he hoped. Leaning on his uninjured elbow, Colt watched her sleep, realizing he wanted this simple pleasure to be his every morning.

Maybe she sensed him watching, because Shay stirred and her eyes opened. Her lips curved into a sleepy smile.

"Good mornin', darlin'."

"Morning, Colt."

He pressed his lips to hers. He believed they were meant to be together. Now, more than ever, he knew she was the woman he'd been waiting for.

"I slept great last night. How about you?" she asked, yawning and stretching her arms above her head.

"Best sleep I've had in years." He kissed her again and then gently tugged her out of the bed by the hand. There was no time to waste, now that he'd made up his mind.

"What are you doing?" she laughed. They were both naked, but she didn't seem to mind. When he bent on one knee and folded her hands into his, her mouth dropped open and her eyes enlarged.

"You know I've never believed in the supernatural, but all that's changed since we met," he said. "Fate has brought us together. Shay, you've made me the happiest man on earth. I love you. I don't want to spend another day without you. Will you marry me and be my wife?"

She nibbled her lip, and tears sprang to her eyes. He felt her hands trembling inside his. "Are you serious?" she whispered.

"As serious as a heart attack."

"What about children? You said—"

"I want children," he assured, squeezing her hands tight. "I want babies with you. We can start trying tonight, if you want."

She chuckled, knowing he was telling the truth and knowing what a good father—and husband—he was going to be. Not afraid anymore, she nodded. "Okay."

His eyebrow lifted. "Okay?"

"Yes. I'll marry you, Colt. I'd be honored to become your wife."

"Yee-haw!" He got to his feet and grabbed her around the waist and planted another big kiss on her lips before lifting her off the ground and swinging her around with his good arm.

"I don't want to waste another second," he said. "Let's buy you a ring and plan the wedding."

"So soon?"

"Honey, it's never too soon to start your life with the one you love."

Shay spied the perfect ring in the first jewelry store they visited. It was a gorgeous emerald-cut diamond in a white gold setting; simple, not too big, and it was in stock in her size.

"Is this the one?" Colt asked, as she admired it on her hand.

She'd seen the price tag, and although it seemed a reasonable amount, she had no idea what his budget was. With her fortune, she could have bought her own ring, but, despite being an independent woman, she was old-fashioned that way. Besides, Colt never would allow it. He'd said as much in the car.

"I know you're filthy rich," he'd started, "but I'll be buying your ring. And I won't be touching a dime of your money now, or once we're married. I know you used some of it to buy the Buckhorn, but the rest is yours to invest, or do with as you please. I want to make it perfectly clear. I'm marrying you for love, not money. I have enough of my own. I can take care of us, and our family. I don't need—or want—a sugar mama."

That last statement had got her to laughing hard. He'd been uninterested in her fortune from day one when she'd told him about it. To hear him reinforce now that he was marrying her because he loved her was all she needed to forget the past and look forward to the future.

"Yes. This is it," she said, feeling her face beaming.

The transaction went smoothly. Colt paid for the ring and she wore it out of the store. "I'll never remove this for as long as I live," she said, climbing into the driver's seat, continuing to gaze at it.

"Maybe I should drive," he said, slamming the car door. "You may wreck us if you can't keep your eyes off the ring and on the road."

She stuck the key in the ignition, and the engine turned over. "I won't wreck us. We both don't need broken arms for our wedding."

"Speaking of the wedding, how soon do you want it to take place? Do you want a big ceremony or a small one?"

The car idled. From the time women were little girls, most dreamed about their weddings. Because of the way she'd grown up, Shay had always thought she'd have a grand wedding and a fabulous reception. But now that she had found the perfect man, and her life had taken such an unusual path, none of that mattered anymore. Colt was a simple man. Her parents were gone and she had no family now, except his, and Frank. Everything had changed since she'd settled in South Dakota, bought the saloon, and met Colt. She no longer needed the things that had once been important. Anyway, Colt had been married once already. Maybe he didn't want another big wedding.

"I don't care if we get married at the courthouse," she answered with honesty. "I just want to become your wife as soon as possible."

Grinning, he said, "I second that last part, but you might regret it later if we don't have a formal ceremony. Anyway, I want to see you in a gown. You'll make a gorgeous bride."

"Thank you, honey."

"And . . . my mama might throw a fit if we run off and elope. She enjoys weddings, and she does like a good party afterward."

What a dummy I am, Shay thought. Of course his family and friends would feel hurt if they weren't invited to their wedding.

"I'm sorry, Colt," she apologized, feeling embarrassed. "That was stupid of me to even think of excluding your family. I never meant . . ."

He interjected. "I know you didn't, sweetheart. I never thought that. I'd take you to the courthouse and marry you this very minute, but I know every woman wants to have a nice wedding. We can look at the calendar and pick out a date. We can make it the day after this cast comes off, if you want."

Careful not to bump his arm, she scooted over to him and gave him a long, passionate kiss. "I like that idea." Another thought occurred to her just then. "Colt, where are we going to live? Your place or mine?"

Scratching his chin, he said, "Good question."

She thought about it a moment. It made sense for her to move into his house since the saloon had no real kitchen or living area. It wasn't a traditional home. When she'd bought the place, her initial thought was to maintain the historical integrity of the building while renovating the upstairs and turning it into a bed and breakfast. A B and B still seemed like a good plan, now that the spirits were gone. She could be there during the day when Colt was working, and hire a manager to handle things at night. At least, that would work until the first baby came.

"Seeing how I'm a Realtor," he said, interrupting her thoughts, "I know all the good deals around. We can sell my place and find our own home, if that would please you. I wouldn't want you to be uncomfortable since I shared the house with Denise."

It was obvious he had only her feelings in mind and wanted to do what would make her happy. Smiling, she replied, "What pleases me is that you would even consider that. I love your house. It'll make us a fine home."

"Okay. That's one big decision made. See how easy this is? Now, there's one more thing we can't put off."

"What's that?"

"Telling my family about our engagement."

With a broad grin she said, "What do you suggest?"

"I was thinking we could invite my folks and Brady and Dawn to a restaurant for dessert after the chuck wagon show tonight. We can tell them all together."

"Great idea."

Everything was moving fast, but it seemed so right. Shay's heart leapt inside her chest.

"I'll call Mama and Brady now. I'll ask them to meet us at the Alpine around eight o'clock."

Shay smiled. "There's one more person to tell."

FIFTY-ONE

"We have some more news, if you can stand it," Colt informed Frank later that day.

"What's that?"

Colt held Shay's hand up to show off her diamond. "I asked Shay to marry me and she said yes. Can you believe that?"

Frank's face broadened into a grin. "For heaven's sakes. Isn't that something? I'm certainly a lucky man. I gain both a granddaughter and a grandson. How'd you manage to rope her, Colt?"

Shifting from one foot to the other, and acting as shy as a schoolboy, Colt said, "I guess it was my natural charm that did it."

"And your good looks," Shay added. "Don't forget your good looks."

Frank laughed and then started coughing and couldn't stop. Colt poured him a glass of water that he sipped at. Once he'd recovered, he said, "Am I invited to the wedding?"

Shay and Colt exchanged glances. She could tell they were thinking the same thing. The wedding needed to be held as soon as possible if they wanted him to attend, because no one had any idea how long Frank would live.

She patted his hand. "Of course you're invited, Grandpa."

His eyes enlarged and she knew he was touched.

"That's the first time I've been called Grandpa. It has a nice ring to it."

Colt grinned. "Shay and I hate to run, but we have a few

more things to do before telling my family about our engagement tonight."

"Well, well. What do you know?" Frank chuckled. "I found out before Chet and Hannah. Hannah won't like that."

"You can say that again, so don't blab," Colt teased.

Frank nodded at Shay. "You made a good choice in Colt, honey. There's no one else I'd rather you hitch your wagon to."

She smiled, mentally picturing that.

"I've known the boy all my life, but it looks like he's become a clumsy oaf as he's aged." Frank pointed to Colt's cast. "You'll have to take real good care of him, you know."

"I will. I promise."

"By the way, did you ever figure out all that ghost business?" Frank's curious gaze latched onto her.

Shay had no intention of exposing the kind of man his grandfather had been, but Frank deserved to know that his own experiences in the Buckhorn years ago had been real. "Yes, we did," she said. "The spirits are at peace now. As is the saloon."

Frank nodded once, and he rested his head against the pillow with his thin lips curving into a smile.

As Shay and Colt walked to the car holding hands, the image of Dean Averill entered her mind. Flowing through her veins was the blood of a murderer. It gave her the willies to think they were related. She prayed Frank would live to see her and Colt married. He didn't have an ounce of bad blood in him, and he deserved some joy in the twilight of his life.

She felt at ease with her decision to keep Dean's actions a secret from Frank. There would have been nothing gained by giving him the hurtful details. She wondered if Frank knew of anything in his grandfather's past that would have made him terrified of fire, but if she asked, then she'd have to explain more than she wanted. That was something else she'd just have to wonder about.

As Shay's dad had told her mom all those years ago, sometimes it's better for the past to remain in the past. What was important was to live for today.

"Hallelujah! Both my sons are marrying," Hannah exclaimed, as she gave Colt and Shay each a big hug. "Do wonders ever cease?"

The six of them sat at a table in the restaurant with melting ice cream sundaes in front of them. Chet and Dawn both looked stunned by the news, but Brady got up and gave Shay a congratulatory kiss on the cheek and whispered in her ear, "I knew it. I can see smitten a mile away."

"When's the big day?" Chet asked, spooning hot fudge and whipped cream into his mouth.

"Two weeks from Saturday," Colt said, beaming like a lighthouse beacon. "The day after I get this damned cast off."

Hannah shot him a look that could have sliced him in half. Then her gaze shifted to Brady and back to Colt. Shay knew what Hannah was thinking; that she was pregnant like Dawn.

Colt immediately cleared up any misunderstandings without embarrassing his future sister-in-law. "We want Frank Averill to attend the wedding, and there's no telling how long he has left. It's going to be a small affair, just family and a few friends."

"Oh," Hannah said, obviously relieved. "Why is it important for Frank to be there?"

"Do you want to tell them, or do you want me to?" Colt asked Shay.

"I will."

He took her hand under the table and held it, bolstering her for the complicated and emotional story she was about to tell.

Once Shay had finished the account, Hannah and Dawn had tears in their eyes, Chet was shaking his head, and Brady's gaze was wide in surprise.

"Oh, honey," Hannah smiled, "I knew you were one of us the first time Colt introduced you." She tapped a finger to her temple. "I have a sixth sense about these things."

Seeing how Dawn remained quiet and looked left out, Shay switched the subject back to her. "Have you and Brady set your date yet?"

Brightening, Dawn answered, "We were going to tell everyone tonight. And then Colt called." She glanced at Brady.

"Go ahead and tell them, baby." Brady patted her arm.

"Tell us what?" Chet asked, pushing his empty bowl back.

"We're already married." She held up her hand that she'd kept hidden under the table all evening. A gold band shone from her left ring finger. "We went to the courthouse today." Brady pulled a matching band out of his pocket and slipped it on his finger.

"Lordy sakes!" Hannah cried.

Colt, who was sitting next to his brother, clapped him on the back, and Chet shook his head again, as if he weren't surprised by anything anymore.

"Why'd you go off and elope?" Hannah wanted to know.

"Neither of us cared much about having a big wedding," Brady said. "And with Dawn expecting and all . . . well, we didn't want to make a fuss."

"It was my idea, Miss Hannah," Dawn offered, looking like a frightened rabbit. It was evident she worried about what Brady's mom thought of her, the pregnancy, and even the kind of home she came from. "I don't want the family . . . you . . . to be ashamed or humiliated. And I didn't want to be walking down the aisle looking like I had a beach ball stuffed in my dress."

Shay's heart went out to her. Dawn had a right to a wedding same as any other woman, pregnant or not, rich or poor. But it seemed she was starting to grow up, since she was taking responsibility for her choices. Brady too.

He said, "The important thing is we love each other and we did the right thing. We're married and we're happy. And we're going to have a baby."

"Hear, hear," Colt said, raising his glass of water. All of them did the same and then clinked their glasses together in a toast.

"To love and marriage," Shay said.

"And to grandbabies," Hannah added, with a wink and a grin. She rose from her chair and gave Brady and Dawn each a warm hug. "Congratulations, son. Welcome to the family, Dawn."

"Thank you, Miss Hannah." Dawn looked like she might burst out bawling.

Hannah must have noticed, because she gave her an extra hug and said, "You can call me Mama, if you'd like."

Relief and gratitude flooded Dawn's face.

"Colt," Brady said, as they all exited the restaurant a short time later, "do you think you can find Dawn and me a little house in town? I've got money saved, enough for a down payment. I was going to buy a new truck but we need our own place. Not too big, but room enough for the baby, and a backyard would be nice, too, so the boy and I can play catch and toss a football."

"How do you know he's a boy?" Dawn asked, elbowing him in the ribs.

"Okay, okay. Even if he turns out to be a girl, we'll still need a yard to play in. Girls like to toss balls, too."

"You're going to be such a good daddy," Dawn said, leaning her head on his shoulder.

Colt shook his hand. "I have a couple of places that would work. Call me tomorrow and we'll set up some times to go look at them."

Shay felt exhausted. Everyone said good-bye outside and she

tossed Colt the keys to her car. "Cast or no cast, you can drive. I'm beat."

He caught the keys. "So am I. I can't wait to crawl into bed."

"Which one? Yours or mine?"

"Ours," he said.

Once they got back to Colt's place, they stripped and got into bed. Shay snuggled next to him. She trailed her finger down his chest to his belly button and further. "You know, I think I've gotten my second wind," she whispered.

He pulled her on top of him with his right hand so she was straddling his legs and she bent and pressed her mouth to his.

"Are you up for a ride?" he asked, fondling her breasts.

Shay arched her eyebrow and flashed him a wicked smile. "Yeah, cowboy. And you won't even have to feed or brush me when it's over."

FIFTY-TWO

Shay strolled down the white aisle runner strewn with pink rose petals with her gaze fastened on Colt. The wedding was being held outdoors, in the backyard of their home. With blue skies and sunshine to spare, the day could not have been more perfect. An intimate group of family and friends were gathered to witness their marriage and were seated in chairs on both sides of the aisle in the grass.

As the Double M Cowboy Band played the romantic George Strait hit "Cross My Heart," with Brady singing the lyrics, Shay kept her eye on her man, who was standing under an arch that was wrapped in white organza and topped with an arrangement of pink roses.

Her heart jumped in her chest at the sight of Colt, so handsome in a suit and tie, and polished black boots. His wide grin and loving gaze were sure signs that he was a man in love.

She felt so beautiful in her wedding gown—a simple but elegant ivory dress with a V-shaped neckline that Colt had helped choose.

When she reached the arch and the song ended, she smiled at Dawn, her matron of honor, and Brady stepped to Colt's side to take his place as best man. When Colt took her hand and the minister began the ceremony, Shay felt contented and fulfilled.

"Who gives this woman to be joined with this man?" the minister asked.

"I do," Frank answered, in a strong voice, from his wheelchair in the front row.

Shay blew him a kiss.

After exchanging vows and promising to love and cherish each other, the minister pronounced them husband and wife and told Colt he could kiss his bride.

The kiss was long and enthusiastic, with Colt's arms wound tightly around her. When they parted, everyone laughed as Colt dove in for a second smooch.

"It's my pleasure," the minister announced, "to present to you for the first time, Mr. and Mrs. Colton Morgan."

The guests clapped as Shay stepped over to her new in-laws and gave Hannah and Chet a hug. Likewise, Colt kissed his mom and shook his dad's hand, and then Shay bent and hugged Frank.

Music began, and their guests tossed handfuls of flower petals at them as the two of them strode, arms linked, down the aisle.

The band entertained the crowd during the laid-back reception held under a canopy. At the end of the evening, Shay and Colt received final congratulations and thanked all their friends and family for sharing the day with them.

After waving good-bye to Chet and Hannah, the last to leave, Colt put his arm around Shay and they sauntered into the house and locked the door behind them. Gifts were stacked on the dining-room table to be opened tomorrow.

"You're the most gorgeous bride I've ever laid eyes on," Colt said, pushing a strand of hair back from Shay's face. "You've made me the luckiest and happiest man on earth."

"Fate brought us together," she said. "Love will keep us together."

He smiled and pulled her close. As his body pressed against her, she could feel he was ready to enjoy a night of lovemaking—as husband and wife.

"Let's get out of these clothes," he said, running his hand under her hair and down her body.

"I'll join in you one minute. I need a drink of water. My throat is parched."

She stepped into the kitchen and filled a cup with tap water and drank it down. A noise from outside captured her attention. It sounded like . . . a bird chirping.

When she peeked out the window above the sink, a bluebird sat perched on the clothesline in the yard. It stared straight at her and continued singing its friendly tune.

"Could it be?" she said aloud.

When it stopped chirping, the bird stared at her a few seconds, and then spread its wings and flew off. She smiled. The bluebird had first come to her in a time of confusion and pain, to teach her how to achieve internal peace, something she'd never have trouble with again.

As Shay stood at the window, she believed the bluebird had been a gift from Denise. Besides Denise's blessing, she also wondered if both her moms had been working some miracles of their own from heaven.

She strolled down the hallway to the bedroom, completely at peace for the first time in years.

Lit candles shimmered on each of the side tables to cast a golden glow throughout the room. Soft music played from somewhere in the distance.

"It's not Paris or Rome," Colt said as he met her at the bedroom door, "but I promise this will be the best wedding night of your life. Let me help you out of your dress, Mrs. Morgan." He skimmed his hands over her hips and up her back. Kissing her mouth while undoing the dress buttons, the gown slipped past her shoulders and she shimmied out of it and let it slide to the floor.

Sweeping her into his arms, he carried her over the threshold to the bed and laid her down.

"Let's make a baby tonight," he breathed.

Shay gazed into his eyes.

When they kissed, something deep inside hinted that together, they'd be able to accomplish anything.

ABOUT THE AUTHOR

Stacey Coverstone is an award-winning, multi-published author of romance novels and a member of Western Writers of America. Married with two grown daughters, she lives on the East Coast with her husband and their menagerie of horses, dogs and cats. Although she has written stories all her life, Stacey was inspired to begin writing western romance novels in 2006 after her husband gifted her with a week at Cowgirl Camp in New Mexico for having earned her master's degree. When she's not writing, Stacey enjoys her animals, camping and traveling with her husband, photography, and creating scrapbooks of her adventures. You can visit her Web site at: http://www.stacey coverstone.com